Secret Circumstance

Marsha Sabin Pester

For Debbie.

Prologue

June, 1885

The trip to Weedy Creek would take almost an hour by horseback, or most of two hours by wagon. Nate crossed several items off the supply list before leaving. Doris wondered what they were. She hoped they weren't critical items she desperately needed. What did Nate know about running a house? He never offered to help with anything inside the house and now, less and less outside. Doris had cautiously given him a letter addressed to her sister,

Susan, now living in California with her husband, Ethan Hayes.

"Please. Let me go with you." Doris begged for at least the tenth time. She hadn't been to town since their unfortunate wedding in April. It was now the middle of June.

"No, woman! I don't want to be stuck drivin' that wretched old wagon. And you can't ride that other horse 'cuz I need it for carryin' supplies."

"Ginger."

"What?"

"The horse's name is Ginger."

"Oh, just shut-up!"

Nate rode hastily towards town. Trailing behind him was Ginger, Doris' once spirited horse. Nate utterly loathed the beast. Unfortunately, he needed Ginger to carry home the supplies. He jerked on Ginger's reins several times as the animal tried to slow down.

Ginger had been Doris' horse since a colt. She loved Ginger. She had even trained her to count, bow and prance. Papa thought this silly. But Susan and Janie, Doris' younger sisters loved to watch Ginger perform.

Just before riding into Weedy Creek, Nate crumpled the letter Doris had written to her sister. He didn't know what was in the letter. Probably just some woman's nonsense. He was going to town to buy supplies, talk to the land agent, have a couple of drinks and enjoy himself. As he thought about his circumstances, he silently admitted the fact that he despised and detested himself for the mess he had made of his life and now Doris' life as well. He also really detested farming.

It was a little after noon when Nate entered the sleepy town. He couldn't cotton why anyone would willingly live in Weedy Creek. It was a dirty, ramshackle, tumbled down dump. Well, if things went his way, he wouldn't be here much longer.

His first stop was the land office. He dismounted his horse, Beacon, and walked up to the land office just as the agent walked out of the door. He closed the door and locked it. "Hello, Nate."

"Howdy, Sam, I just got ta town. I want ta talk ta you about the farm."

"I'm just closing to go home for lunch. You'll have to come back in an hour."

"Oh, come on, Sam. Can't we do business now?" Sam Johnson was a middle-aged man, who had lived in Weedy Creek since his folks had arrived before Weedy Creek was incorporated. He had inherited the land office business from his father. He pretty much knew everything about everybody in town.

"Nate, are you sure Doris wants to sell? I've always thought she really liked living out on that farm. After all she was born there. I've never heard her express any desire to move."

"Sure, she wants ta sell. With all that's happened in the past couple of years there's jest too many sour memories. It makes her depressed. We're goin' out to California where her sister lives. She's real anxious to git goin'."

"I've told you this before. She'll have to come in and sign the transfer papers herself. Sorry, your name's not on the title."

"How 'bout givin' me a few dollars in

advance? Ya know the place will sell real fast."

"Nate, I just can't do that."

Sam got on his horse and rode away leaving Nate standing in front of the locked office. Nate angrily made his way to the saloon. The cheery piano playing "Rag Time Cowboy Joe" did nothing to change his sour mood as he entered the building. He walked to the bar and ordered a whiskey, telling the bartender to leave the bottle.

"Hey, Nate, it's been a long time. I heard rumors you were hangin' out in these parts." Nate turned to see Dan Reynolds, an old riding partner from back in Kansas.

Nate hesitated before replying. "I've been workin' on a farm a-ways out of town, but, I'm gittin' tired of livin' in this one-eyed town. Me and my woman are selling out and moving ta California."

"Are ya now? Let me buy your thirst." The bartender poured each a whiskey; they picked them up along with the bottle, walked over to a corner table, and sat down. "This is my brother Herb. Herb, this here is Nate Clarkson."

Nate touched Dan's arm. "Quiet, Dan. I'm goin' by jest Clark now."

"Don't matter ta me none what handle yer usin'."

Herb was a rough-looking kid about sixteen. His almost colorless blue eyes narrowed as he gave Nate a hard stare. Although the brothers bore a close resemblance, Dan was bigger and harder looking. It was obvious that someone had once broken his nose. His long greasy hair was starting to thin. Both brothers had the same colorless blue eyes and sallow skin. Smirking Dan informed Herb. "This is the fellow I've been tellin' you about, Herb. Nate and I rode tagether in Kansas. We made some real dough. Didn't we Nate?" Nate, looking uncomfortable nodded at Dan.

In a quieter tone Dan continued, "Nate, I'm formin' a gang for a real special job. How's 'bout comin' in with us? It's a chance ta make some big dough."

"Yeah? Tell me 'bout it."

"There's this bank in Ardmore Bend. This feller I met in the lockup knows for sure they will have at least twenty-five thousand dollars, maybe more, in their safe at the end of the week. It's ours for the takin'."

"Can't say as I wouldn't mind ponderin' on that. I'm real fed up with farmin'. Like I said, my woman has this place outside of town. We're fixin' ta sell. I could use all the cash I can get for a grub stake in California. How long would I be gone?"

"Why, you could join us and be back in a couple of weeks. No one will be the wiser. You'd have the money from the bank and from the farm. That'd be a real nice stake for Californee. I hear this bank's a real pushover."

The three men sat drinking. Dan continued to brag to his brother about the two outlaw's former exploits. Nate kept looking around hoping no one was listening. It irked him that Dan was over elaborating on what really had happened. After a few more drinks Nate finally spoke up, "Okay, Dan I'm in. Let's get out of here."

Dan wasn't ready to leave just yet. "What's yer hurry? Here! Have another! It's on me.

They drank for several more hours before finally leaving the saloon. Nate unhitched Ginger and giving her a slap on the rump, barked rather drunkenly, "Git, you worthless nag." The three mounted their horses and left town.

They rode hard through the early evening and kept riding until past midnight, stopping only to rest their horses. They finally arrived at a dilapidated shack. Waiting inside were three men who looked like they hadn't shaved or bathed in weeks. The smell of body sweat and other bodily odors were overpowering.

Nate immediately recognized one of the men, Monte. He was the head of the gang. He would never be considered handsome or even good looking. He just looked mean and evil. He was about twenty-five, over six feet tall, muscular and broad-shouldered.

The area under his gray eyes bagged from lack of sleep. Dirty brown hair hung past his protruding ears. His shirt was torn with missing buttons. Greasy blue jeans looked like they could probably stand up by themselves. "Well, well, well, if it ain't Nate Clarkson. Haven't seen you in a pig's eye."

"Hey, Monte. Didn't know you were out."

Monte gave a belly laugh. "Sort of helped myself ta git out. Law ain't built a jail yet that can hold Monte Sterling." He laughed at his own joke.

Monte introduced the other two men. "This is Earl Lang." Earl looked to be about twenty. Sad green eyes stared out of a face so long it appeared someone had pushed the two sides together. He had bucked teeth and a sulk on his face that made him look like a baby with a bellyache. His ill-fitting clothes were little more than rags.

"The fellow sittin' on that bunk is Lloyd Higgins, my cousin."

The first thing Nate noticed about Lloyd was his whopping belly. He was sitting on the only bed, sucking his teeth as he picked them with his tongue. The springs sagged as though about to give way. Lloyd's neck was a pouch of fat with heavy jowls hanging down on either side. His short stature only added to the appearance of his round body. Nate felt sorry for the man's horse. Nate guessed Lloyd was probably thirty-five or forty. The man's obesity made it hard to tell. Lloyd's clothes were in a little better shape than Earl's but still ragged-looking. Nate thought they looked handmade.

The handmade clothes made Nate think of Doris. He wondered if there was someone like Doris waiting at home for Lloyd. Nate didn't want to think of Doris. He shook the disturbing thought away.

Monte explained the setup. "This Friday, the bank at Ardmore Bend will have at least twenty-five thousand to pay off a government contract. It's for horses bought from a local rancher."

Herb asked, "How do ya know?"

"Jest who do ya think you are, snot nose? I've got my contacts."

"Easy, Monte. This here's my brother. I'm jest learning him the ropes," replied Dan.

"Well, this ain't no school and I ain't no teacher. So, jest keep him out of my way." Herb appeared like he wished he could melt into the wall.

Monte continued, "Dan and I can ride ta town late morning ta wait for the train. The rest of ya start comin' in one or two at a time sometime after one o'clock. We'll hit the bank soon as the money's delivered. It's comin' on the afternoon train. Two government men will be carrying it. As soon as the men deliver the money and leave the bank, me, Dan, Lloyd and Nate will go in the bank. You young'uns hold the horses. We'll be in and out 'fore anyone realizes what's happening. Any questions?" No one said anything. The six men ate a silent supper of cold canned beans.

All except Lloyd bedded down on the floor of the shack. Lloyd slept in the only bed. Nate didn't sleep much that night. He lay listening to the other men snore. He realized he utterly reviled himself.

Monte and Dan rode into Ardmore Bend late Friday morning to watch for the arrival of the train. Just after lunchtime, a light mist started. By half past one it was a heavy downpour. Neither Monte nor Dan had rain slickers. Their moods were as black as the storm clouds.

Lloyd was the first of the other four to arrive. He stopped in front of a saloon, dismounted and heaved the horse's reins over a hitching rail. The horse snorted in relief. Walking into the saloon for a drink, he stood at the bar near the front. From there he could see the bank. He watched Monte and Dan loitering near a feed and grain store pretending to be interested in some garden tools.

Earl and Herb arrived next. They hitched their horses across the street from the bank and sat on a bench out of the rain. Nate rode in ten minutes later, nervously waiting on his horse two buildings down from the bank, as rain ran off his hat and under his rain slicker.

The train arrived at twenty minutes after two. Two burly guards got out and walked over to the bank each carrying a handle of a strong box between them. Only minutes later they came out of the bank and crossed the street. They gave Earl and Herb inquiring looks as they entered a café.

Monte got on his horse and rode over to the bank. Dan followed shortly after him. By ten minutes to three, the six men had gathered in front of the bank. Herb and Earl held the horses as instructed.

Monte, Dan, Nate and Lloyd went into the bank. They didn't bother to cover their faces. Other than one old lady, they saw only two tellers behind a counter with metal bars across its windows.

Dan shouted, "This is a holdup! Stay where you are!" The lady made a dash for the door only to be grabbed by Lloyd. He shoved her back toward a wall, and she fell against Dan. He hit her hard with his gun. She fainted and Nate grabbed her before she hit the floor. Blood splattered the front of Nate's shirt. He lowered her to the floor and stood staring at her.

Slinging saddle bags over the counter, Dan yelled, "Snap out of it, Nate! You, clerk there; fill these bags nice and full with that government money. Make sure ya don't miss a dollar."

The clerk quickly stepped into the vault and filled the bags. A revolver was concealed on a shelf, not visible to the outlaws. The clerk picked it up and slid it under the saddle bags. He shot at Dan as he handed the bags over the counter. The second clerk reached for a gun hidden under the counter, discharging it in the outlaws' direction.

Nate saw Dan go down. Fear mixed with rage came over him. He fired two shots at the first clerk and saw two bright red spots blossom on the man's shirt as he fell to the floor, dead. He fired at the other clerk who stood dazed as he watched his fellow clerk fall.

The woman slowly awakened and crawled sluggishly to the door, hoping to escape. Lloyd saw her movement from the corner of his eye. He turned and fired at her. She moaned and slumped to the floor.

Nate yelled at Monte, "What ya doing, jest standin'! Why ain't ya helpin'?" Monte moved over to Dan. He wasn't dead but gravely wounded. Nate grabbed the saddle bags and helped Monte drag Dan out the door. The men managed to get Dan on his horse and Nate slung the bags in front of Dan.

The other outlaws were already riding away. Nate heard gunfire coming from behind him and from the far side of the street. He saw the two government men firing in their direction. He felt a burning pain penetrate deep in his side. The gunfire continued. Dan's brother, Herb, slid from his horse. His boot caught in the stirrup. The last thing Nate saw of Herb was him being dragged through the mud in the street. None of the outlaws dared stop to help him. They were making a fast exit through the pouring rain.

The Ardmore Bend's sheriff quickly formed a posse. They had no trouble following hoof prints in the mud.

After riding for what seemed to Nate like forever, the outlaws stopped. Dan could hardly stay in his saddle. The posse was closing in. Earl, Lloyd and Monte had stopped some distance in front of Nate and Dan. Nate could see them talking but could not make out what was being said. He saw Monte pull his gun out of the holster, point it at Dan and heard the report. As Dan slumped over his horse, Nate felt another bullet hit his left arm. Somehow, he managed to stay in the saddle.

The three remaining outlaws were coming back towards Nate. "Get the money," one of them yelled. Nate knew they were going to kill him and take the money. Grabbing the reins of Dan's horse, he high-tailed it into hills north of the road. Now, besides the posse chasing him, the three outlaws were closing in on him. Nate looked back at his friend, "Hang on, Dan. Don't give up."

He saw a fast-flowing creek. Still holding onto Dan's horse, he slowly walked the horses into the creek, hoping it wasn't too deep. He was unable to see the other outlaws or the posse. But he could hear the pounding of several horses in the distance. It didn't matter if they were the posse or the outlaws. Both wanted him dead. He had to get away. Dan was getting weaker; he was barely able to hang on to the saddle horn. Blood was flowing freely from the new wound. Nate himself was struggling to stay in his saddle. His side and arm burned such as he had never experienced before.

Nate stopped in the middle of the creek. The rain had finally ended. The sound of the horses' hooves grew fainter. To his relief at last, he could hear nothing except the gushing water. He decided to risk getting out of the creek. He had no idea where he was, not even which way to go to get back to the farm. He let his horse do the leading. After a few miles, Dan slipped

off his horse. Nate stopped and looked
briefly at Dan's body, and then rode on, still
holding onto the reins of his friend's horse.

Chapter 1

1862-85

Doris stood on the front porch shading her eyes with her hand as she watched Nate ride away. She remembered the stories her parents, Norman and Mae Kepler, had about arriving at this farm. They were homesteaders. They had traveled across the prairie from Indiana through Illinois and Iowa by covered wagon in the spring of 1862 to claim free land in Nebraska, through a federal land grant. At first Papa wanted to continue on to California to look for gold. But they were farmers, not miners. Momma said they had found their gold here.

Momma and Papa had three daughters. Doris was the oldest, born in 1863, ten months after her parents arrived from Indiana. Her sister, Susan, was just fifteen months younger. When Doris was ten, Janie was born. Momma was the most surprised of all the family. She used to laugh and say for the first three months, she thought she just had the flu. Momma was sure she would never have another baby.

The first house was a "soddy," built by cutting blocks of soil containing grass with roots and piling them on top of each other. The roof was a mat of mud, brush and branches.

Doris could remember yellow and pink

flowers blooming in spring in the blocks
of sod. It was very pretty. She would
pick them and take the flowers into the
house for Momma. One time at supper
a clod of mud fell from the ceiling right
onto her dinner plate. Some of her friends
told horror stories of snakes getting
into their houses. Bugs and mice were
constant problems.

Papa grew corn, sorghum and wheat, and
raised cows, chickens and hogs. Momma
had brought apple, peach and cherry
trees with her from the east. She had a
real gift for growing plants. Momma and
Papa were wise in choosing the location
for their homestead. A cold stream
meandered through the northern section
of the farm. To Doris' remembrance, it had
never gone dry.

Doris' daydreams returned to the present.

She drew in the warm June air. Wild blackberries and huckleberries still grew down by the creek. They were in blossom now. With enough sun and the occasional shower, the yield this summer should be very good.

Besides Momma's cherished flower garden, she had a large strawberry patch and a vegetable garden. Mae and her daughters were well known for putting up more than a thousand jars of fruits and vegetables each year. They even sold several hundred to Mr. McCormick, the general store owner. He supplied sugar, salt and jars on credit to the Keplers. He charged his customers a penny deposit on each jar to encourage them to return the empty jars. Glass jars were a new invention and very precious.

Doris had long ago given up trying to

compete with her sister, pretty little Susan. Papa said Doris was "big boned." She wore her straight brown hair in a bun. Doris did have very dark blue eyes – the first thing people noticed about her. Everyone else in the Kepler family had brown eyes. It bothered Doris until Momma told her that her papa, Grandfather Hooper, also had had blue eyes the same shade as Doris'.

Susan was the prettiest of the three sisters. She was really quite beautiful. She was petite, with an hour-glass figure. Her corn-colored hair shone like gold in the sun. It was long and naturally curly. She wore it loose down her back, always with a ribbon or bow. She had a heart-shaped face, very white teeth and a porcelain complexion. Susan knew she was beautiful and prided herself on her good looks.

The youngest sister, Janie was so cute.

She had a square face with a dimple in each cheek. Freckles ran across her nose. Her hair was a wild mixture of curly, red-gold tangles. Her happy personality overshadowed any defects in her looks. She loved playing outside and got very brown in the summer. Momma kept urging Janie to wear a hat but as soon as she was out of Momma's sight, off came the hat.

After eight years of living in the soddy, Doris remembered waking up to a lot of noise in the yard. Three men, a father and two sons, had arrived with a wagonload of lumber drawn by a team of draft horses. The family was finally going to have a real house, a simple clapboard frame structure. On the first floor was a parlor, dining room, kitchen, and Momma's and Papa's bedroom. The upstairs was one large space. Papa said since there were only girls, he couldn't see any need to divide the area into rooms.

At first only Doris and Susan shared the upstairs. Each sister staked out a portion of the upstairs for her own. By resourceful manipulation of two dressers, a chest of drawers and an armoire, a semblance of privacy was achieved. Pity the sister who ventured into another's space without asking for permission to enter.

When Janie was two, the older girls had to repartition the upstairs to make room for her. Doris didn't mind so much. The area was really quite large. Susan was irate. She complained for a week while she repositioned first one piece of furniture then another. Finally, Papa stepped in and did the rearranging as Susan sat on her bed with her arms crossed and a most unladylike pout on her face. Thereafter,

Susan habitually complained about the mess in Janie's area.

Each sister decorated her individual space. Doris, the ever practical one, hung old blankets on her two walls. She reasoned they would help keep the cold out in winter and the heat out in the summer. Susan cut pictures of pretty ladies from old Montgomery Wards' catalogs, and with a mixture of flour and water, pasted them all over her wall space.

At the age of four Janie, pestered Papa into painting the two walls in her area white. She then drew fanciful pictures on the walls. One had a horse with wings. Papa said it was Pegasus. Doris was always amazed at how much Papa knew. Janie had drawn several flowers with fairy faces in another area. Beside the fairy flowers she drew a river with flying fish. She never stopped drawing on her walls. The whole family agreed Janie had a clever hand.

Those were happy years, even though Momma made sure the girls had their share of chores to do.

Doris most liked working with Papa. She learned how to care for the farm animals which included watching for illnesses and injuries. He taught her to ride a horse with and without a saddle. She had no way of knowing at the time how important that would be. They had a lot of father-daughter talks while working together.

One Christmas when Doris was about eight-years-old she was very angry. She was milking a cow. Papa bent down beside her, placing his hand over hers. "Doris whatever you are upset about shouldn't be taken out on poor Bess." Doris relaxed telling him, she didn't get the part in the school play she really wanted. She was given a smaller part. Papa said, "It really doesn't matter. You do the best you can, in the part you have been given, as if you are doing it for Christ. Remember, only what's done for Christ will last."

On her tenth birthday, Papa gave Doris her own shotgun. He taught her how to use it and care for it. She brought down her share of pheasants, quails, rabbits and other small game. She wanted to learn how to shoot a revolver, but Papa said no to that idea.

Doris really didn't enjoy housework. Momma, however, insisted she learn to cook. Momma was a good pie maker and the family could always tell when Doris had made a pie and not Momma.

Susan was the daughter after Momma's own heart. Even as a toddler she had stood on a chair with her little apron on, helping Momma bake cookies and cakes. All the girls had to help clean the house. Janie did most of the dusting. She was such a happy child; she made up songs and sang them as she dusted.

The two older girls fought like all sisters. Janie would stand by and watch, wide-eyed. Doris remembered one time throwing a hairbrush at Susan. It hit her in the ear. Doris knew it had hurt because Susan's eyes had filled with tears. But Doris didn't feel bad. Susan had taken Doris' favorite hair comb without asking and had lost it.

That night Doris was washing dishes and Susan was drying. Susan took the kettle of water off the stove to rinse the dishes. She grinned, "I wonder if this water is hot!" With that she poured a few drops on Doris' backside. Doris screamed. Momma and

Papa came running from the living room. They were very angry. Momma put wool fat on the red spot while Papa spanked Susan. Susan also had to wash and dry the dishes for the rest of the week. Doris chuckled as she recalled the incident. It served Susan right, even though the water hadn't really been very hot.

There were times when Susan was just plain mean. She teased Doris about her name, saying it was a boy's name. The only other person they knew whose name was Doris was Mr. Doris Palmer, a man from England. One day Momma overheard Susan teasing Doris. She grasped Susan by her collar and sat her down.

Momma took a deep breath before speaking in a quiet voice, "You are correct that sometimes a boy is named Doris. In England both boys and girls are given that name. My grandmother, your great-grandmother was named Doris. She was born in England. To be able to come to America she hired on as an indentured servant for seven years. She was the most kind and gentle person I've ever known. I loved her dearly. That is why I named my first child Doris. It is wrong to tease anyone about their name. Babies don't name themselves. It is no different than teasing someone because they are left-handed or tall or brown eyed. I won't have it! Do you hear me?" Susan bobbed her head.

Chapter 2

June 1885

Doris looked around the farm. Nate had been gone more than a week. What a mess her life and the farm were! She remembered when the farm had been considered one of the prettiest places in the county. Now it was falling apart. Half of a hinge on one of the barn doors was no longer attached. Momma's flower garden was just a weed patch. Once, Momma had grown so many flowers. The pretty little white, pink and purple crocuses were the first to appear in the spring, sometimes even through the snow. The tulips and jonquils would be the next to bloom. Momma had flowers blooming all through the growing season – columbine, phlox, chrysanthemums, and others that Doris couldn't recall. Momma had furnished the altar flowers for the church from late April until frost. There had always been bouquets adorning the house in summer.

As Doris continued to look about the farm, she noticed a board was missing from the front porch railing. How fast things fall apart, thought Doris.

Doris sighed. She had tried so hard to keep the weeds out of her mother's strawberry patch, without much success. There hadn't been many berries this spring. However, she was proud of the vegetable garden. She had already harvested some early peas. The other plants were up and looked healthy, even though this spring had been unusually wet.

Doris finished milking the only cow left on the farm. Nate had sold all the livestock except the cow, a couple of pigs and some chickens.

She carried the milk to the kitchen and strained it into a crock. She let it set long enough for the cream to rise. Then she skimmed the cream off the top and poured it into a separate container. She carried the two containers to a spring house where milk, cream and butter were kept in a box with cold spring water running through it.

Doris returned to the house walked through the kitchen and into the dining room. Her eyes fell on a wedding picture of Susan and Ethan. Once again memories came flooding back.

Doris sat down on a dining room chair, her shoulders slumped and she cried, remembering all that had happened in the past twelve months.

Chapter 3

1884

Susan and Ethan Hayes had married in March, 1884. Doris had been secretly in love with Ethan. She had dreamed of marrying him. They had grown up together and were in the same grade in the one-room school. He would tease her until she cried. Susan was two grades behind them. Doris was flabbergasted when she realized it was Susan and not her to whom Ethan had given his heart. She cried herself to sleep the night Ethan asked Papa's permission to marry Susan. How her heart ached as she watched Susan preparing her trousseau. She couldn't even bring herself to talk to Susan. Susan couldn't understand what was wrong with Doris. She seemed to have no inkling of why Doris was sulking.

One day Papa was going to town, and he told Doris to come with him. That was a real surprise. Usually Momma went with Papa, while she and her sisters were left at home to see to the chores. Only later did Doris realize that Papa understood her hurt and wanted to comfort her.

Doris cherished that trip to town. They rode in the wagon and lunched beside a small creek. Again, Doris was surprised, because they generally stopped at the Dodd farm, which was the next farm east of the Kepler's farm.

Papa and Momma had known Arnold and Harriet Dodd back east. They had five children. The oldest, Randall, was the same age as Doris, but she didn't know him very well. He left school early to work with his father. He was shy and seldom left the Dodd farm.

The memory of the afternoon by the creek was precious to Doris. She remembered the bright azure sky. There was not a cloud to be seen. A warm gentle breeze had kissed her cheeks. Papa had commented, "This sure is unusual weather for March. Only last week we had that terrible ice storm. I wonder if it is some kind of sign of what the summer is gonna be like? Can't remember what the almanac said. Guess I'm getting old."

"Don't say that, Papa. You're not old. Old is like Mr. Hayes."

Papa gave a hearty laugh, "Sweetheart, Mr. Hayes is a year younger than me."

"Oh! Well, he looks a lot older," Doris replied with chagrin.

"He's had a hard life. It's weighed him down some." Papa became serious. "We all face problems and we have to make choices to deal with those problems. We also have to live with the consequences from those decisions. Some of the decisions Mr. Hayes made were not good ones. Life has been more difficult for him than it's needed to be."

They talked a little more about life's problems and decisions people must make. Finally, Papa said, "Doris, I know you are upset about Susan marrying Ethan."

"Why should I care? They're in love with each other. So that's that." Having declared this, Doris began to cry, "Oh, Papa, my heart is breaking. I can't face them. I heard Susan asking Momma to wear her wedding dress. I always thought it would be me first."

"Yes, daughter, I figured you'd be the first to wed. You must put your faith in God and trust that He has a better plan for you. He does, you know."

"No, I don't know. I don't know anything except I'm angry. I'm so angry, I wish I could pour boiling water on Susan's rear!" Papa laughed and laughed until tears ran down his face. Doris smiled. "You know what?"

"No, what?" asked Papa.

"The time Susan dumped the hot water on me – well, it really wasn't very hot. I just carried on to get her in trouble." Doris began to laugh also.

When they had finished laughing, they continued to eat the lunch Momma had packed for them. Before starting on to town, Papa reached into the wagon for his Bible. Papa was in the habit of reading the Bible after each meal. This time was no exception and he read Psalm thirty-seven. Doris stopped listening after verse four: "Delight thyself also in the Lord: and he shall give thee the desires of thine heart." Oh, how she wanted to believe that verse!

Papa and Doris arrived in town in the early afternoon. They first stopped at the bank. Doris was surprised. Why would Papa be going to the bank? Papa told Doris to stay in the wagon. He wasn't in the bank very long. When he returned, Papa drove onto Mr. McCormick's general store.

Mr. McCormick was a good man and about Papa's age. Doris realized many of the men in town must be about the same age as Papa. Weedy Creek was the town established soon after the arrival of the Keplers, the Dodds, the McCormicks and the others from the wagon train. Most of the families wanted land, but some, like Mr. McCormick, started businesses.

Mr. McCormick was a kind man who made good choices in his life. Doris knew there were many times he had carried a family if they were having a tough time. Mrs. McCormick was not the same. She had a long sour face with cruel looking eyes and lips perpetually in a frown. If she heard her husband allowing a family to put off paying their bill, she would press her lips together, place her hands on her hips and refuse to speak to her husband for days.

Doris followed her papa into the store. There stood a man she had never seen before. Strangers were unusual in Weedy Creek. He was rather good looking. But not what could be called handsome. He stood just a little taller than Papa. His very dark hair looked as though it had just been cut. His mustache was also well trimmed. The black, serious-looking eyes gazing at Doris made her feel very uncomfortable. She wondered if there was some Spanish blood in him. He had broad shoulders; the sleeves of his faded, but clean, shirt were strained tight by bulky muscles. She guessed him to be about thirty. He looked strong and tough. He was, however, very polite to Papa and even to Doris. He stepped away from the counter. "Sir, wait on these fine folks first. I ain't in no hurry."

Mr. McCormick filled their order. Next Papa did another odd thing. He handed Doris a small black coin purse with silver fasteners. She could tell by its weight it held several coins. "I'm going to see Doc Little. Momma asked me to get her a tonic. You take this money and buy yourself some material for a new dress. If you want, you can see Mr. Mason about new shoes. I'll see you in an hour in the café."

Doris was startled. Never before had Papa done anything so unusual. Then his words about Momma penetrated her brain. "What's wrong with Momma? I knew she wasn't up to her usual self. I just thought it was spring fever."

"No, nothin's wrong. She probably just has spring fever, like you said," replied Papa.

Papa left. Doris stood staring at nothing until Mrs. Ross came up behind her. Unpleasantly Mrs. Ross snorted, "Excuse me, Doris, and please step aside so Mr. McCormick can wait on me."

"Oh, excuse me, Mrs. Ross. I'm just wool gathering." Mrs. Ross disliked the Kepler family with a passion. Doris quickly stepped aside remembering why Mrs. Ross so disliked her family.

Mrs. Ross had a daughter, Laura, two years older than Doris. Laura was short and husky with a ruddy flat face and washed-out pale eyes. She was also very mean-spirited. During her school years, Laura bullied the other students, particularly Susan. Finally, one day Doris and Susan had had enough. At recess that day, they waited behind a tree. When Laura came out of the school, they jumped out and knocked her down.

Doris sat on her chest while Susan flopped across Laura's legs to help hold her down. Doris pummeled Laura. The other students ran over to the turmoil making a circle around the fighting. The children were shouting, "Get her Doris." "Hit her in the nose." "Hold on Susan."

Miss Schooks was writing the afternoon assignments on the blackboard and heard the loud commotion out on the playground. She placed the chalk on the tray and hurried out to see what was happening. Moving the children aside to get to the center, she was very surprised to see Doris on top of Laura. Doris felt a strong jerk as she was pulled off Laura. Susan, seeing Miss Schooks, let go of Laura's legs and stood up. Laura lay on the ground holding her bloody nose and crying.

Miss Schooks looked at Doris at first not sure what to say. This was the first time she could ever remember Doris behaving in such a manner. She finally found her voice. "Margaret, take Laura to the pump. Help her to get cleaned up." Still holding on to Doris, Miss Schooks propelled her into the school as Susan followed.

"I am so upset with the two of you. Of all the children, you are the last two I would have expected to behave in such a manner." Doris started to say why she beat up Laura but, Miss Schooks stopped her. "I don't care why you feel justified in behaving as you did. You are wrong."

The schedule for the afternoon was forgotten. Miss Schooks spent the rest of the day reprimanding the class for their ungentlemanly and unladylike behavior. Several stern stares were directed in Doris' and Susan's direction.

Laura sat with her hands primly clasped on her desk top, looking, for all the world, like a wounded princess. Miss Schooks saw this and leaned down close to her face.

"And young lady, don't you think I am not aware of your shameful behavior. It will stop right now. Do you understand?" Laura hung her head and nodded.

The teacher didn't have much sympathy for Laura, but felt she had to punish the sisters. She kept them after school and made each write ten times on their slates, 'It is wrong to solve a problem by beating someone up.' She knew when they got home late, their mother would question why they were late. They would probably be punished again.

Miss Schooks was right. Mamma was watching for her daughters. She was waiting at the door when they arrived. "You girls are late. I can see by your clothes that something happened at school today." How did Momma always know when things weren't right? The sisters looked sheepishly at each other. "Well, I can see something's not right. Come into the kitchen and sit down." Momma handed each daughter a glass of milk. "Let's hear about it, Doris."

"Momma, Laura Ross has been mean to Susan for so long. I told her over and over to stop it and to leave her alone. Well, today I just had enough. I beat her up."

"I helped," piped up Susan. This was no sooner out of her mouth when there was loud pounding at the front door. Momma went into the living room and opened the door. Mrs. Ross and Laura, wearing a black eye, were standing on the porch.

Before Momma could utter a word, Mrs. Ross began bellowing at the top of her lungs. "Do you know what your wicked daughters did to my Laura today? Look at her! They beat her up! She has a loose tooth! What if it comes out? The two of them ganged up on my poor Laura. Why, there's no telling what might have happened if Miss Schooks hadn't heard my poor Laura crying and stopped them."

Papa heard Mrs. Ross' angry rantings and came to the house from the barn to investigate. Momma tried to calm Mrs. Ross without success. Finally, Mrs. Ross finished her outburst with, "If they ever touch my Laura again, I'll take a switch to them myself." She grabbed Laura, none too gently, and briskly walked to their buggy.

Doris retold Papa what had happened at school. By the time she finished, Papa was laughing so hard he had to sit down.

Momma put her hands on her hips and said, "Really, Norm. That's enough."

"Mae, you know Laura is a spoiled brat. She's been asking for a good beating for a long time."

"Be that as it may, I'll not have my daughters fighting like two ruffians. Doris, Susan, tomorrow you will go to school and in front of Miss Schooks, you will apologize to Laura."

"Apologize!" Both girls wailed.

"Yes. Also tell Laura that she is never to bother either of you again."

"What will happen if she does?" asked Susan.

"Never you mind. You let Laura worry about that."

Laura never harassed either of the sisters again. Momma and Mrs. Ross had not spoken kindly to each other since that day, except to greet one another politely in public or at church.

Chapter 4

1885

Doris finished musing over the past and walked over to the sewing area. While looking at the various bolts of material, her eye caught a sky-blue fabric with little pink roses surrounding yellow centers.

"That one would look real nice on you. It would bring out the blue in your eyes." Doris turned to see the stranger standing near her. She blushed self-consciously. It was the first time a man had ever said anything like that to her. She didn't reply but made her purchase and quickly left.

Holding her package tightly, she walked over to see Mr. Mason, the cobbler. She thought to herself how nice it would be to have a pair of dress shoes. Her best friend, Wilma Smith, had three or four pairs of shoes. But her father was a lawyer. It seemed Wilma had on a different pair every time she went to church or to a dance. Doris had never had more than one pair at a time in her life. As she entered the cobbler shop, she glanced behind her to see the stranger watching. She was so embarrassed; she hoped Mr. Mason hadn't noticed.

"Well, Miss Doris, what brings you here today? Don't tell me those shoes I sold you last fall have already worn out." Mr. Mason was one of the older men in town.

He had come with his wife and children
to Weedy Creek just after the town had
been incorporated in 1869. Mr. Mason was
about Papa's height only heavier, with a
large belly. He had a jolly face and always
seemed happy. His hands always looked
dirty; Momma said it was from the shoe
dye. His wife had died after the birth of
their eleventh child several years ago. Doris
could only remember his wife as always
expecting another baby.

"Oh, no, Mr. Mason. You make very good
shoes. See, they're fine." She lifted her
foot to show him. "I'm looking for a pair of
dress shoes."

"Well, I may just have the pair for you."
He set a pair of white shoes with little
heels on the counter. They were the most
beautiful shoes she had ever seen. They
were so dainty. They tied at the side with

yellow ribbons and there were other yellow ribbons fashioned in the shape of roses in the center of each shoe. "I made these for Mrs. Canfield. When Mr. Canfield came in to pick 'em up, he said they were too fussy and refused to pay for 'em. Try 'em on. I'm sure they're your size."

Doris admired the white shoes. They were impractical. But she thought how well they would look with her new dress. If she wore her boots on the way to church and put these on before going in, well... she just had to have them. "How much are they, Mr. Mason?"

"Seeing as they're left over or second hand, you might say, I'd let you take 'em for $2.00."

"Two dollars! That's a lot. Would you consider $1.00?"

"No, I couldn't go that low. How about a dollar and four bits? That's a very good price, Miss Doris."

Doris chewed her lip. She really wanted those shoes. "All right, a dollar and a half it is." She was floating on air as she made her way to the café to meet Papa.

Susan was jealous when she saw the shoes. "Doris, where did you get the money for the shoes?" Doris refused to tell Susan. "Oh, Doris, those shoes would look so nice with Momma's wedding dress. Please let me wear them. Please, please." Doris really didn't want to let her. "Doris, all I have to wear are these awful brown shoes." She picked up a pair of scruffy, worn-out shoes. "Can you imagine how they will look with a wedding dress?"

"I thought Momma had a pair she said you can wear."

"Her feet are so small; I can barely get my big toe in them." For being so petite, Susan did seem to have unusually large feet. "Please, Doris. I'll do the dishes from now until my wedding day. I promise."

Doris hesitated for several seconds. Finally, she said, "All right, on one condition."

"What?"

"You leave Momma's dress here when you go to California. I'm hoping Janie and I will wear it someday."

"Oh, I'm figuring to have a daughter who would one day wear it to her wedding." Susan looked forlornly at Doris.

Doris almost gave in. "No, if you want to wear my shoes, you must promise to leave the dress here."

"Oh, all right, I promise," Susan answered sourly.

Susan looked beautiful on her wedding day. Momma's dress was made of light dove gray silk satin. Tiny gathers at the waist fell gracefully down the dress. The sleeves were long and tight, and slightly puffy at the shoulders. The neckline was high. Momma had used several shades of pink glass beads to decorate embroidered roses of various sizes on the front of the dress. Green leaves and vines were embroidered among the roses. Around each cuff were more embroidered pink roses and green leaves. Susan had replaced the yellow ribbons on Doris' shoes with pink ones. She had also removed the yellow roses from the center of each shoe.

Doris' friend, Wilma Smith and her mother

had decorated the church with bunches and bunches of spring flowers grown in the Smith's yard. Mrs. Smith was famous for her flowers. She had won many blue ribbons at the yearly county fair. Momma had learned years ago not to compete with Mrs. Smith.

Doris was the maid of honor and wore her new dress. She knew it was the loveliest thing she had ever had and was very proud of making it. The dress buttoned down the front with gathers around the waist. The square neckline was low cut. Papa had questioned if the neckline was just a little too low. Momma had found some white lace in her sewing supplies for Doris to trim the dress. To make Papa happy, Doris cut two pieces of the lace into triangles. She sewed the bottom side of each triangle to each horizontal side of the neckline. Next, she sewed the second side of each triangle to the vertical sides of the neckline ending at the shoulders. Papa was satisfied with the addition of the lace. The two pieces met in the middle over the buttons.

The sleeves ended at the elbows. Doris divided the remaining lace into two equal parts and gathered each piece. She sewed one gathered piece to each sleeve. They hung delicately over her elbows.

Wilma Smith offered to let Doris wear a pair of her shoes. They were a bit too big, but Doris wore them anyway. She stuffed a cloth in the toe of each shoe, which made them very uncomfortable. Her feet hurt all day.

The day after the wedding Susan and Ethan left on the train for California. After the family and friends said their good-byes at the train depot, Momma came over to Doris and said, "That was really nice of you to let Susan have your new shoes. I was very surprised." Doris just stood there with her mouth open, staring at Momma without replying.

When she finally got home, she ran into the house. She looked everywhere she could think of. She went through all the dresser drawers and under her bed. Next, she looked through Susan's area. She even looked around Janie's space. Both her shoes and Momma's wedding dress were gone! "Why, the little snot! I hope she has twelve sons!"

Chapter 5

1884-85

In September of 1884, Janie cut her leg while playing outside around an old broken plow. It didn't seem like a bad cut. Momma washed it and covered it with a dressing for a couple of days. Everyone forgot about it.

A week or so later, Janie began to sweat and run a fever. She refused to drink water. She complained it hurt to swallow. One day Papa came into the house, causing a draft in the room. Janie's body started to spasm. Each day her illness became worse and worse. She had fits. Any touch to her body caused her to stiffen. Eventually, her back arched and she had a terrible grimace on her face. One day Papa brought the wagon up to the house. "Mae, Doris, get in the wagon."

"No, I won't," replied Momma. "I need to stay with Janie."

"Don't argue! Do as I say!" Papa's tone of voice upset Doris. He was always so quiet. Doris could not remember him ever speaking cross to Momma. Doris quietly climbed in. Momma stood on the porch with her arms crossed in front of her staring at Papa. She began to cry. Slowly, her body relaxed in defeat and she climbed in beside Papa. He gave Momma his handkerchief and put his arm around her. She put her head on his shoulder and started sobbing. They just drove around for an hour or so. Doris couldn't understand why. When they got back to the house, Janie was dead.

The people in the community were so very compassionate and comforting. Even so, living through the funeral and burying Janie was the hardest thing the family had ever faced. At the funeral dinner, held in the church basement, Wilma took Doris to another room and whispered, "I heard my papa telling Mr. Getz that Janie had lockjaw. Mr. Dodd smothered her to put her out of her misery. That's why your papa had you and your momma take that buggy ride." Doris didn't believe it, but was too afraid to ask Momma about it. She had heard rumors of this happening to other people.

Momma was shattered. The sparkle she radiated whenever she entered a room was gone. She didn't seem to care about anything. Momma didn't complain, but Doris knew she was also in physical pain. Most of the work around the house was now left to Doris. Doris didn't protest or mind. Her heart ached for her parents and for herself. She felt anger at Janie's dying.

About Christmastime, a terrible sickness lay on Weedy Creek. Papa had gone into town to get Momma more tonic from Doctor Little. A week before Christmas, Papa started coughing and running a fever. Doris was terrified he might have lockjaw. She questioned Papa and he reassured her he hadn't cut himself. He said it was only a cold. She did all that she could to help him. She applied a mustard plaster to his chest. Tearing up a flannel sheet into squares, she heated one at a time and rotated them to cover the plaster. It didn't however, seem to help relieve his congestion.

As the cold winter days passed, he coughed more and more. Sometimes, especially at night, he coughed so hard it almost seemed he was going to strangle. Momma helped warm flannel packs for his chest so Doris could get some rest. Both she and Doris took turns boiling water and setting the kettle by his bed trying to help him breathe.

Early on a cold morning, two days before Christmas, Doris came downstairs to relieve Momma who had been sitting up with Papa since midnight. Momma looked sadly at Doris through puffy, red rimmed eyes. Papa lay peacefully on the bed his eyes closed and hands folded. Momma looked at Doris. "He just gave a soft moan about two o'clock and quit breathing. He was so worn out from struggling to catch his breath."

They sat all morning beside the deathbed. Finally, Momma sighed, got up and told Doris to ride over to the Dodd farm. They would need the Dodds to help them get Papa to town. She dressed warmly as the day had turned bitterly cold. Her horse, Ginger, was not eager to leave the cozy barn.

Doris couldn't understand what was happening to her family. She thought maybe God was punishing her for something she had done. She was still angry because of Janie's death and now, papa's passing. How could a loving God allow her to suffer so much?

Rev. Rockwell came to visit Momma and Doris three weeks after Papa's death. He brought some pain medication with him for Momma. Her pain was getting worse and she was weakening. Doris was afraid Momma was not going to get better. While Momma slept, the pastor and Doris sat talking. "Brother Rockwell, what's happening? Doesn't God care? Where is He?"

"Doris, I don't know why God has allowed your family to face so much sorrow. He knows you're hurting. It's all right to be angry at God. He can take it. He loves you more than you can ever understand. Romans 8:28 tells us, 'And we know that all things work together for good to them that love God, to them who are the called according to his purpose.' God can take all that has happened to you and use it for your good. Your job is to trust Him and believe His promises. That is the beginning of healing. There was nothing you could have done to change what has happened.

It will take a long time to recover, maybe years. You can survive this. May I pray for you?"

Doris nodded and bowed her head.

"Heavenly Father, we know you love and care about us. You sent your Son, Jesus, to die for us. He lived on earth as a man. He cried when his friend died. You understand Doris' sorrow. We ask that she would feel Your arms around her. May she trust You, and find the peace that passes all understanding. We ask this in Jesus' holy name. Amen."

They talked on for some time. Doris felt less guilty, but her sorrow was still so great she thought her heart would break. Doris wasn't sure God was going to bring anything good out of all that had happened. She wasn't even sure she loved

God. She did not know that more sorrow
still lay ahead.

Chapter 6

February, 1885

On February 2, 1885, Doris sat at the kitchen table drinking tea. She had come in from gathering wood from the grove of trees beyond the creek. Her hands were cold. She wrapped them around the mug trying to warm them. Momma came slowly into the room. "Momma, you should have called me. I would have helped you get up. Let me get you a cup of tea."

"I'm fine, dear. I don't want any tea just

now. Sit and rest. This is a special day. Do you know what day this is?"

"Yes, of course. It's my twenty-second birthday."

Momma smiled and handed Doris a small box.

"The day you were born was much like this one. It was sunny but biting cold. Papa had gone to get Mrs. Dodd. She was expecting Randall, her first. Neither one of us knew much about what to do. She was an only child and I was the youngest in my family. Of course, we both had watched animals being born. But they seemed to have such an easy time of it. Adults never talked much about birthing around children. I guess we still don't.

"I'd been having pains for a day and a half. It was like you knew how cold it was and just didn't want to leave your warm, cozy nest. Papa arrived with Mrs. Dodd. Mr. Dodd came over later after he'd finished his chores. Poor Papa and Mr. Dodd stayed out in the barn most of the time. About two hours after dark, with one last push, there you were. You were the most beautiful baby I had ever seen. I loved you from the first moment I held you. And oh, how you could cry! Your lungs would pierce the air with an earsplitting wail. Papa said he thought you were mad to have been born. At first, he was afraid to hold you. I guess he thought you might break."

Both Momma and Doris laughed. "The next time Papa went into town he brought back what's in that box. Open it, sweetheart."

Doris lifted the lid. In the box was a small pair of earrings of ivory and pink cameo. The cameos were carved into hummingbirds drinking from bell flowers. Each cameo was surrounded by a lacy, scalloped setting in gold. Hanging at the bottom of each earring was an amethyst stone.

"I want you to have these, Doris."

"No, Momma! They are your treasure."

"Doris, I know I'm dying. These are all I have to give to you. Papa gave them to me when you were born. They should be yours. Please take them.

"There is something more we need to talk about. When your Uncle Bob was here, I signed papers to put the farm and my savings in your name. And I want you to sell this place."

"Oh, Momma no! I love living here."

"Doris, listen to me. You know you can't

live here alone. We haven't been able to keep up with all the work that needs doing. There is no way you can do it by yourself."

"I can hire some of the Bradley kids to help."

The Bradleys were a poor family living west of the Keplers. Mr. Bradley's first wife had died. There were three boys from that marriage. He and his present wife also had a number of children, who always appeared hungry. Several times the Keplers and other families had helped them with food and other necessities.

"That won't do. The Bradleys need their children to help at their place. Besides, where would you get the money to pay them? No, honey, sell out. Mr. Dodd has been after this land for years. He's asked me twice since Papa passed if I'd sell. He'll be fair in his dealings. We've been friends a long time.

"Another thing, you should marry. I've watched the young men when we've been in town. With just a little encouragement on your part, any one of them would jump at the chance to spark you. Take that boy, Randall Dodd. He's just three months younger than you. He's quite a looker and, more important, he's a fine young man. There's the possibility that Mr. Dodd might let the two of you live here if you two were married."

"But I don't love him, Momma. His pa took him out of school after just four years. I hardly know him."

"Doris, I hardly knew your papa before we married. My papa, Grandpapa Hooper, came to me and said Mr. Kepler had asked if I'd marry his son. Well, you can imagine my reaction. I said about the same thing you just said. My papa replied, 'Mae, Norman Kepler is a good Christian. He's stable and a hard worker. He'll make you a good husband. You won't go wrong hitching up with him. You can learn to love him after you're wed.'

"Well, I prayed about it. I decided if your papa wanted to marry me, he had to ask me. The next Sunday, I was coming out of church. He was standing by a big oak tree between the church and the cemetery. He looked so handsome standing there. For some reason, I remember how straight his back was, just like a soldier. Rays of light came through the tree and made his slicked down hair shine. There was a group of young men standing a-ways from him. At first, I thought he was going to join them. I sent up a quick prayer for him to stay by the tree. As I started to walk over to him, my sister started walking towards me. I lifted another prayer to heaven, and my ma called her away.

"I walked over to your papa. 'Norman,' I questioned, 'is there something you want to ask me?' He just stood there, a-staring. I thought maybe I was making a fool of myself. Then he got down on both knees, took my hands and started rambling. I don't remember a word he said except, 'marry me.' All the people standing in the church yard started clapping and laughing."

Both women laughed at Momma's story. "Doris, love did come."

They heard a horse riding into the yard. "I wonder if that's Mr. Dodd or one of his boys." Momma said the last part with a twinkle in her eye, that Doris had not seen since before Janie's passing.

They heard heavy boots on the porch, then a knock at the door. Doris got up to open the door. There stood the stranger whom Doris had seen in town. "Good afternoon, Miss. My name's Nate Clark. Doc Little asked me ta bring your ma this medicine."

"Ask the young man in, Doris."

"Oh, I'm sorry. Please come in. Let me take your coat. It is so nice of you to bring Momma's medicine so far and on such a cold day. Would you care for a cup of coffee?"

"That sounds mighty fine, miss."

"Come into the kitchen and meet Momma." She preceded Nate into the kitchen. "Momma, this is Nate Clark. Mr. Clark, this is my momma, Mrs. Kepler."

"Hello, Mr. Clark. Thank you for bringing

my medicine. Sit down. Have you had anything to eat?"

"Well, no, ma'am, I ain't."

"Get Mr. Clark some of that chicken stew you made us, Doris." Doris did as Momma asked.

After eating, Nate said, "Ma'am, I couldn't help but notice your wood pile is gettin' low. In kindness for the good meal, I'd like ta stock it up."

Chapter 7

Nate stayed on. At first, he slept in the barn. Doris had been sleeping in Momma's room to be close by if Momma needed help during the night. Momma suggested Nate move into the upstairs room. She figured since Doris wasn't using it, there was really no sense for Nate to be sleeping in a cold barn.

Nate didn't ask for any pay. This was good because there was none to give him. He really was helpful even though he went into town frequently. Momma said since Nate wasn't really a hired hand, they had no say in what he did. A couple of times Doris was sure Nate had come in drunk. She wanted to put a lock on the bedroom door, but she knew she couldn't. The door had to stay open. Momma needed the heat from the fireplace. It seemed she was always cold.

Many nights Doris spent on her knees begging God to heal Momma and not let her die. Not yet! Not so soon after all that had happened. Where was God, didn't He care?

One night as Doris was once again pouring out her heart to God, she felt the whisper of a still soft voice, "Doris, your mother is not going to get better. I will be here for her and for you. I will hold you in My strong right hand. My grace is sufficient for you. Trust me. My thoughts are not your thoughts nor My ways your ways." From that day on, Doris did everything she could to please and comfort her mother.

In mid-February, Doris had Nate move Janie's bed next to the fireplace for Momma. Doris slept in a chair next to her. As long as Momma was alive, Nate was mostly pleasant. Day by day Momma got weaker and weaker. It was difficult to get her to eat.

One Tuesday afternoon there was a knock at the door. Doris almost collapsed when she opened the door and saw Mrs. Ross standing there. "Mrs. Ross! Please come in. Let me take your coat. Momma, look who's here." Doris and Mrs. Ross walked over beside Momma's bed.

"Hello, Hazel, what a surprise!"

"Yes, I suppose it is. Mae, I knowed you've been sick for some time. I should have come before now. I brung you some chicken soup and a loaf of bread. Here, Doris." Doris took the gifts and set them on the dining room table. "I figured you might not have time to make bread being busy carin' for your ma.

"I come to tell you I'm sorry for the time we had our falling out. I knowed my Laura was a difficult, strong-willed child. Neither her Papa nor I was much good at making her mind. It were easier jest to let her have her way. I even knowed she had been unkind to Susan and I did nothing to stop it. I was wrong, and I'm sorry."

"Mrs. Ross, please sit down. Let me get us some tea." Doris picked up the soup and bread and hurried to the kitchen to prepare tea. She returned moments later carrying a tray with the tea items. Doris poured Mrs. Ross a cup and one for her Momma.

Momma needed Doris' help and only took a couple of small sips, before refusing anymore. Doris set the cup down.

"I brung a hymnal from church."

Doris lifted a quick silent prayer. "Oh, Lord, please don't let her start singing."

With a slight smirk, Mrs. Ross said, "I can't sing, as everyone knows. But these hymns are really beautiful poetry. If it would be a comfort to you, I'd like to read some."

"I'd like that very much, Hazel. And thank you for coming. Your words do my heart good. I should have tried harder to heal our differences."

"That's enough said about the past. Doris, if you got something to do, I can sit here for a while."

"I'll be in the kitchen if you need me." She

had dampened some clothes for ironing earlier in the morning. She put two irons on the stove to heat. While she waited, she poured herself a cup of tea and cut a slice of bread. Mrs. Ross was right: Doris hadn't had time to bake bread. She was so tired. Nate didn't do much to help with the farm labor any more. Besides doing most of the outside work, she had the inside work and the care of Momma. Once she had eaten, she folded her arms in front of her on the table and laid her head on them. She only meant to rest a few minutes.

The next thing she knew, someone was shaking her. "Doris, wake up. It's getting dark. I have to leave."

"Mrs. Ross, I'm sorry. I didn't mean to fall asleep. Thank you for coming. I'll see you out." Doris saw that Momma was sleeping as they passed her bed on the way to the front door.

"I'd like to come again, maybe in two or three days. I'll sit with your mother so you can have some time to yourself."

"Thank you, Mrs. Ross. I'd appreciate that."

More visits by Mrs. Ross never happened. Time for Momma had run out.

Chapter 8

The night Momma died Doris remembered the awful storm. The rain came down in sheets. Doris looked out the window several times during the night but it was so dark she couldn't see anything. About two o'clock a large limb came crashing through the kitchen window. Doris was trying to stuff rags into the hole when Nate came into the kitchen. He told her to go back to sit with her mother, he'd take care of the window. It was one of the kindest things he had ever done. She just hoped no more windows would be broken.

Near morning Momma opened her eyes and lifted her arms. She said, "You've come for me. I've been waiting. I knew you'd come." With that she breathed her last and joined Papa and Janie in eternity.

Doris sat by the bed weeping. She cried over and over, "Oh, Momma, oh, Momma, what am I going to do?" Finally, she sensed Nate near her. He was folding Momma's arms.

"I've het some water so's ya kin worsh yer ma. I'll hitch the horses so we can take yer ma ta town."

Doris washed Momma. She hadn't realized how thin Momma had become. When she had finished washing, she went into the bedroom to get Momma a dress. She saw the sky-blue dress with the pink flowers surrounding yellow centers. Her last act of kindness to her mother was to let Momma wear her cherished dress into eternity.

The ride to town was agonizing and cold. They stopped at the Dodd farm only long enough to tell them of Momma's passing. A short while after leaving the Dodd farm, Nate cleared his throat and said, "With yer ma gone, it ain't right for us to be livin on the farm alone. It would be best if we got married."

Doris wasn't sure she had heard him right.

"Did ya hear me? I know it may seem wrong to be talkin' about gettin' married so soon. But what other choice do ya have?" She would later remember those words so clearly.

They arrived in town in the late afternoon. The few people that were out on such a glum day stopped and stared as the wagon went by. Most knew what it carried. The first stop was the funeral parlor. Arrangements were made to have the funeral the next day. The mortician insisted that it was too soon. Doris didn't care. She just wanted the funeral over. Finally, he agreed to have things ready by the next afternoon. Several men living in town volunteered to get word about the funeral to out-of-town folks. Nate then dropped Doris off at the Smiths' house. She didn't see him again until after the funeral dinner.

Wilma gave Doris a hug. "I'm so sorry 'bout your momma. Whatever are you going to do now?"

"Nate asked me to marry him. He says it won't be right for us to stay at the farm alone."

Mrs. Smith was listening from the kitchen. She put down the rolling pin she had been using to roll out a pie crust and went into the living room. "You surely aren't serious! Why, Mr. Smith told me he saw Nate drinking in the saloon. He said that Nate even got into a fight over one of the women that works there. You know what kind of women they are!"

"So, what was Mr. Smith doing in the saloon?"

"Well, I never!" Mrs. Smith turned on her heels. As she left the room she said, "Remember, 'Marry in haste, repent at leisure.'"

The rain and cold continued the next day. Despite that, Doris was surprised and pleased at how many people came to the funeral. Even all of the Bradley family were present. Ungraciously, Doris figured it was for the dinner after the funeral.

Doris looked at Momma one last time before the casket was closed. Momma was beautiful. She looked peaceful. Doris whispered, "I love you, Momma. Tell Papa and Janie, I love them too."

Neighbors and friends rallied around Doris, setting a fine funeral dinner and offering to help however possible. Behind her back, the ladies whispered about all that had happened to the Kepler family. They felt sorry for Doris and at the same time were thankful it wasn't them dealing with such tragedy. The men wondered what Doris would do now. Some shook their heads at the thought of her living on the farm with that no-good man, Nate Clark. Most thought Mrs. Kepler had been very foolish to have allowed him to stay on at the farm. One man, a regular customer at the same bar Nate frequented, voiced the opinion that he thought Nate was on the run from the law. One bachelor expressed the hope of getting Doris to marry him.

Mrs. Rockwell, wife of the pastor, took Doris aside during the funeral dinner. "Doris, Mrs. Smith came to me quite concerned. She said you are considering marrying Nate Clark."

Doris was furious to learn Mrs. Smith was gossiping about her. She had all but decided not to marry Nate. She didn't love him nor did she trust him. She didn't quite know what came over her. "Yes, I am, as a matter of fact!"

"I think you should wait for a bit. You are under a lot of strain just now and may not be thinking clearly. You really don't know much about Nate. He's just a drifter."

"I resent Mrs. Smith spreading gossip about me and Nate."

"Well, she did say some worrying things about him. What would it hurt to wait just a couple of months? You are welcome to live with us. Nate could look after your farm 'til you decide. We could ride out every week or so and look in on things."

"Thank you, Mrs. Rockwell. I appreciate your concern, but I have decided." Rev. Rockwell was standing at the other side of the room with a group of men. Doris called out to him loud enough for all to hear, "Pastor, Nate and I want to get married. Can you perform the service tomorrow?"

The pastor walked over to Doris, took her by the elbow and escorted her to his study. He shut the door, "Doris, I don't believe I can in all good conscience marry the two of you. I just don't feel right about doing it. Besides it being much too soon after your ma's passing, you don't know Nate well enough. Sadly, I don't believe he is a good man. Please sleep on it tonight. You may feel differently in the morning. You and Nate come to my office tomorrow at nine o'clock. We'll pray and talk about your situation."

Doris decided to stay at the hotel instead of returning to the Smiths. She knew staying at the hotel would start tongues wagging. She also went to the bank to get some money. She was surprised at how much Momma and Papa had put aside.

That night alone in the hotel Doris climbed into bed. She began to cry. At first it was just soft weeping before changing to mournful heart wrenching sobs. "Oh, God where are You? Are You real? What am I to do? I don't want to marry Nate. I don't want to go to California. Oh, what, oh, what, am I to do?"

Her crying spent; she lay listening to the night sounds. Music was coming from a saloon. Voices of people walking on the board walk could be heard, if not understood. Several horses and a couple of wagons went by. Was that knocking? Someone was knocking at her door. She didn't want to talk to anyone. Maybe it was Nate. She sure didn't want to see him.

The knocking came again. This time a little harder. "Miss Kepler, please open the door. I need to talk to you."

"Go away. I don't want to see or talk to anybody."

"Please. It's important."

Groaning, Doris picked herself up from the bed and dragged her weary body to the door. Doris gasped. Standing in the hall was, what her mother would have called, a woman of the evening. The first thing Doris noticed was the woman's very low cut, very red dress. The dress sparkled in the lamp light and scarcely came down to the woman's knees. Her shoes were red with gold buckles. Her hair was also red, done up in an outrageous mass of curls. Several fancy gold embellishments held the coif in place. She did have lovely dark brown eyes, high cheek bones, a flawless complexion and full lips colored bright red. Red dangly earrings touched her bare shoulders. Doris didn't know what to say.

The woman finally spoke. "Honey, I know I don't have no right coming here after you just planted your ma. I just felt like I had to say somethin' about Nate. I work at the saloon Nate likes to drink at. He's there now, talkin' about you. He's talkin' about you two gettin' hitched. I just want to warn you, don't marry that man. He's not a nice person. He'll make your life miserable. You'll regret it the rest of your life."

Doris stood in the doorway gawking at the woman in red. She couldn't think or get beyond all the red. "Well, Honey, I've got to go. Consider yourself warned." Having said that, the woman turned on her heel and walked away. Doris closed the door and leaned against it starting to cry once again. Was the woman telling the truth or was she jealous and wanted Nate for herself? Walking slump-shouldered to the bed, she flung herself on it.

It was the next morning before she saw Nate again. He came into the café as she was eating breakfast. He looked a little bleary-eyed. "I didn't know you checked into the hotel. I went to the Smith house lookin' for ya."

"I'm sorry, Nate. I didn't see you around

town or I would have told you." She started to tell him she had withdrawn money from the bank then stopped. She wasn't sure why.

"So, what's your answer to our weddin'?"

"Yes, Nate, I'll marry you. But Rev. Rockwell has refused to perform the ceremony."

"We'll go see Noah Chadwick; he's a justice of the peace and willing to do about anything for money."

Chapter 9

The wedding night was a nightmare. They ate supper alone in their hotel room. Then Nate left. Doris waited for him until midnight then decided to go to bed although she slept fitfully. She was upset and irritated. This wasn't what she had expected. Nate eventually returned. He was drunk and smelled like liquor. Nate flopped down on the bed and rolled over on top of Doris. He kissed her softly at first, then hard on the mouth. He started groping her. Doris didn't know what she was supposed to do. He was very rough; he was hurting her. Suddenly he flung himself to the other side of the bed, swearing under his breath. Doris wasn't sure what he had said; it sounded like "I can't do it."

She lay in the bed humiliated, not daring to move. Nate began to snore noisily. It reminded her of Papa's snoring. The sisters used to lay upstairs in their beds and listen to their papa. That had been a pleasant sound. The only pleasant thing about Nate's snoring was that he was asleep and not touching her. She lay awake all night. She was demeaned and scared all at the same time. She realized she had made the worst mistake of her life.

Eventually the morning activities began to stir. She could hear birds chirping, doors banging, and a horse being hitched to a wagon. The window was open a crack to let in fresh air. Two men were talking just below it. She recognized the first speaker. It was Jimmy Murphy. Papa had sometimes hired him to help with special projects on the farm.

"Man, that Clark sure got drunk last night. Ya wouldn't know he had a piece of jam like that Doris waiting for him up in the hotel. I sure wouldn't have been letting her wait like that!" Both men laughed.

The second one, Doris couldn't place his voice, replied, "Well, they've been living on the farm together for some months now. Maybe last night wasn't that special." The men laughed again as they walked away.

Angry, Doris got up and dressed as quietly as possible. She left the room and went to the hotel café. Two waitresses were serving breakfast. Doris had gone to school with both of them. The older waitress had quit after the fifth grade;

the younger one had finished the eighth grade with Doris but had not gone on to high school.

The county high school was in Stoneville, fifteen miles from Weedy Creek. In fact, Doris was the only one in her eighth-grade class to graduate from high school. This had required her to board at her aunt's and uncle's home in Stoneville. Susan had started high school two years later but was so homesick she dropped out.

The older waitress came over to Doris. "Where's your hubby, Doris? Sleepin' in?" The younger waitress heard this and giggled. Doris felt her cheeks warm.

"Bring me a cup of coffee. Where my husband is, is none of your business." She sat drinking coffee for almost an hour. After her third cup she knew that she could wait no longer. "Please bill the coffee to my hotel room." She gave the rude waitresses a hard stare and returned to her room.

Nate was still sleeping. Doris had been taught not to touch a sleeping man to wake him. He could very likely come instantly awake, fighting or pointing a weapon. Still, she managed to say, "Nate, Nate. Get up. We need to get back to the farm. There are animals that need care."

Nate opened his bleary, bloodshot eyes. He looked around as though he wasn't sure where he was. Then he slowly sat up, not looking at Doris. Grabbing his pants, he finished buttoning them, picked up his war bag and walked out of the room.

As she waited for Nate, Doris took the time to pack her few belongings. To her surprise when Nate returned, he had shaved and combed his hair. Without looking at Doris he picked up her satchel and said, "Let's go." They stopped only long enough at the hotel desk to pay their bill, which Doris had to pay. Nate said he didn't have any money.

They didn't go into the café for breakfast. Doris was glad of this. She didn't want to face the waitresses again. She was sure if she tried to eat anything, she would throw up.

The ride back to the farm was done in silence. They did not stop at the Dodd farm. Doris was hopeful no one would see them pass.

Doris was dreading the coming night. When it did come, the strangest thing happened. Nate got up from the supper table and went upstairs. Doris went into the room she had been sharing with Momma and waited for Nate. He never came. Nor in the weeks that followed did he ever come to her bedroom. Doris wondered if there was something wrong with her. Was she so repulsive that Nate regretted marrying her? At the same time, she was relieved. Although she had grown up on a farm and knew about animals, she was ignorant about how husbands and wives acted towards each other in private. Momma never talked to her about such things. She wondered if Momma had talked to Susan before she got married.

Nate went to Weedy Creek frequently and even began drinking at home. He had found Doris' coin purse containing the money she had withdrawn from the bank. Most of the money was now gone. Doris could not deny that Nate was lazy. She continued to do the majority of the chores.

Less than a month after the wedding Nate started harassing Doris about selling the farm. Doris realized, that was why he had married her. He really didn't care one bit about her. He just wanted money. She refused to sell. It was during a heated argument that he first hit her. Mrs. Smith's words of warning came back to her: "Marry in haste, repent at leisure." Doris decided Mrs. Smith was right after all.

Doris stopped her contemplation and came back to her present situation. She flopped the wedding picture of Susan and Ethen down on the table so hard the glass broke. Sighing she walked outside.

Chapter 10

June, 1885

Ignorant of Nate's whereabouts or his criminal activities, Doris spent the day doing her chores with his fate never far from her mind. She spent another fitful night wondering.

Nate rode on into the night. The rain had stopped for several hours, and then started again. There was no moon; it was pitch black. Nate's side was bleeding more now. He stopped and tried to wrap an extra shirt he had with him around his waist, without much success.

"I'm so tired. I can't keep my eyes open. Beacon, I hope you know where we are, because I got no idea." Beacon trotted on through the dark night.

Nate realized he must have been sleeping when he almost fell off his horse. It was just before dawn.

A voice came out of the blackness, "What's you want, mister?"

"I need help. Please help me."

"Yeah, you one of them sidewinders that robbed the bank and killed the clerks? They said a couple of you was shot."

"No, no. I'm just lost. I ain't robbed nobody."

"You look like yer shot up to me. Jest you ride on."

"I can't."

Nate could see the old man now. He was holding a shotgun. The man started to raise the gun in Nate's direction. Nate instinctively pulled his gun and shot the old man. Not even looking at him, Nate spurred Beacon up to a nearby house.

With excruciating pain, Nate dismounted. His legs wouldn't hold him and he fell into the mud. He lay there waiting to see if anyone would come out of the house. No one did. Weary and weak from loss of blood, Nate crawled onto the porch, rested a few minutes, and then made it into the house. There was a small fire in the fireplace. The warmth felt so good. He saw a half-eaten bowl of oatmeal on a table.

As he began to eat the oatmeal, he thought about his life. **What happened to me? Where did I go wrong? I had a good family. I shouldn't have turned out this way, killing an old man for a half-eaten bowl of cold oatmeal. My name—Nathaniel—a gift of God. Some gift I was.**

He remembered his mom and dad. **Pop was a barber and a good one. He always talked to me about coming into the barbering business when I was older. Ma helped out that old lady Ambrose in her millinery shop. Ma was really talented about designing hats with feathers and little flowers.** Even in Nate's misery he chuckled as a memory returned. **One time when Ma was gone, Hank and I put on some feathered hats Ma had just finished decorating. We raced around the house pretending we were fierce Indians. Ma**

124

was as mad as a wet hen when she got home. He smiled at the memory.

His mind kept racing: **Our family went to church every Sunday. Why, I even won a prize for memorizing Bible verses in Sunday school. What were they? I remember there was a bunch of 'em. I had a hard time memorizing those verses, but I wanted the prize. Can't even remember now what the prize was.**

The first verse was about everyone bein' a sinner. For all have sinned, and come short of the glory of God.[1] Well I sure do fit that one.

The next one, oh, why am I trying to think? I'm so tired. Yeah, now I remember. Our sins have to be paid for. For the wages of sin is death; but the gift of God is eternal life through Jesus Christ our Lord.[2] I sure seem ta be payin'.

But the teacher said it wasn't physical death the Bible was talking about. It's eternal death and that Jesus has already paid for them on the cross. That's it. Something about believin' in Jesus and confessin' our sins. If thou shalt confess with thy mouth the Lord Jesus, and shalt believe in thine heart that God had raised him from the dead, thou shalt be saved.[3]

Well, I reckon I've come too far for even God ta save me now. Oh, how I wish I could see my folks. I wonder if Hank went inta the hair-cuttin' business with Pop. Why did I have to be so pigheaded? I'm so tired. If I could jest lie down in that bed for a few minutes. Better not. I've got to git goin'. Those men, they'll find out about the farm. I've got to git there before they do.

Nate managed to get out of the chair and out to the porch, where he could see the horses by the water trough. He gave a weak whistle and Beacon trotted up. The Morgan followed. "Thank you, Lord." The words were out of his mouth before he realized he had said them. Nate tied the Morgan's reins to Beacon's tail, and had to use a large rock in the front yard to mount Beacon.

As he rode out of the yard, he saw the old man lying in the mud. He cried great heart-wrenching, heaving cries. "Oh, Lord, I'm sorry for all my sins. I'm so sorry. If you can forgive me, please help me to get to Doris before those men do."

With that he laid his head on Beacon's neck and fell asleep.

---

1. Rom. 3:23 (KJV).

2. Rom. 6:23 (KJV).

3. Rom. 10:9 (KJV).

Chapter 11

June, 1885

Doris was in the chicken coop gathering eggs. "You chickens have sure been doing a good job laying. I don't know what I'm going to do with so many eggs. Might as well take some over to the Bradley family. Don't really care for Mr. Bradley or those boys of his. I do feel for Mrs. Bradley. She's not much older than me, but birthing a baby every year sure has aged her. I remember when she married old Mr. Bradley. She wasn't more than fourteen or fifteen, and him already having three or four young'uns from the first Mrs. Bradley."

Doris heard hoof beats in the yard. She went to see who it was. "Hello, Sheriff. What brings you out this way?"

"Doris, when was the last time you saw Nate?"

Doris' face became worried. "It's been about two weeks. He went to Weedy Creek to buy supplies. I expected him to be gone only a couple of days. About four days after he left, Ginger – that's my horse – came home. Nate had taken her with him for carrying supplies. What's wrong?"

"I'm sorry to be the one telling you. He's been named in a bank robbery in Ardmore Bend."

"Ardmore Bend? Isn't that in Colorado? That can't be!"

"I got a telegram yesterday naming him as one of the robbers. Two bank tellers and a lady customer were shot and killed."

Doris sagged and felt light-headed. The sheriff jumped off his horse and helped her into the house and sat her down in an overstuffed chair. He went into the kitchen and poured her a glass of water from a pitcher on the table. After giving the glass to Doris, he continued, "Before I came out here, I went through some old 'Wanted' posters."

He withdrew a poster from his vest pocket, unfolded it and held it up for Doris to see. "Isn't this Nate?"

"It looks somewhat like Nate, yes. But it says this man's name is Nathaniel Clarkson."

"Doris, I believe this is Nate. He's just

dropped the 'son' from his last name. He's wanted for bank robbery in Missouri. There's a reward on him. Are you sure Nate hasn't been around here?"

"Yes, Sheriff. Like I said, I haven't seen him for going on three weeks now."

"You'd best pack a few things and come back to town with me. You know, Doris, you may not even be legally married. There's a rumor he was already married when he married you."

"Not legally married!" Doris sat in her mother's chair stunned. **What more can happen to me?**

"Sheriff, there is something I need to do. I'll get ready and come in with the wagon tomorrow."

"Doris, I don't think that is wise. There are three outlaws left, not counting Nate.

If they should come here and Nate's not with them, there's no telling what might happen to you."

"How would they know to come here? Surely, Nate wouldn't tell them about me."

"You don't know that for a fact. Besides, word gets around pretty quick about things like this. Now get some things together and come along."

"No, I must do a couple of chores first. Please be so kind as to stop at the Dodd's farm on your way back to town. Tell them to expect me. I'll stay there tonight and come to town in the morning."

"It's against my better judgment, but all right."

The sheriff left. Doris sat in the chair. **There's no way I'm going to town and have Mrs. Smith and those other old biddies** say, "I told you so, I told you so." I'll pack the wagon with as much from the house as I can and go to Darley and sell the stuff. I'll send Susan a telegram to let her know I'll be coming by train for a visit. Then I'll write Mr. Dodd and take him up on his offer to buy the farm.

She felt guilty as she made her plans, but she also felt relief to learn that she most likely wasn't really married to Nate. She would have to make sure that was true.

Early that evening as Doris was trying to decide what to take with her, she again heard horse hooves. This time they were coming from behind the house. She went out the screen door. She saw Nate fall off Beacon to the ground. He screamed in pain.

"Nate. Oh, Nate."

Nate heard Doris' familiar voice. "Doris, git out of here. You have to git."

"Just hush. The sheriff came by looking for you. He told me all about the robbery and the killings. Let me help you into the house."

"I can't make it, Doris. I can't."

"Yes, you can. You've made it this far. It's only a few more feet."

Doris tried her best to support him as he weakly staggered into the kitchen. He collapsed onto the floor.

"Let me help you get out of these dirty clothes. We've got to get your wounds taken care of."

"No, Doris. Just git me a drink of water."

She got a cup from the cupboard and poured water from the pitcher. Nate did not have enough strength to lift his head. Doris dripped water into his mouth.

"Doris, I know I'm dyin'. The pain is awful. A bullet's still in my side. It hurts so much. I'm hit in the arm, too. I can't even feel my fingers. Oh, Doris, it's worse than anything I've ever felt. Get me my bottle. It's behind..."

"I know where it is." Doris got up and retrieved a whiskey bottle from where Nate had it hidden. Again, she slowly dripped the liquid into Nate's mouth. This started Nate coughing. Blood oozed out of his mouth. He started crying. He was the most pitiful man she had ever seen. She wasn't sure what to do. Her heart ached for him, for herself, for the lies, for the hurt and for what should have been. Her feelings were so muddled. She was angry for the way Nate had treated her, for marrying her when he already had a wife. Yet she was also so very sad.

She knew he was dying and decided to make his passing as easy as she could. She tried to give him more whiskey but he couldn't take it. She got up, wet a towel in cold water, and began wiping his face.

"I have to tell you some things before I die." Haltingly Nate began to talk, "I've got ta make things right with you Doris."

"Please don't talk, just rest. I'll do what I can to ease your pain."

"Please, listen. Yer not gonna like what I have ta say. We ain't rally married."

Doris had been kneeling beside Nate. She leaned back on her heels. "I know we're not, Nate."

"It was all a lie, Doris. My name's not Clark.

It's Clarkson. I already got a wife and even a son in St. Louis. Please, write her. Her name is Rachel. Just tell her I'm dead. Don't tell her who you are. I know I'm askin' a lot of you. Say you will, please."

"I'll try," she replied, very reluctantly and not very truthfully.

"Doris, I'm so sorry and 'shamed of how I lied ta ya and how I treated ya. Ya deserve better than a wretch like me."

His voice became so weak Doris could hardly hear him. She had to bend close to his face. "You have ta git out of here. The other men are comin'. Don't be here when they git here. Just leave. Yer not safe here. I'm so sorry, Doris." He looked at her tear-stained face and closed his eyes for the last time.

How long Doris continued to sit on her

heels, staring into nothing, she didn't know.
She was so tired. Her heart was heavy.
She couldn't think. Slowly she got up and
walked into the bedroom. She fell across
the bed and she cried herself to sleep.

The next morning Doris awoke and felt the
warm sun shining on her. She lay there just
soaking in the warmth. Her head ached.
Her back hurt from helping Nate into
the house.

She sat up on the side of the bed and
looked into the dresser mirror. She was
shocked at what looked back at her. Her
eyes were mere slits, the lids red. The bun
at the back of her head was lopsided and
falling apart. Hair hung in sweaty strings.
Her dress was covered in a dark brown
stain –Nate's blood.

Then she heard the horses whinnying. "Oh,

those poor creatures. They've been out there all night."

She quickly got up and walked into the kitchen. There lay Nate so still, his life all gone. She returned to the bedroom and grabbed a sheet. Just before she draped it over him, she looked at him one last time. "Why, God, why? Why is all this happening?"

Again, the horses snorted. She covered Nate and went to help the horses. They needed water and feed and a good rub-down. Those things she could do.

In the barn she removed the saddle from the Morgan and the saddle bags fell off. Some of the money spilled out. **Paper money? I've never seen paper money before. Well, I'm not taking this money to the sheriff. Likely as not, very little, if any, of it would ever get back to the bank in**

Ardmore Bend. I've got to think. I've got to have a plan.

After seeing to the needs of the horses, Doris started to walk back to the house. She had to get herself cleaned up. There was an indoor pump in the kitchen, but to use that would require her to step over Nate. She just couldn't bring herself to do that. However, near the remains of the soddy was the old pump, now used to water the garden in dry weather.

Outside the back door of the kitchen were a wash-up pan and a bar of soap. She found some rags in the barn to use for drying herself. After fetching the pan and soap Doris walked to the outdoor pump, filled the pan with water then carefully walked around the house to the front door. She deliberately kept her eyes off the entrance to the kitchen and went into the bedroom. Stripping off her garments, she scrubbed herself clean in the cold water, wishing she had time to wash her hair. Instead, she brushed and brushed and brushed her long hair.

While cleaning herself up she formed a plan. **I've got to see that the money gets returned to the bank in Ardmore Bend. I can hitch Beacon and Ginger to the wagon. Even going easy, we should get there in a few days. Maybe I'll just let the Morgan go. He's probably stolen anyway. He can find his own way home.** She hurriedly dressed in clean clothes and pinned up her hair.

Doris returned to the barn and picked up the money. She put it back in the saddle bags, and heaved them over her shoulder. Hurrying to the house she tossed them over the back of a chair. She tried not to look at the shrouded Nate, but walked into the bedroom and removed pillowcases from the bed pillows to use for carrying her supplies.

Momma had a cedar chest given to her by her parents as a wedding gift. In the bottom of it was a black tin box containing important papers, including the deed to the farm. She removed the deed and stuffed it into her pocket. As she was about to leave the bedroom, Doris noticed the yellow ribbons from her shoes hanging on the edge of the dresser mirror. Without knowing why, she grabbed them and stuffed them in her dress pocket.

What am I going to do about Nate? I can't just leave him here. She stared at the shrouded figure. **Why did I ever marry you?**

Then she remembered Rachel, Nate's "real" wife. The anger she had been dealing with welled up more powerfully than she had ever felt before, penetrating her whole being. She took several deep breaths and sighed. Softly and with great sadness, she said, "I guess Rachel has a right to know what happened to you. I'll send her a telegram when I get to Ardmore Bend. I've still got to do something about your body. I just can't leave you lying here like this. How long will it be before someone comes here looking for me and instead finds you?"

She finally decided that on her way west to Darley she would ride over to the Bradley farm. **I'll hide Beacon and the wagon in the woods while I'm there, so they won't suspect me of going anywhere. I'll ride Ginger onto the Bradley place and tell them that Nate has had an accident. And I need their help getting him to town. I'll ask them to meet me at my house and**

quickly ride away before they have a chance to ask any questions.

She knew this didn't make much sense. The Dodd farm was closer to her farm and on the way to town. She was hoping that out of curiosity the Bradleys would go to her farm.

Chapter 12

Doris returned to the barn carrying one of the pillowcases. She was about to release the Morgan when once again she heard horses coming into the yard.

"Hey! Nate. You in there? Nate, this is Monte. You there?"

Three outlaws cautiously approached the house, dismounting near the porch rail. Doris was terrified. Now what was she to do? All her supplies, including the little money she had, were still in the house in the other pillowcase. She knew she couldn't stay. She slowly walked the three horses out a side door which was away from the view of the house. She reached the woods without being seen. She led the three saddleless horses into to a small ravine fastening their reigns to some brush. She climbed the rise, and resting on her stomach, watched the outlaws.

She could barely hear the men in the house. "What's that on the floor there?" asked one of the outlaws.

"It looks like a body wrapped up," replied another. He approached Nate and drew back the sheet. "Well, will you look-see here. It's Nate. He's dead! There's the saddle bags, see if the money's in 'em."

"They're empty, Monte."

Monte walked over to Nate's body and gave

it a kick. "Wad ja' do with the money? Earl, Lloyd, look around see if you kin find the money. Look at this on the table. 'Pears someone was fixin' ta leave. This here's women's stuff."

With a lot of noise, banging around and yelling, they found nothing. "Curse you, Nate Clarkson!" shouted Monte. "Earl, go upstairs and have a look. Maybe the woman's hiding up there."

Earl took the stairs two at a time. He looked under the beds. He could see there was no other place to hide so he pulled open the drawers dumping them on the floor. Coming down the stairs and almost tripping over his own feet, he told Monte, "Ain't nobody up there and nothin' worth takin'. I say we torch the place. That'll teach 'em ta try ta cheat us!"

"Go ahead, set fire to this place! Wherever

his woman's hiding, there won't be any reason for her ta come back."

Fleeing the blaze as they set the house on fire, the men ran outside to safety. They headed to the barn, rummaging through it, looking for the money. With no success, they set it on fire and rode away.

"Where ya 'spose the woman went, Monte?" asked Earl.

"If she has the money, she either went ta give it ta the sheriff or she's keepin' it. Let's ride into Weedy Creek first. We'll keep an eye on things, see what we can learn."

Doris waited with tears flowing down her cheeks. All she had in the world was going up in flames. Momma's beautiful things, all the lovely pictures Janie had drawn, were gone forever.

Doris stayed hidden, not daring to move.

Just as she decided that it was safe to ride out, several of the Dodds, having smelled the smoke and seen the fires, rode into the yard from the east. This was followed by the Bradleys coming from the west. Doris moved a little deeper into the woods. She could see the people but not hear them. Most of the fire had burnt itself out. They walked around the house pointing to various items. They stood where the kitchen door had been for some time, talking. Doris figured they could probably see the remains of Nate's body and wondered what was going on. She hoped she didn't get the blame for his death and the fire. After about an hour everyone mounted their horses and left.

Doris still waited. She wanted to go back to see if she could salvage anything. She started for the barn as darkness was coming on. Again, she heard somebody coming. She edged back into the woods. It was two of the older Bradley boys. They dismounted, went into the smokehouse, and in a few minutes came out, each carrying hams and bacon.

"Those little thieves," Doris said to the horses. Then she decided, **"Oh, what does it matter! That family's so poor; they need the meat."** After they left, Doris waited until total darkness.

A slip of a moon gave just enough light for Doris to see. She went to the root cellar, since the boys hadn't thought of looking there. Candles were stored there to be used in case of an emergency. She lit two. She found jars of jam, several jars of green beans, tomatoes and applesauce, half a gunnysack of onions, and a few potatoes left from last year's harvest.

The root cellar was also used as a storm

refuge. Momma had stored several old blankets there, to be used if needed. Doris carefully wrapped the glass jars in a blanket. Once outside she looked at the wagon; it was burned beyond use. Making do, she tore a blanket into strips. She wrapped the strips around the jar-filled blanket, and tied it so that it balanced onto Ginger' back. She hoped she had wrapped them adequately.

On impulse she decided to look in the smokehouse. Maybe the boys had missed something. At first, she didn't think anything was left. Then she spied some bacon, which she wrapped in another blanket and rebalanced the load for Ginger. She was about to leave when she remembered the chickens.

In the chicken coop she found a couple of cages. She managed to get a dozen chickens into each cage. She knew the eggs would break so she didn't bother with them. After dragging the crates outside, she ripped another blanket into strips and used them to tie the crates onto Beacon. He didn't like it one bit and pranced around in disgust.

Thus prepared, she would have to ride the Morgan without a saddle. Before leaving, Doris walked around the house trying to see if there was anything of use, she could salvage. There was nothing. She had no money and no change of clothing. Standing on a tree stump, she managed to get on the Morgan's back. She silently thanked Papa for insisting she learn to ride well, even bareback. Grabbing the reins of Ginger and Beacon, she trotted out for the last time. She rode for as long as she could. Finally, she could go no farther. She slid off the horse, tethered all three horses

to a tree and lay down on the grass. Doris
was instantly asleep.

Chapter 13

Doris awoke to the smell of coffee and frying bacon. As she sat up, she saw what at first, she thought was a small man. This person was dressed in dirty, patched, blue jeans, and a faded flannel shirt that appeared to have been red at one time. A very large sombrero made it difficult to see any telltale features. When the stranger spoke, Doris realized it must be a woman.

"So, yer awake. Thought you were gonna sleep all day. You must be Doris Clark or Kepler."

"How is it you know my name?"

"Huh, the whole county's lookin' fer you. I was in Weedy Creek yesterday afternoon. Just as I was fixin' ta leave, a farm kid came flyin' in shoutin', 'The Kepler farm's been burnt and there's a body in the house!'

"He told the sheriff his pa didn't think it were you. It looked like a man to him. You should have heard the people start squawkin'. Most think it were your husband. One old woman said you probably kilt him, his being so mean and all. Then the sheriff said your husband was wanted for robbin' a bank and killing two clerks.

"That caused more speculation. Folks think maybe you were hidin' him and them hoot owl outlaw friends of his showed up and kilt him for runnin' off with the money and snatched you. 'Bout that time the sheriff quieted them down and said he'd ride out with the coroner to have a look-see.

"Now c'mon over here and git yerself some breakfast. When your done eatin' you can tell me what really happened. It's my coffee but your bacon. As Doris got up, she saw the horses had been unpacked. They were contentedly munching grass. The chickens had been let out of the cages and were pecking for bugs.

"Thanks for looking after the animals. I was just too tired last night."

As Doris approached the woman, she thought she must be about her mother's age. However, this woman's skin was very wrinkled and brown. Momma had always taken great care to keep her skin from the sun; it had been smooth and very pale. The woman's hair appeared to be white, what little Doris could see under the sombrero.

Doris sat down on a log near the fire. She was hungry. Her last meal was breakfast yesterday. She was curious about this woman and also very thankful for her help.

"My name's Rose Elder." Rose held out her hand. Doris had never shaken anyone's hand before. She wasn't even sure which hand to use. Since the woman held out her right hand, Doris also extended her right hand. Rose squeezed it so hard Doris thought her fingers were going to break.

As they ate, Doris told Rose the whole sad story. "The man in the fire was my husband. He was all shot up and died a few minutes after getting home. The sheriff told me about him being a bank robber and a killer.

"I was in the barn getting ready to leave when the other robbers rode in. I hid in the woods and watched as they burned the house and barn." She began to cry. "Everything I have in this world is gone. Everything!"

"Now don't be cryin'. It ain't good to hold onto things too tight. Life shouldn't churn around stuff."

"But I have nothing! I don't have any family. I don't even have a friend." Doris' face was wet from tears and her nose was running.

"I can be your friend, Doris."

Doris gathered her skirt and cleaned her face and nose with it. She looked at Rose. "Thank you, Mrs. Elder. I can really use a friend right now."

"Call me Rose. So, what happened to the bank money? Did it burn up?"

"No, I hid it. I'm going to Ardmore Bend. I'm going to let them know at the bank where it is."

"You know them hoot owls are lookin' for ya. If they find ya, you'll be in a heck of a lot of trouble. The best thing ya can do is ta jest tell the authorities. Let them handle it."

"I know I should do that. I just wanted to get away. Doing this seemed to give me a purpose. You understand, don't you?"

"Reckon I do. However, you do know yer in Kansas? You've been riding southeast. Ardmore Bend is northwest."

"It was dark when I left. I didn't know where I was going. I guess I'm lost."

"You could take a train to Ardmore Bend. That would be faster and much easier on you."

"I don't have any money."

"You could sell your horses."

"I figure the Morgan is stolen. I'd planned to let him go and find his own way home. After I couldn't use the wagon, I needed him. I don't have the bills of sale for the other two. They got burnt up."

"I'd say yer in a fine fix."

Doris felt uncomfortable with all the talk about her situation. So, she changed the subject. "What are you doing out here alone?"

"I'm lookin' for my daughter."

"You lost your daughter! How awful. How long has she been missing?"

"Ten years."

"Ten years!"

Rose gave a small chuckle. "Here, have another cup of coffee and I'll tell you my sad tale." Rose poured each of them a cup of coffee. "Sorry, I don't have no milk or sugar."

"That's all right. I don't mind it black."

"Well, this is my story. About ten years ago my husband wanted our Saree to marry the town blacksmith. Her pa thought the only purpose for a woman was ta marry, have babies and take care of her man. Saree had just turned fifteen. The blacksmith was a widower with a new baby. Saree wanted no part of him or the baby. The blacksmith was a nice enough fellow. Saree jest wasn't ready for a husband or baby.

"My husband, Elmer, got real mean with Saree. He told her she would marry the blacksmith. The morning he planned ta take her ta town, she was gone. I was beside myself with fright. I was gone three days lookin' for her. When I got back, Elmer was sick in bed. Doc said he'd had a heart seizure. The last words Elmer spoke to me was that he was sorry and I was to find Saree and bring her home. Then he died.

"I'm letting a nice couple sharecrop my farm. They pay my share ta the bank. Whenever I'm a-needin' cash, I send the bank president, who happens to be my sister's husband, a telegram. He telegraphs the money, to the local bank in the town I'm stayin' at, for me."

"Where have you been looking for Saree?"

"Oh, honey. I been from Texas to Wyomie and Mississippi to Californee and 'bout all points in between."

"How do you go about asking for her?"

"I go ta a town and looks over the saloons and brothels."

"Why would you look in places like that?"

"Cuz, I figure a gal with no education ain't gonna get no other kind of job."

"What are you going to do when you find her?"

"I'm gonna put my arms 'round her, tell her I love her, and I want her ta come home."

The conversation stopped; each woman lost in her own thoughts. Finally, Rose said, "What do you say we ride on tagether? I haven't been ta Ardmore Bend in several years."

"I'd like that," replied Doris. "I do need to go to some town and send a couple of telegrams. I'll have to send them collect.

But I'm sure the people I'm sending them to will pay."

"I'll pay for the telegrams."

"No, that's not necessary! I know the people getting the telegrams. I'm sure they'll pay."

"Colby is north of here. If you don't mind staying there for a day, I'll send one ta my brother-in-law. I'm gettin' short on funds. I'll have him telegraph me some money. Also, I'm thinkin', are your horses broke ta pulling a wagon?"

"Yes, both Ginger and Beacon are. Why?"

"We can buy us a wagon. We could let that Morgan go; he'll find his way home like you said. Letting your horses and my horses trade off pulling, we could make pretty good time."

"That sounds like a really good idea to me. I'd appreciate that."

"Well, the day's a-wastin'. Let's get the horses ready. We should be there by supper."

The two rode mostly in silence. Doris was getting sore, as she wasn't used to riding horseback for so long, especially without a saddle. She finally had to ask Rose if they could stop and rest. "I'm sorry, child. Should have appreciated you needed ta stop."

They rested for a couple of hours, ate cold bacon left over from breakfast and drank water from a nearby creek. Then they traveled on. They neared Colby in the late afternoon.

"It'll be best if we don't take all the horses ta town with us. We'll leave the extry horses hidden. If we ride in trailing three extry ones, it might raise questions."

Rose had two horses with her and Doris had the Morgan, Ginger and Beacon. They found a place near a small stream, and the area appeared secure. They hobbled the extra horses front to back, to keep them from wandering away. The horses would be able to move enough to graze and get water.

They rode slowly into Colby. It was unusual for two lone women, one wearing men's clothing and another riding saddleless, to ride into a town far from civilization. Several people stopped and stared at them, but no one questioned them. They went first to the telegraph office.

Doris had never sent a telegram. Rose wrote out hers first, as Doris watched. When Rose finished, Doris asked the agent for two sheets of paper. She had been thinking all day what to say in the telegrams; now she carefully wrote out the words. The first one read:

Frank Dodd,
Willing to sell farm for price offered earlier. Send money to me care of Ardmore Bend, Colorado. Will send deed by return mail. I am fine. Going to California to live with Susan.
Doris Kepler Clark

The second one was similar:

Robert Hooper,
Closing bank account. Send money to me care of Ardmore Bend, Colorado. I am fine. Going to California to live with Susan. Doris Kepler Clark

Rose then handed the money to the telegrapher.

Doris thought she needed to explain to Rose why she hadn't requested money be sent to her in this town.

"Rose, I'm afraid to let anyone know where I am until I get to Ardmore Bend and talk to the bank president."

Rose called over her shoulder as she started for the front door. "Honey, don't you trouble yerself. What's ever ya do is fine with me."

She opened the door, then slammed it shut, whispering to her friend, "There's three rough-lookin' men out there checkin' out Beacon. I think they might be the outlaws. Quick, back slang it."

Doris quickly figured out what that meant. They ran through a curtained door located at the back of the room. The telegrapher yelled, "Hey! You can't go out that away. That's private. It's for company men only."

Rose and Doris ignored his commands. They entered an area that appeared to be living quarters. There was a narrow bed along the right wall. Near the back were a small table and two chairs. A dry sink sat under a small, curtainless window. Next to the sink was a door. Rose turned the handle. It was locked. She muttered under her breath.

Doris looked wildly around. In her fright, she spied a set of keys hanging on a hook near the dry sink. She grabbed them and passed them to Rose. Rose started trying one key after another, muttering after each failed attempt. The third one unlocked the door.

They hugged the side of the building as

they slunk through an alley separating the telegraph office and another store. Rose peeked around the corner of the building. She could hear the three men talking. Earl was saying, "Monte, I'm sure that's the gelding Nate was riding."

"It sure looks like it. Git down and take a closer look." Earl did as he was told.

"I think so. Ya suppose the woman's 'round here?"

"You knot head. The only way ta find out is ta look! We'll try the general store first." The other two outlaws dismounted. The three walked two buildings down to the general store.

Rose saw their chance. "Quick! Get on your horse. Don't ride fast. We don't want to attract attention." They made it to their horses without being spotted. They walked the horses past the last house before starting into a gallop.

Doris looked behind her. "Rose, I think they're following us!" Both gave their horses a kick. After about a mile, Rose spotted a barely visible trail leading into dense woods. They followed it. A short time later, Rose got off her horse. She went back over the trail, covering it with brush. The three outlaws missed the trail and galloped past. Doris and Rose waited until dark before returning to the other horses. They ate a cold supper of green beans, applesauce and water. As they were finishing, Rose declared, "I got an idea. Tomorra' I'll go ta town with my two horses and wait fer my money. Those men don't know what I look like. You'll have ta stay here by yerself. Can you do that?"

Hesitantly, Doris said, "Yes, of course."

"Now, after I git my money, I'll buy a wagon and if I got the time, I'll go ta the general store and git us some grub."

Chapter 14

Rose left for town just after dawn the next day. She took her two horses to use to pull the hoped-for wagon.

Doris didn't know what to do with herself. She brushed down each horse using bunches of dried grass. Then she went to the creek and washed herself the best she could without any soap. She gathered twigs and small limbs for a fire. She didn't eat any lunch. Finally, she decided to prepare a good supper for the two of them. Rose had a pot and a frying pan in her supplies. Doris carried the pot to the creek and filled it with water. She built a fire. As the water was heating, she looked over her chickens and chose one.

After wringing its neck, she hung the chicken by the legs from a tree branch to drain the blood. When the water started to boil, she dunked the chicken in the boiling water to help remove the feathers. Doris had plucked many chickens and was done in just a few minutes. Next, she dumped out the water, took the pot back to the creek, rinsed it out, and refilled it. She put the pot back on the fire. As the water heated, she gutted the chicken, cut it into pieces and put them in the pot. She let the chicken cook for quite a while. Meanwhile, she peeled several potatoes, needing to cut out many bad spots. She cut slits in a couple of the chicken pieces to see if they were cooked through.

Satisfied they were almost done, she put lard from Rose's supplies in the frying pan and placed the pan over the fire. When the lard was melted and hot, she added the chicken pieces to it. She tossed the potatoes into the chicken broth. She was thickening the broth for gravy when she heard a wagon coming.

Doris was so scared she didn't know what to do. She ran deeper into the woods, trying to hide.

"Hey, Doris! Where ya at?" It was Rose. Doris slowly came back to their campsite. "I've been smellin' that chicken for half a mile. Is it ready?"

"Yes, it is."

Rose was sitting in the funniest-looking wagon Doris had ever seen. She walked around the wagon, giving it a close inspection. It was made from two short, very old, wooden water troughs. One long side of each trough had been removed. The troughs had then been attached together length wise. This made the bed of the wagon. It was bolted to a four-wheeled frame. An old church pew was nailed to the frame in front of the trough boxes. Someone had upholstered the pew in red-flowered material. Stuffing was coming out of several torn places. A small door had been affixed sideways to the frame about two feet in front of the pew to form a dashboard. There were no springs on the wagon to soften the ride.

Rose started laughing at Doris' perplexed look. "There weren't no regular wagons ta be bought. I got a good price fer this one. Seems the owner died of lead poisoning. The hostler said he tried playing poker with a cold deck."

"What's a cold deck?"

Rose laughed again. "He was cheatin' and got shot. Look at all the room in the back for carryin' our supplies. I sold one of my horses. Figger, we don't need it. I also got us rain slickers and tarps to cover our supplies."

Just then a dog's head popped up from under the pew.

"Is that a dog?"

"Yeah, it's a dog. It follower'd me for a couple of miles. Then it ran around the wagon and sat down in the middle of the road jest whinin'. So, I gave him a drink and put him in with me. He might make a good watch dog. I believe he's hungry."

Doris gave the dog some chicken scraps, careful not to include any bones. She looked him over. He wasn't a big dog.

His coat was a pretty brown and black with just a bit of white above the nose and he looked reasonably healthy. She wondered who he belonged to. Was some boy crying because his pet hadn't come home that evening? Or had the dog run away because of mistreatment?

"He needs a name."

"What?"

"The dog needs a name."

"Colby."

"Colby?"

"Yeah. He's from Colby. So, we'll call him Colby."

"All right. Here, Colby. That's your name, dog." Doris held out a scrap of skin. Colby came over to her, wagging his tail, and took the skin.

"I got somethin' else ta show you," stated Rose. She reached into the buggy and pulled out a large package. After unwrapping it, she held up what appeared to be a skirt. "This here's what's called a divided skirt. See?" She held the skirt so Doris could see it was actually a pair of very wide pants. "Bought both of us one." With that, Rose commenced to remove her trousers and donned the skirt. "Also got me a new shirt," Rose said as she pulled out a bright yellow-flowered shirtwaist. "Here's your skirt. Got you a new shirtwaist to." She tossed the two items to Doris.

The divided skirt was the same as Rose's. However, the shirtwaist top was gathered at the yoke. It flared out, ending about mid-thigh. "Go ahead; try 'em on."

Doris hesitated. "Let's eat. I'll put them on later."

"Doris, I know your secret. It's okay. Put the clothes on."

Just then Colby began to bark and growl. "Now what you suppose is wrong with the pup?"

They heard hoof beats. Rose yelled out, "That's far enough, mister! There's nothin' here you need or want. If you don't move on, I'll sic my dog on ya. He'll eat ya alive."

A lone horseman rode up. "You sic that mongrel on me and I'll shoot him. He's the town tramp. Looking at Doris he asked, "Is your name Doris Clark?"

Rose spoke up before Doris had a chance to answer. "Who's askin'?"

The man pulled back his vest to reveal a badge. "Name's Sam Bennett, Sheriff Bennett." The sheriff looked to be in his late thirties, with graying hair at his temples. He had permanent wrinkle lines on each side of his eyes. "I just arrested one of the lawbreakers that robbed that bank in Ardmore Bend. Said Mrs. Clark knows where the money is. Described you, ma'am."

Doris folded her arms above her protruding belly, holding her upper arms with each opposite hand and spoke up. "I'm Doris Clark. How did you know where to find us?"

"Twern't hard. Saw your telegrams. Been watching Mrs. Elder all day."

"That's against the law. That telegraph man had no right ta show you them telegrams," voiced Rose with her hands on her hips.

"Oh, for crying out loud, he's, my brother. Shows me everything. Now about that stolen bank money, Mrs. Clark."

"The money was in the saddle bags. The last time I saw those bags they were hanging over a kitchen chair. Those thieves went through my house before setting it on fire. So, the saddle bags must have burnt up if the outlaws didn't take them."

"That's not the story I got. I'd like you to come to town with me. We'll get this story sorted out. Leastwise it isn't safe for you out here."

Rose suddenly had a shotgun in her hands. "She ain't goin' nowhere with you. She ain't done nothin' wrong. Now you can jest turn that horse of yours and head back ta town."

The sheriff sat his horse, staring at Rose then at Doris. Doris reminded him of his sister. They looked to be about the same age. It angered him to think of a similar thing happening to his sister. Doris didn't deserve being chased by the law or the outlaws. For all he knew she was telling the truth. But if so, why was she running?

He thought about the election he'd be facing in the fall. He didn't want to have on his record a showdown with a woman old enough to be his mother and a woman that looked to be fixing to birth a baby. His opponent would have a grand time with that. He turned his horse around and headed back to town. He decided he'd just telegraph the U.S. marshal and let him handle the situation.

"Don't be coming back or hidin' in wait. This may be a mutt, but I'll set him on you. And don't be takin' the word of an outlaw before a good Christian woman!"

The sheriff shook his head and continued back to town. When he was out of hearing range, both started to laugh. Colby sat on his haunches with his head cocked, looking from one woman to the other.

"Reckon we best not stay here. Sheriff will likely be back with help. Let's eat fast and pack up. I hate to do it, but it's probably best if we let the Morgan go, like you been thinking."

They ate a hurried supper and packed their belongings onto the buggy. They tied Ginger and Rose's horse, Molly, to the back of the buggy. Beacon was hitched to pull the buggy.

Rose slapped the Morgan on the rump. "Go on, git, go home." The Morgan trotted a short distance before stopping to watch them leave, then turned and followed behind.

Chapter 15

Late in the night they came upon a deserted farm. Both were exhausted. There was a collapsed soddy house not far from the road. They saw a wooden barn beyond. One wall of the barn was partly missing, as were the barn doors. Rose drove the buggy into the barn. Both women got down.

"Doris, look around for a lantern. Watch out for snakes. Better we stay in the center, away from corners." Doris found a lantern hanging on a center post. It still contained a small amount of kerosene.

She rummaged through their belongings and found some matches. She was thankful Rose seemed to know what supplies to carry; however, she reasoned after ten years on the road that should be no surprise. They first saw to the needs of the horses, including the Morgan.

"Rose, this Morgan wants to stay with us. I'm thinking maybe he could be used to pull the buggy. Tomorrow how about hitching him to the buggy and see how he does?"

"Good idea! Now let's get some rest. I'm all done in."

During the night rain started, but the women were so fatigued the rain didn't wake them. They had packed the supplies so that an area was left in the center of the wagon for sleeping. Colby slept on the pew.

Near dawn Doris awoke. She didn't move for fear of bothering Rose. Listening to the drip of water was soothing. However, she could wait no longer to get up. As quietly as possible she got out of the wagon. To her relief, Rose didn't stir. Doris changed quickly into the divided skirt and new blouse. The blouse draped gracefully to her mid-thighs. The skirt was very comfortable.

She wondered what Momma would have thought. Momma never allowed her daughters to wear overalls, even when helping with the harvest. She smiled as she readjusted herself. **So, Rose knows my secret, does she? I wonder.**

When she was confident that she had herself "put together," she cleared an area of debris just inside the missing doors' opening. Next, she built a fire using pieces of dry wood she found lying about. They had a little water with them, which Doris used to make coffee. Then she sliced off some bacon and began frying it.

Colby jumped out of the buggy and ran barking towards the back corner of the barn. This awakened Rose.

"Is that coffee and bacon I smell? My, my, what a night! This day doesn't look to be buildin' up to be much better." She climbed out of the buggy. "Well, look at you. If you don't look smart!"

Just then Colby came running out with a rat in his mouth. "Get out of here, dog. Get away from me with that thing!"

Doris began to laugh. "Rose, what did you mean last night when you said you know my secret?"

"You know what I mean. Didn't you say

you'd only been married a couple of months? And except for the first night when Nate was drunk as a skunk and most likely not up to doing much lovin', your husband slept alone upstairs? Don't worry, child, your secret's safe with me." She gave a little laugh. "If that coffee and bacon's ready, let's eat; I'm hungry."

After breakfast they packed up. This time they hitched the Morgan to the buggy. He didn't fuss or buck. He gave the impression of being at home in the traces. The other three horses were tied to the back of the buggy. Colby, minus the rat, sat on the seat between the two women. The rain didn't seem to bother him.

"Do you know where we are, Rose?"

"I got a fair idea. I think – I hope, that is, we're still goin' northwest."

The make-shift buggy with two women, a dog and three horses hitched behind made an odd picture traveling down the muddy, rutted road. About midmorning the road was so muddy the Morgan was having a hard time pulling the buggy. Rose guided him to a grassy area beside the road. "Reckon we best wait out this storm." They stayed in the buggy. Both were thankful for the slickers.

"If this rain don't stop, we'll likely be eating a cold lunch. I sure could use a cup of coffee."

"I kept what was left from breakfast. It's cold, of course."

"I've had worse than cold coffee. Pour me a cup, if you don't mind." Doris poured both of them a cup. They sat and sipped in silence. Each was lost in her own thoughts.

Finally, the rain stopped. "Must be about eleven," volunteered Rose.

"How do you know that?"

"Ain't you never heard, 'Rain before seven, stop by eleven?' My granny used to say that every time it rained of a mornin'. Shore wish I knew where we are. Seems like we should be comin' ta some town. Once we cross the Republican River, I know fer sure we'll be in Nebraskee. When we do get ta a town, if you don't mind, I'd like ta stay a couple of days. Check out where my Saree might be."

"I could help you!"

At this suggestion Rose gave such a hearty laugh that it woke up Colby, who had been asleep in the back on top of their supplies. "You'll do no such thing! Remember there are still two outlaws a-lookin' fer you."

"There must be something I can do."

"We'll get us a hotel room. You can stay there and look out the winder."

"Oh, Rose, I want to be useful."

"You are, child. Yer a joy to be with. It gets mighty lonely traveling by myself. You help with the cookin' and takin' care of the horses. I'm glad yer with me."

"Thank you, Rose. That's one of the nicest things anyone has ever said to me."

"Now, let's not get syrupy. I think I'll try drivin' this buggy along the side of the road. The grass might be easier goin'."

They made slow but steady progress on the grass. Finally, they reached higher ground and were able to use the road. They stopped twice to change horses. The second time they stayed long enough to eat a jar of applesauce. It was just getting dark when they saw the lights of a town. They decided to chance going in. A sign over the livery stable read "McCook, Nebraska."

Chapter 16

The hostler was a friendly man. He talked nonstop, asking many questions as he saw to the needs of the horses. Doris found out that Rose was very adept at getting around these questions. She even persuaded the hostler to let Colby and the chickens stay at the stable with the horses.

"Where's the best hotel?"

"Down the street on the other side."

"Thank you kindly, sir." Being called 'sir' caused the man to stand a little taller.

The hotel clerk was reluctant to rent the two women a room.

"Well, now, ma'am, we don't generally let rooms to single ladies. Are you traveling by yourselves? Haven't you got a man to look after you?"

"Look, mister, there's jest the two of us. We don't need a man to look after us. We're decent women. We don't drink, smoke or have men visitin' us, so we won't be causin' you any trouble. We're hungry and tired. We need a room for two nights. We also want a tub of water – hot water that is, prepared for us after we eat supper. So, jest hand over the key."

The clerk could hear his mother's voice in Rose. Without another word, he gave her the key to a room and began readying their bath.

They ate supper in the hotel dining room. The waiter apologized that the only item on the menu was beef stew. It sounded wonderful to both Doris and Rose. The other diners stared at the two. It didn't seem to bother Rose, but Doris was very uncomfortable. They did not linger at their table. After a bath, they fell into bed and were asleep immediately.

Rose gave Doris a stern warning the next day before starting out to search for Saree. "You stay in this room. There are still two men out there somewhere, lookin' for you. I'll be back at lunch time. Do you promise?"

"Yes, I promise," replied Doris.

Doris did her best to occupy her time. She sorted and washed their few clothes. When Rose arrived for lunch, the room was strung with rope and hanging clothes. They dined once again in the hotel dining room.

Once again, the only item available was beef stew.

"Rose, I just can't stay in that room any longer. I must get out if only for a couple of hours. Don't you think it would be all right if I walked down to the stable and checked on the horses and Colby? The hostler will be there."

"We'll both go. The hostler might even know something about my Saree."

It felt so good to Doris to be out of the hotel room and walking. Colby ran up to them as they entered the stable.

"Hi, Colby. Did you miss us? Have you been good?"

"That dog's 'bout the best dog I ever knowed," expressed the hostler. "Would ya be of a mind ta sell him?"

The two women looked at each other and said in unison, "No."

"I figured as much. I'm goin' down to the café ta get me a bite of lunch. Be back in about an hour."

After he left, Rose walked over to Molly and started rubbing her down. Doris was about to look in on Ginger when she felt a rough grip on her arms.

"Well, lookee who we got here." Earl had her held tightly by both arms now. She could smell his foul breath, rank with liquor and rotted teeth. It almost made her gag.

"Let me go!" shouted Doris. Earl just laughed. Colby came running out of a stall when he heard Doris. "Get him, Colby!" cried Doris, but Colby sat down and just looked at her.

"Sic 'em, Colby!" bellowed Rose as she

came at them brandishing a pitchfork. Colby flew at Earl, getting a vicious hold on his right leg. Earl gave a painful howl. He still held Doris as both fell to the floor. Doris felt her left arm twist.

"Get that dog off me 'fore I shoot him!" Earl yelled as he let go of Doris and reached for his six-shooter. Doris rolled away as she saw Rose running at Earl with the pitchfork. One tine went through Earl's right hand, pinning it to the hard dirt floor. He gave another painful howl. Colby was still ripping at his leg. Earl was swearing up a storm as Monte entered unseen though a side door. He had a revolver in his hand.

"What's going' on here?" called a voice from the stable entrance. It was the deputy sheriff, the hostler and a couple of other men. Monte slithered back out the door.

He quietly mounted his horse and rode out of town.

"This man tried to bushwhack us. We're just tryin' to defend ourselves," uttered Rose.

"Call off the dog," ordered the deputy as he pulled the fork out of Earl's hand.

Doris grabbed Colby by the neck. "Let go, Colby. Good dog."

"Oh, these women are tryin' ta kill me, sheriff. I ain't done nothin'. I jest came in here ta ask a question and they attacked me."

"Not a very likely story. Bill, go get the doc," said the deputy to one of the bystanders.

"Sheriff, this man is one of the outlaws that robbed the bank in Ardmore Bend several weeks ago," Doris revealed.

"Then you must be Doris Clark."

"Yes, I'm Mrs. Clark, but I had nothing to do with the robbery. I'm just trying to get to my sister's."

The doctor arrived as Doris was speaking. "Couple of you men, carry this man over to my office. He's going to need stitches."

"You'd better go with him, sheriff. He'll bolt the first chance he gets," expressed an irritated Rose.

"You ladies staying at the hotel?" Both nodded. "Go back there and don't leave 'til I have a chance to talk to you."

Doris and Rose walked back to their hotel, holding tight to each other. Colby was close at their heels.

"Rose, I'm so scared. What are we going to do?"

"We're goin' to pack up and leave."

"But the sheriff said to wait."

"Forget the sheriff. We've got ta look after ourselves. That other outlaw is around somewhere."

As they started to climb the stairs to their room, the hotel clerk saw Colby and roared, "You can't take that dog up to your room. It ain't allowed!"

Both women ignored him. Rose locked the door after they were in.

"Git them clothes off the line. Pack up." Fortunately, the weather had cleared. It was a warm day and the clothes were dry. "We'll sneak out the back door and take the alley ta the stable. Hopefully, we can hide in the stable 'til night. The hostler should be gone by eight or nine. We'll go south and east for a day to throw off anyone that might be trying ta foller us."

They hurriedly packed their few things. Rose peeked out the door of their room. No one was in the hall. Quietly, they walked down the back stairs. They could hear the clerk talking to someone. "Yeah, they came in 'bout 10 or 15 minutes ago. They had a blasted dog with them. They're in room 10." A deputy started up the front stairs as Doris and Rose left by the back stairs. The clerk yelled after the deputy, "And tell them to get that dog out of here!"

Again, their luck held. No one was in the alley to see them go to the livery stable. The hostler was busy in the tack room as they quietly entered. They hid behind a pile of hay until the hostler went home for the night.

Rose stretched as she stood from her

hiding place. "I'm gettin' too old fer playin' hide and seek."

"I'm sorry I've brought all this misery on you."

"Oh, don't pay me no mind. It's really kind of excitin'! That is, as long as we don't get ourselves shot."

They secured their belongings to the buggy and checked their supplies. The chickens were surprisingly content, still in the cages. The Morgan was harnessed to the buggy. Rose opened the stable door and looked around. It appeared safe to leave. She opened both doors as Doris drove the buggy with the other horses tied to the back and Colby sitting beside her. Rose closed the doors and climbed aboard the wagon.

Chapter 17

Once again, they traveled through the night. It was at least a warm, beautiful night. Doris looked up into the heavens at all the stars. She remembered something Janie had said once when the family was returning home from a party at the Dodd farm.

"Momma, heaven must be a beautiful place."

"Why do you say that, Janie?" responded Momma.

"Because, look at the pretty nails God used to build it."

Doris smiled at this memory. Oh, how she missed her family! Tears began to roll down her checks. She tried not to let Rose know she was crying. But Rose sensed her sorrow. She pulled the buggy to a stop, set the brake and wrapped the reins around it. Then she reached into her war bag to retrieve a large red handkerchief which she gave to Doris.

"Here, darlin'." She put her arms around Doris, holding her. Doris laid her head on Rose's shoulder and began to sob.

"I'm so miserable. I miss Momma and Papa and Janie and even Susan. I just can't help crying. I want them back." Rose didn't say anything. She just held Doris tight, letting her cry herself out. Finally, Doris heaved a great sigh and sat up. She blinked back the tears and blew her nose. "Thank you, Rose. I believe God sent you to me. Or maybe He sent me to you."

"Darlin', that's real nice of you to say. Listen! Do you hear water running? There's a stream near here some place. We best camp 'til morning. We'll be needin' water."

Rose pulled the wagon to the side of the road. They climbed into the back and lay down on their makeshift bed.

"Do you have any idea where we are, Rose?"

"I've no idea. Tomorra' will be better, though." Then she laughed. "I don't know how things could git much worse."

It was only a matter of minutes before Doris heard the rhythmic sound of Rose sleeping. Sleep did not come quickly to Doris, however. Her mind was a battlefield.

What am I going to do after this is over? I really don't want to live with Susan and Ethan. I would be miserable seeing them together every day. But what can I do? What would I do for a job? At least there will be some money to keep me for a while. I should give half the money from the farm and savings to Susan. That would sure be a surprise to her. It was her last thought as she drifted off to sleep.

Something was licking her face. She opened her eyes to see Colby's tongue. "Get off me, you silly dog."

Rose was laughing. "I set him on you to wake you up." She sat by a fire, frying fish.

"You've been fishing?"

"Yep. That's a might pretty stream. Clear as crystal. Got enough fish so we can take extry for lunch."

"Have you figured out where we are?"

"I think we're back in Kansas."

"Oh," groaned Doris.

"Now, I could be wrong." This made Doris laugh.

After breakfast they started west. Today Ginger had the first round of pulling the buggy. She was actually prancing as though happy to be useful. A short time later a small town appeared in the distance. Doris was driving as they came to a grove of trees.

"Pull inta that wood," uttered Rose. I'll put on my man clothes and ride Molly inta that town. I'll find out where we're at. Look over our supplies. If I go inta the store to buy things, it'll only be natural ta make small talk. If you don't mind, I'll jest take a few extry minutes to look for Saree."

"Of course, I don't mind, Rose." She knew it wasn't safe for her to go in with Rose. The authorities would have been notified to be looking for them. It made her angry. She hadn't done anything wrong, but they were treating her like one of the robbers.

Rose rode swiftly off. She did look like a man from a distance. She slowed Molly into a trot as she neared the town, which really wasn't much of a town. It consisted of one main street and one street at each end. One building served as the general store, post office, saloon and hotel. That was the biggest building in town. Rose figured the whole town was owned and controlled by one person. There were only four or five other small buildings. None were painted. She didn't see a bank or stable. She rode up to the general store. A sign over the false front read "Barker

Ridge." She dismounted, secured Molly to the hitching rail, and entered the store.

A cold potbelly stove occupied the center of the room. Along the right wall was a bar, where a couple of cowboys stood drinking beer. Both turned to look at Rose as she entered. She returned their look with a cold stare. Between the bar and the stove were four round tables; all were empty. At the back of the room an unused piano sat near stairs leading to the second floor. On the other side of the room was a counter identical to the bar. It served as the general store area. Tucked in the corner near the front door was a caged area. A sign at the top of the cage spelled out U.S. Post Office.

"What kin I help you with, mista ... I mean, ma'am?" An older man was standing almost unseen in the back corner behind the general store counter, putting material on a shelf.

"I'm needin' two pounds of flour, one pound each of cornmeal and sugar, two pounds of coffee and a half pound of salt." She saw a jar filled with an amber liquid. "Is that honey there?"

"It sure is. Preacher raises bees. It's been blessed!"

"Give me a jar of it. And throw in a bag of that hard rock candy, too."

The store owner filled her order. "That'll be $2.35."

Rose pulled out her pocket purse to pay, she stopped. "You got any revolvers?"

"Sure do. Right over here." They moved down the counter a few steps. Under a glass case were several revolvers.

The owner raised the glass lid and lifted out a Colt single-action army revolver. "Now this here one is a real nice piece. I ain't had it too long. A feller came in 'bout a month ago. He was lookin' ta trade for a rifle."

Rose recognized the gun. It looked like the same kind her husband had used. "How much?"

"I'll give ya a good deal. This revolver, a box of ammunition, and this here belt for $25.00."

Rose didn't know if that was a good price or not. "I'll take it for that price if ya give me two boxes of bullets and a box of those 12-gauge shotgun shells sittin' right next to 'em."

"Well, I won't be making much on this sale, but all right."

Rose was about to pay for the second time when she saw a small flat-crown Stetson hat. It was black felt wool with a wide brim and a leather chin strap. Pointing to it she asked, "How much for that hat?"

"Now I've had that while. It's kinda small so I can give you a good deal, say $10.00."

"I say $5.00."

"No, I can't do that. I'll split it: $7.50."

"Total her up."

"It all comes ta $44.85."

Rose handed him two twenty-dollar gold pieces and a five-dollar gold coin. "Ya can keep the change if ya forget I was ever in here."

"Lady, I never seen ya in my life."

Rose collected her purchases. Before she

walked out the door, she turned to the two cowboys and said, "Fellers, I know how ta use this gun and I'm real good at aimin'. If you don't want ta be looking at daisy roots, I suggest ya forget ya ever seen me." As she packed the supplies on Molly, she couldn't hold back a laugh. She had never shot a revolver in her life!

Rose rode slowly out of town going in the wrong direction to get back to the camp site. She didn't trust the cowboys. At a bend in the road, she guided Molly into a coppice, down into a gully and waited. Sure, enough the two cowboys came riding by. They missed the turn where Rose was hiding. As soon as they were out of sight Rose hurried out of the gully. Back on the road, she put Molly into a fast trot back towards Barker's Ridge. Skirting around the town, she rode to the campsite.

Chapter 18

Doris was at odds as to what to do while Rose was gone. She walked around gathering wood. They could take the wood with them. She had had a dream last night. All day she had been trying to decide if she should tell Rose about it. Maybe she would tonight over supper. The chickens had been in the cages for some time. Doris let them out to look for bugs. She decided to cook bacon and eggs for supper. There was a bit of cornmeal so she could make hoe cakes.

She had no idea how long Rose would be gone. She thought it would be all right to fry the bacon. Next, she made the hoe cakes. Only after Rose arrived would she fry the eggs. To make the hoe cakes she heated water. After measuring out about two cups of meal, she poured the hot water over it. Next, she added enough cold water to thin the mush and stirred it. She removed the bacon from the frying pan, and dropped dollops of the batter into the bacon grease. When the first side was brown, she flipped each cake over to brown the other side. She couldn't help but think how good some honey would taste on the cakes.

Doris had just finished the last cake when Colby growled. Doris turned around, fearing the last outlaw, Monte, had found her. Instead, standing near the wagon was an Indian woman with a cradle board on her back holding a baby. Behind her were two small children. The children hugged their mother's legs, peeking out from behind each side. The woman didn't look to be more than twenty. Her small face made her black eyes seem large. They were serious-looking, unhappy eyes. The mother and her two children were remarkably filthy and looked like they were starving. Doris hesitated. The Indian woman pointed to the bacon, "Please, my children are hungry. Please, would you give them something to eat?"

Doris picked up the plate and urged her, "You eat some, too." The woman and the two older children sat down and devoured the bacon almost instantly. Next, they gazed at the hoe cakes. Doris handed the cakes to them. While they were eating the cakes, Doris gathered eggs and cooked those for the hungry family. Finally, they seemed to be satisfied. The woman skillfully removed the baby to her lap and began nursing the infant, who clearly was also very hungry. The two children continued to hug their mother. "Thank you so very much. You have saved my children and me."

"What are you doing out here? And where did you learn to speak English?"

Doris heard a horse coming from the direction of town. She hoped it was Rose. As the horse cleared a rise in the road, Rose came into view. Doris sighed with relief.

"What we got here?" Rose questioned. Doris quickly explained the situation. Rose looked at the poor family. "So, you speak English. Your children look like half-breeds. Is their father white?"

"Yes. We were married, but he is dead now. His family will not allow us to remain with them. I am trying to get back to my people."

Doris looked at Rose, "What should we to do, Rose?"

Rose didn't answer at first. She stood with her hands on her hips and chewed her lip. "Make up a bundle of food to give them. I bought some more cornmeal. Cook up more hoe cakes. I'm thinking we ought to give them a couple of chickens, too.

"Rose, I want to give them Beacon. He reminds me too much of Nate. He's ornery and doesn't like being hitched to the buggy. " She turned to the woman. "What is your name?

"My name is Grace."

"Grace!"

"Yes, I am a Christian. My people are Christians."

"Do you know how to ride a horse, bare back?"

"Yes."

Doris walked to Beacon then led him to Grace. "Well, I'm going to give you this horse. He can be irritable and he's strong-willed. Do you think you can handle such a horse?"

"Yes, I can make him obey me. You are so kind. I do not deserve such help."

Smiling at Grace, Doris replied, "Yes, I believe you do. Besides, if we only helped those who deserve it, hardy anyone would ever be helped."

Doris wrapped the cakes in a rag, and grabbed two chickens, tying their legs together. Rose walked to Grace and gave her two five-dollar gold pieces. "Here, take these."

"No, I cannot. You are too generous."

"Take 'em. You'll need money ta buy food fer yer young'uns and maybe a little oats fer the horse."

With tears in her eyes Grace smiled as she accepted the gifts skillfully arranging them on Beacon. He pranced around disliking the smell of the chickens. Grace grabbed his ear and said something into it. This settled Beacon down. Neither Rose nor Doris heard what she said.

Rose lifted first one child then the other onto the horse and behind the squawking chickens. Grace positioned the cradle board on her back. Taking the reins of the horse, she started to walk back into the woods. Before disappearing, she turned and softly voiced, "God bless both of you. I will pray you have a safe journey wherever you are going".

Rose had been traveling for ten years and was not surprised meeting this Indian family. She shrugged it off and unsaddled Molly, "I sure am hungry. You got anything left?"

Doris laughed. "Just give me a few minutes. Bacon, eggs and hoe cakes coming right up!"

Rose finished seeing to Molly and began putting away the supplies while waiting for supper. She put the honey on a stone by the fire.

"Honey! Rose, you're a wonder. I was thinking how good some honey would be with the cakes."

After supper Rose got out the new hat. "I got somethin' for you, Doris." Doris looked at the hat with pleasure. It was a little big, but would be just fine.

"Rose, this is wonderful. Thank you so much." She gave Rose a big hug. "You are so good to me. I really don't deserve your kindness. I wish I could do something to repay you."

"Now hush. Ain't you just cooked me the best supper ever? What more could a body ask for?"

"Rose, I had a dream last night. It was very special. Could I tell it to you?"

"Why, of course you can."

They were sitting near the fire, drinking coffee. Evening had come on and it was getting chilly. Each woman was wrapped in a blanket. Anyone seeing them from a distance might mistake them for Indians.

Doris began to talk about her dream. "I was standing in a mist. I couldn't see any trees or buildings or anything like that. Then I saw my sister, Janie, coming towards me. She was dressed in a white, shimmering gown trimmed in blue. She had a blue cord wrapped around her waist. Blue had always been her favorite color. Her hair sparkled like the sun. She looked so happy! She didn't say anything, just took my hand. We walked together for a bit. We saw other people and children along our walk. Janie looked at me and said, 'These are my friends.' Then there stood my momma and papa. Both were young and healthy. Papa's hair was dark like I remember him when I was little. He looked strong and fit. Momma wasn't sick! She smiled at me.

There were no wrinkles on her face. She wasn't in pain."

Doris couldn't hold back the tears as she continued telling her dream. Rose opened her blanket and encircled both of them in it.

"Then Janie let go of my hand and took Momma's hand. The three of them walked slowly away together. Just before they disappeared, Papa turned around, smiled at me and waved. It was such a nice dream. So special I didn't want to wake up."

"That was a gift to you, Doris."

"I know, Rose, I know. Sometimes I wish I could just go to heaven and be with them. I'm so scared. I don't know what to do. I really don't want to go live with my sister. I don't know how I'd make any money. I don't want to end up like you think your Saree might have."

"Don't worry 'bout tomorrow. Tomorrow will take care of itself. There's enough trouble for today. That's what my Granny always told me."

"That's from the Bible. I don't think she quoted it exactly."

"It is? My granny was one for havin' someone read the Bible to her. She couldn't read nor write."

"Yes, I heard our pastor preach on that scripture once. I didn't know what it meant then. Now I do."

"Well, what it means to me is don't you worry 'bout what's goin' ta happen. As long as yer with me, I won't let nothin' bad happen to you. Now, let's get some sleep."

Chapter 19

Doris and Rose had been traveling for two days, detouring around towns and most farms. Today it had been raining since early morning.

"I feel guilty that you haven't gone into the towns to look for Saree," Doris said.

Wiping rain from her eyes, Rose responded, "Now, there's no reason ta be feeling that away. I was in these parts jest a few months ago. No one had any information about my Saree.

"So much for my granny's old wives' tales about rain stoppin' by eleven if it starts by seven. Looksee, there's a farm. I believe we can chance askin' ta stay in the barn for the night."

The farm couple would not hear of the women sleeping in the barn. Their four children stared wide-eyed at the women but asked no questions.

"Take the ladies to your room, Caroline," directed the mother. Looking at Doris, the mother continued, "I'll have one of the boys bring you some water to wash up."

The girl talked as she showed Doris and Rose her room. The only privacy was an old blanket hanging between the bedroom and the entrance to the combination kitchen, living room.

"My name's Caroline. I'm eight." She was

tall and slender. Her long golden hair, with its two braids, was tied up around her head. She had bright blue eyes with flecks of green and a long neck. She wore a much-patched flour sack dress under a dingy, gray apron.

Just then the oldest boy came into the room carrying a large bowl in which sat an ewer of water. "This is Sam. He's older, but he don't talk much." Sam was a head taller than Caroline, also a blonde, with hair that hung in his blue eyes. His pants were patched and, since they stopped about three inches above his ankles, it was obvious he had outgrown them. Both children were barefooted. Sam blushed and left the room.

"Caroline, once you get the ladies settled, please help me put supper on the table," called the mother.

"Supper will be ready in a minute," stated Caroline as she happily scampered out, pleased to have company to break the dull monotony of her usual routine.

"Thank you kindly. Ain't she the prettiest thing!" declared Rose.

Ignoring Rose, Doris exclaimed as she started to wash, "The water's warm!" After cleaning up, Doris and Rose came into the main room from the children's bedroom.

"Welcome to our home, ladies. We enjoy having company. And we haven't even introduced ourselves. My name's Ben Van der Waal." Ben, husband and father, was very tall. His head almost reached the low ceiling. Like his son, he wore patched bibs and a patched shirt. His coloring made it easy to see where the two children got their blonde hair and blue eyes "This is my lovely wife, Beatrice."

Beatrice looked tired and worn out. It was obvious she was expecting a fifth baby. Her dull, brown hair was thinning. Doris was surprised to see a sparkle in the pale blue eyes as they intently scrutinized the two travelers.

Ben continued, "You've met Caroline and Sam. The one hiding behind his ma is John." John looked like a smaller version of his older brother. "The baby's name is Jane." At this Doris' heart flipped.

"Supper's about ready. I hope you like beef stew and corn biscuits," announced Beatrice.

"We really like beef stew," replied Rose with a sweet smile. Both women had to admit that Beatrice's stew was much better than that served at the hotel.

Rose excused herself to go out to the

wagon. She brought back the sack of rock candy and gave each person a piece. Then she handed it to Beatrice, "Keep this for the children fer special times." The room was quiet as all sat enjoying the unexpected treat. The children's faces glowed with pleasure and sticky goo.

The two boys were told to sleep on the floor in the kitchen area so Doris and Rose could have a bed. As were most beds, this one had a mattress filled with corn husks. Doris thought she heard a mouse moving around in it. Colby had been banished to sleep in the buggy, which was good. Doris knew he would be poking his nose in the mattress to find the mouse.

The following morning, they were served a breakfast of cornmeal mush. Beatrice was busy at the stove while Ben was helping to feed the baby. Rose took the opportunity to slip a five-dollar gold piece under her bowl. She smiled, "Boys, I sure appreciate you giving up yer bed for us. To show my appreciation here is a penny for each of you." The boys were so pleased they sat staring at their open hands holding the pennies.

Doris likewise wanted to do something for the Van der Waals. She remembered the yellow ribbons from her shoes. They were somewhere in her belongings. "Excuse me, there is something I need from the wagon." She hurried outdoors, stepped up onto the wagon and rummaged around. Rose and the boys followed her out.

"What are you doin', gal? Yer messing up all our stuff."

"I'm looking for something. Here they are." The yellow ribbons were still in her dress pocket. She had forgotten that she had left them in the pocket when she washed the dress. She did her best to smooth the wrinkles out of the ribbons and went back into the house.

"Caroline, I want to give these to you for being so kind and helpful to us." Caroline took the ribbons and stared in wonderment at them.

"Thank you, Miss Doris. They're the prettiest things I ever did see."

Just before leaving, the farmer handed a bone to Doris for Colby. "You might need this. That dog appears real high-strung. You sure are welcome to stay an extra day. This is foul weather, especially for this time of year. I can't remember a wetter summer."

"We need to be going. Thank you again for all your kindness. You have a wonderful family. I hope you are always as happy as you are today."

Ben scratched the back of his neck, not quite understanding Doris' comment.

The rain continued coming down in sheets. The wind was fierce. Thunder was followed by lightning. By late afternoon, the clouds were so dark it gave the impression that evening was coming on. The Morgan was pulling the buggy. He seemed restless and was prancing around. Rose was driving and was having difficulty managing him. "I think it might have been better to have waited this day out," she stated.

The buggy was just cresting a hill when both women let out a scream. Coming at them were what seemed like hundreds of stampeding cattle.

The cattle drive had begun, several weeks prior, from the Circle G Ranch in Texas.

Chapter 20

1864-65

The Circle G Ranch was owned by Howard and Patricia Gibson. They and their two sons, Blake and Walt, had immigrated to Texas in 1852 from western Tennessee. A third son, Mark, had been born a year after they arrived in Texas.

Their ranch was rather small by Texas standards. Unfortunately, Howard was not a good caretaker of his land, lacking common sense and good insight. This often led to irresponsible decisions. He did not know how to read nor write, which hindered his business transactions. Some people thought him dull and took advantage of him.

It had been sheer luck Howard had been able to hold onto his ranch. The main reason for this was due to two benefits. One was water, a precious commodity on any ranch, and the other was the rights to government grazing land.

The two older sons, Blake and Walt Gibson, were conscripted into the Confederate cavalry during the Civil War. Their younger brother, Mark, was only thirteen and allowed to stay home.

Blake, married to Catherine, had an eight-year-old son, Tim. Walt, two years younger than Blake, was not married. A neighboring rancher's son had gone with the two brothers to fight. His name was Jim Johnson, whom everyone called J.J. The three young men were close friends.

These three Texans participated in a battle known as the Camden Campaign. It was a drive by the North to gain control of Louisiana. Beginning in late March, 1864, a Union force of 8,000 men marched southeast from Little Rock to Arkadelphia, Arkansas. The first encounter with the Rebel cavalry occurred on April 1, followed by several skirmishes during the following days.

The most intense fighting began on April 17. The Union army was running low on supplies and their commander sent a unit of men and wagons into the country to forage for food. They gathered what crops they could and then plundered the area for other valuables.

On the morning of April 18, the Confederate generals positioned Rebel cavalrymen to block off the return route of the Union wagons. Included in the Rebel force were Choctaw Indians. The Rebels crushed the Northern army, made up of both black and white infantry units. All the wagons and horses belonging to the North were either destroyed or captured. Many of the blacks were killed and scalped by the Rebel-hired Indians as revenge for Union pillaging in the territory.

The Union army's casualties amounted to 300 men killed, wounded or missing. The Confederate casualties were about 145.

Unfortunately, one of the Confederate casualties was Blake. During the severe fighting, a Union sharpshooter had taken aim at Walt's head. Just as the sharpshooter fired, Walt moved ever so slightly and the bullet penetrated Blake's chest. Walt never knew the bullet meant for him had hit his brother. He saw blood soaking into Blake's shirt. Blake was on his back, gasping for breath. Red-tinged foam bubbled from his lips with each breath. Walt picked him up and ran for safety away from the intense fighting.

As Walt was carrying an unconscious Blake, he suddenly came face to face with a "blue belly." The Yankee was black, just a kid. He didn't look much older than Mark, Walt's younger brother. But this kid held a rifle with a bayonet attached. Instinctively, Walt kicked the rifle out of the boy's hands. The startled boy gritted his teeth and charged Walt. Walt quickly dropped Blake as the boy flailed a right fist at him. Walt blocked the fist with his left arm and at the same time shoved his right knuckles into the kid's belly, doubling the boy over onto his knees. Walt didn't want to kill the boy unless he had no other choice. He heard the boy say, "Please, Mista', don't kill me." Walt sighed and picked up the rifle. He saw that the rifle was useless. It wouldn't have fired, even if it had been loaded, which it wasn't.

Blake groaned in pain. Watching the boy, Walt went to Blake. His wound was bleeding badly. Walt once again tried to stem the blood without success. Walt felt helpless. He looked at the boy. Every instinct in his body said to kill him. The boy sat on his haunches staring at the two brothers.

Running feet, over crunching branches, sounded in the woods. Another black Yankee came to a stop in the clearing. He seemed not to notice the Rebels. His eyes were wide and focused only on the other

Union soldier. "Moses, the rebels has Injins with 'em. They be killing and scalping us colored folk!" Then he saw Walt and Blake. Walt glared at them for an instant, then said, "Go on, git!" The two boys took off into the woods, heading north.

Almost immediately two Choctaw Indians appeared. They took in the death scene. One said something in his own language pointing in the direction the two Yankees had taken. The Indians took off at a fast trot following the broken trail.

Moments later Walt heard two horrific animal-like sounds. He lifted his head to the sky and cried, "How long, oh, Lord, how long?" He buried his head in his now dead brother's shoulder and cried with great shaking sobs. The two Indians returned to the clearing. Each had a black curly-haired scalp attached to his belt.

Shortly after dark, another figure walked into the clearing. He slowly approached Walt, kneeled down and placed his hand on Walt's shoulder. Walt looked up, his eyes red and swollen. "He's dead, J.J. My brother's dead."

"I'm awful sorry, Walt. Let me help ya carry him back."

"No! He'll only be dumped in a pile with other dead men."

"All right, I'll go find a shovel and we'll bury him right here, where he died."

As J.J. dug the grave, Walt started to make a cross. "Walt, it might be better not ta mark the grave. If the blue bellies come this a-way, they might not treat the grave too kindly."

"No one will know where he lies."

J.J. pointed to a nearby tree. "Jest cut his name and the date on that big oak. Some day after this war's over, you can bring Catherine and Tim ta visit."

Chapter 21

The last battle in which Walt and J.J. took part occurred October 25, 1864. It happened at Mine Creek, Kansas. The Confederates had managed to capture a Union supply caravan of wagons ten miles long. They were withdrawing south to Texas to take the badly needed supplies to soldiers and hungry civilians. At Mine Creek they were met by two brigades of over 2,000 Union cavalrymen, considerably less than the Confederate cavalry, which totaled 7,000.

Each side formed a defensive line. The Union cavalry charged, although outnumbered three to one. They had breech-loading carbines, while the Confederate soldiers were armed with long muzzle-loading rifles. These were almost impossible to reload while the men were still on their horses. Union soldiers could fire multiple times while the Rebels were trying to reload once. Many Rebels fired once, before fleeing on their horses. The remaining Rebels used their rifles as clubs. The fighting turned to hand-to-hand combat while the men were still on their horses. It was one of the largest cavalry engagements of the Civil War.

Walt was using his rifle with the bayonet fixed to defend himself against a Union sergeant when he was walloped across his upper back by a second Union soldier. He fell off his horse onto the wet, muddy field, caused by the rain of the previous night. Several prancing, excited horses stepped on him. Their hooves were tearing his shirt and cutting into his back as he lay stunned. Only the soft mud helped reduce the impact of the blows. He tried to move away from the fighting. His bleeding back was hurting almost unbearably. He wondered how many bones had been broken by the horses' hooves. The pain was so intense he thought he might pass out. Suddenly two strong hands grabbed him and started pulling. He yelled in pain, and fainted.

It was pitch-dark and raining when Walt next opened his eyes. Clouds obscured any moon there might have been. He started to move. A gentle hand touched his chest and a low voice whispered close to his right ear, "Stay still, Walt." The voice belonged to J.J.

"Yer hurt bad. The blue bellies are holding us prisoners. Here, take a swig of this." It was whiskey. Walt didn't like the taste of whiskey but took a big drink just the same.

A second voice spoke up. This one Walt did not recognize. "The Yankees ain't watching close. They jest tryin' ta keep dry. They can't see any more than we can. Several men have already escaped. If we're gonna go, now's the time."

"Help me with my friend."

"Leave 'em. Most likely, he's gonna die anyway."

"No, I won't leave him. We made a deal. Now help me."

"He's right, J.J. Just leave me. I hurt too much ta move."

"No. You, mister, grab his left side."

The stranger sighed and took a rough hold of Walt.

The pain was so bad Walt had to grit his teeth and purse his lips not to cry out. The trio moved quickly away. There seemed to be no pursuit. Dawn was just breaking the horizon when J.J. spied a small hollow in a cluster of rocks. It was just large enough for the three to lie down out of the rain. Walt went in first, followed by J.J., then the stranger. J.J. gave Walt another swallow of whiskey. He was instantly asleep or passed out. J.J. didn't know which.

Walt awoke to warm sun on his face. It felt so good. Both J.J. and the stranger were gone. Walt lay perfectly still, listening. He heard the sound of singing birds and a babbling brook. It was all so peaceful. He heard another sound and turned his head to see J.J. coming towards him.

"Mornin', private, are ya ready for some breakfast?" He handed Walt a small, wormy apple. Walt took it and ate the whole thing, worm, seeds and all. J.J. handed him a second apple. After both had eaten what passed for breakfast, J.J. helped Walt to the creek for a drink.

"What happened to the other guy?"

"Don't know. When I got woke up this mornin', he was gone. Reckon he thinks he kin make better time by hisself."

"Where's he from?"

"Don't know that either. Don't even know his name. He jest said he was gittin' out and would help me with takin' you."

"What did ya have ta pay him ta help?"

J.J. looked at Walt for several seconds before answering. "I give him my mouth organ." J.J. prized his mouth organ. He had been popular around the camp for playing it. A man could name any song and J.J. would play it.

"I'm sorry, J.J. When we git out of this, I promise ta buy you another one."

"Mouth organs can be replaced. Friends can't. Now we best git. The place is crawling with blue bellies."

Chapter 22

J.J. and Walt walked day after day in a southwesterly direction, trying to make it back to Texas. Several times they had to scramble into briars and brambles to avoid being caught by a Yankee patrol. A Confederate troop passed them within hearing distance late one afternoon – an opportunity to get back into the war. Whereas Walt wasn't able to return to the fight, with J.J. it was a different matter. He had decided the war had to be almost over and the South had lost. He wasn't going back, ever.

Walt found himself having to ask J.J. to stop and rest numerous times. His whole body ached. He still wasn't sure that some bones weren't broken. J.J. used the rest periods to forage for food. At an abandoned house he found a rusty kitchen knife. Up until then neither man had any weapon. J.J. had reached the point where he could sneak up behind a squirrel and club it. Once he killed a snake. The two men had never realized how good a snake could taste.

More and more Confederate soldiers were deserting. They had not received any pay for several months. There were marauders committing unspeakable acts. Soldiers who had been good moral men were now turning to outlawing, robbing, killing and worse. People did not trust drifters. Citizens lived in fear of any stranger coming onto their property.

The two men had been walking for over a month when late one day they noticed a seldom-used trail leading into a forest.

"I wonder where that path goes. Maybe there's a place ta rest fer the night."

Walt was glad J.J. had suggested this, as he was once again utterly exhausted. They turned and walked through the woods to a clearing. They saw a small cabin leaning as though it might collapse at any moment. A barn stood a short distance from the house. It looked to be in worse shape than the cabin. The sound of someone chopping wood was coming from in back of the cabin.

Both soundlessly stepped around the cabin. An old woman was trying to chop firewood with a rusted dull axe. J.J. cleared his throat. The woman dropped the axe and picked up an ancient muzzle-loading gun. The men doubted it would fire. If it did, it would probably do more harm to the old woman than to them. "You can just turn around and go back where you come from. I've got nothin' left. The likes of you has already taken all I got." As she was talking, Walt slumped down into the dirt, and hung his head.

"We ain't here ta steal or harm ya. We're jest tryin' ta git back home ta Texas. My name's Jim Johnson. Folks call me J.J. This is my friend, Walt Gibson. To my mind you could use some help with that wood. Do ya suppose we could chop kindling for ya in payment for a meal?"

The old woman looked at J.J. He looked to be taller than her late husband who had made their door especially high so he didn't have to stoop entering the cabin. What weight J.J. carried, which wasn't much, was all muscle. His dark hair was long, dirty and uncombed. He had a long, shaggy beard and his clothes were little more than rags. He was probably in his late twenties or early thirties, but right now he looked to be a hundred.

The man sitting on the ground looked worse. Walt had lowered his head to his chest. As he raised it, she looked at his sad brown eyes. His hair and beard were also dirty and badly matted.

"Looks like your friend there can hardly breathe. Don't think he's going to do much choppin'. Well, come to the cabin. Best you eat first, then work."

The two men followed the woman to her porch. They stopped as she started to go into the house. "We ain't fit ta step inta your house, ma'am. It would be better if we stay out here."

"Shucks, dirt can always be cleaned away. Come on in."

With grateful hearts, they sat down on the kitchen chairs. The room was warm. It felt so good. A pungent live chicken smell permeated the room.

"My name's Minnie Jones. Just call me Minnie. Sorry 'bout the smell. I keep my chickens in this room most of the time. The deserters took my team and wagon, my pig and most of my chickens."

As she was talking, she put a large iron frying pan on the stove. Then she plopped a good-sized spoonful of bacon grease into the pan. Just the aroma of the grease cooking smelled good to the men. Minnie next reached to the back of the stove and picked up a large bowl full of cornmeal mush. She poured heaping cups into the frying pan to make pancakes. As the men ravenously devoured the cakes covered with molasses, Minnie cracked eggs into the same pan.

She gave each man four eggs apiece. "Sorry, I ain't got any coffee. Ain't had any for two years now."

Minnie sat down as the men ate and listened quietly as they told her their story.

When they finished their tale of woe, Minnie shared her own story. "My youngest, George, got kicked in the head by a mule while he was still in army training. Pa brought him home. We tried so hard to save him. Even paid for the doc to come help him. But the doc said there weren't nothin' he could do. George's head was busted. He died and we buried him in the family plot jest the other side of the woods. Our oldest son was killed at

Gettysburg. Were either of you boys there?" Both men shook their heads.

"Then some men came and made my husband and the only son we got left go with them ta fight. My husband was killed at a place called Manassas. Ever hear of that place?" This time the men nodded. "I heard my second oldest son, Delbert, is a prisoner in a Yankee camp. I can't be sure. It's just what some of the fellers that have come back have told me."

The men were surprised when she told them she was only forty-two. She looked at least sixty. Her hair was all white; her face was brown and swathed with worry lines.

J.J. stood up. He couldn't bear anymore. "I'm sorry ta hear about your losses, Miss Minnie. I hope your son makes it home soon. He shore will be comin' ta some mighty fine grub. Ya got a whetstone I kin use ta sharpen that axe?"

"Look in the barn. There used to be one out there. Like I said, most everything of value has been taken. While you chop, I'll see to Walt's wounds."

Walt sat in the warm kitchen; it was making him sleepy. He wanted so much to be of help. His guilt was overwhelming. He could hear J.J. chopping. In the next room Minnie was tearing cloth into strips. She returned to the kitchen carrying strips of printed cloth and a jar of wool fat.

"This is sure good of ya, Miss Minnie. I wish there was some way ta thank ya proper like."

"Don't worry 'bout it. Take your shirt off and let me see that back." She gently washed his back and neck, then poured alcohol into the wounds. It hurt something fierce. "I know this is painful, but it has ta be done. Have ta keep the infection out. You should have had this stitched up. Too late now! It ain't healing right."

When Walt's back had air-dried, Minnie covered a flannel cloth with wool fat and placed it over the wounds. Next, she used the strips of colored cloth to wrap the whole area. Walt wondered if she was going to choke him before he realized she was very skilled in what she was doing.

"I reckon ya done this before."

"Raising three sons and caring for a husband teaches a body many things."

Finally, she was satisfied she had done all she could for Walt. He slowly got up and went outside. He could see a pile of split wood around J.J.

Walt painfully began to pick up pieces and stack them close to the house. He wondered if he would ever be free of pain. The men worked mostly in silence until nearly dark. It was then that the old woman came out of the back door.

"Supper's 'bout ready. Time ta worsh up."

The men looked at each other and smiled for the first time in many weeks. Minnie had made cornmeal mush pancakes again, served with molasses. This time instead of eggs, there were strips of fatback.

The men sat at the table as Minnie cleared the dishes. Both volunteered to help. She declined their offers. "I know ya boys are anxious ta get home. But would ya be willing ta stay for another day? My sons' wagon that my husband made as a Christmas present is round here somewhere. I don't think it's been took.

You could use it ta carry logs from the woods. I'd sure appreciate it."

J.J. and Walt looked at each other. Walt spoke up. "I could use another day of rest. I've been spyin' that gun of yerns. It needs a good cleanin'."

J.J. inquired, "Where would I look fer the wagon, Miss Minnie?"

"In the mornin' look in the barn. Be careful, though, it's 'bout ta fall down."

"We noticed that," J.J. said. All three chuckled. That night the men slept in front of the fireplace. It was the first warm sleep they had experienced in months. Neither heard the chickens cooing.

J.J. made several trips back and forth to the woods, using the little wagon he had found under a pile of rotting gunny sacks. Walt was correct that Minnie's gun wouldn't shoot. He carefully disassembled it, cleaned and oiled each piece then put it back together. When finished with the gun, he went outdoors to begin stacking firewood.

Near dinner time J.J. thrust the axe into a log and stood up straight. "Walt, is that chicken I smell cookin'?"

"Yes, I surely do believe it is."

"Do ya suppose Miss Minnie is cookin' one?"

"That sure would be nice! God sure was good leading us to this place."

Once again Minnie came to the door. "Sons, you done enough work. I got hot water aplenty. If ya bring in that worsh tub hanging there, after dinner you can git a proper bath."

The men didn't need to be told twice. Walt put the wagon and axe away while J.J. retrieved the tub. They washed their hands and faces at the outside basin before going in. Sitting on the table was a platter of fried chicken, gravy and the ever-present fried mush. They could only stare.

"Well, fellers, sit down 'fore the gravy gets cold."

They sat down and Walt spoke up. "Ma'am, I'd like ta give a prayer of thanks, if that's all right with you." Minnie nodded. "Dear Lord, we thank You for bringin' us to this fine woman. We thank You for Your blessings of this day. Thank You fer this fine meal and again for this dear lady. We ask You ta have mercy on her son Delbert and bring him home safely ta his ma. We ask this in Jesus' name. Amen."

Once the kitchen was cleaned and the

washtub filled, Minnie said, "Before you take your baths, I got somethin' for you." She left the room and returned with an armload of men's clothes. "Yer welcome to look through these duds. Some was my husband's and others was my boys'." She set them on the table, along with rags what passed for towels and again left the room.

Both men had a bath in the washtub and picked out a shirt and pants from the homemade clothes. Walt put on a brown cotton shirt with patches at the elbows. The pants were faded-blue denim bib overalls. One knee had a plaid patch. They were much too long. He removed them and cut off the end of each leg. He was glad the pants were bibs, so he could tie knots in the straps.

J.J.'s shirt was brown of the same cotton material as Walt's. It also had patches at each elbow. The pants were regular denim blue jeans, with a length that fit better. J.J. was a very tall man but extremely thin. He didn't have a belt to hold up the pants, but he remembered seeing an old rope in the barn. He retrieved the rope and cut a length long enough to use as a belt. He wound it through the loops of the pants and knotted the ends together. The waist of the pants almost looked like a woman's gathered skirt when he tightened the rope.

The next morning Minnie surprised the men once again. She gave each a yannigan bag made of muslin with straps for carrying it. J.J. could haul his on his back, but since Walt could not do that, Minnie had fashioned his to be tied around his waist. It held a change of clothes, a couple pieces of chicken, and several hard-cooked eggs. J.J.'s held the same items plus cornmeal and a small slab of bacon.

As they left, Minnie made a parting promise: "I'll be prayin' for ya boys ta make it home."

"Thank ya, Miss Minnie, ya really shouldn't be givin' us this food. Ya need it yerself," Walt said as he stood and opened the door.

Minnie started to reply but Walt held up his hand to silence her.

Standing at the edge of the farm yard was a young doe.

Quickly, but barely moving his arm, he said, "Miss Minnie, real easy like, hand me yer gun." Without questioning why, she did as Walt asked. Walt carefully lifted the gun, took aim and squeezed the trigger. The doe staggered and fell. J.J. ran to the doe and began to field dress it.

The men did not leave that day as planned. They stayed on another day to butcher the venison. Miss Minnie had an old smokehouse that needed to be repaired. By late afternoon J.J. and Walt had it in working order and began smoking some of the meat. The meat wouldn't be done soon enough for them to take any with them, but it would see Miss Minnie through the winter. For supper that night they all enjoyed fried venison steaks. Minnie also roasted a large piece of the venison.

The next day as the two left, besides what was already in their bags, Minnie had added a large portion of roasted venison for each. The leaving was hard. The three realized they likely would not ever see each other again.

Day after day the Texans continued walking. There was panic in the South. No one really knew what was going to happen. Farmers sometimes ran J.J. and Walt off, often at the point of a gun. They learned that by volunteering to do some work, they were more likely to get fed. That is how they went: chopping wood, mending a fence, repairing a roof. They worked, begged, hunted and sometimes stole their way across Kansas, Arkansas, the Indian Territory and finally into Texas.

Chapter 23

The day Walt walked onto the Circle G Ranch was forever burned into his mind. The big house looked deserted. There were weeds where once his ma had planted flowers. No lights shone from any window of either the big house or from Catherine and Blake's smaller house. No smoke rose from any chimney. He hadn't seen any cattle since coming onto the Gibson land.

Walt knew things were bad. Times had been hard even before he had joined up. There had been drought conditions since late in the 1850s. In 1864 the drought had resulted in the loss of the entire wheat crop and people lived in fear of starving to death. Walt had heard rumors that in February some troops had been given furloughs to go home and replant the wheat.

Blake's wife, Catherine, has seen Walt coming. She had just milked a cow and was returning to her house from the barn. At first, she thought it was Blake. When she realized it wasn't, she dropped the pail she was carrying, spilling the precious milk on the ground and crumpled to the earth on her knees. The most horrific scream Walt had ever heard came from deep within her chest. She bent to the ground and pounded her fists into the dirt. Alerted by the scream, her father-in-law, Howard, had seen her go down and ran to her. He tried his best to calm her and helped her into the main house. She continued to sob, holding tight fists close to her chest and looking up to the ceiling. For days she refused to eat or see anyone. Her son, Tim, sat outside her door crying, "Please, Mommy, please let me in."

A week later the community held a memorial service for all the men who did not come home. Catherine did not want to go. Her mother-in-law, Patricia Gibson, came into her bedroom.

"Catherine, you git out of that bed. Wash yerself and put on clean clothes. We're all mournin' Blake's death. I know you are more than the rest. But you have a son who's mournin' too, and needs comfortin'. You must brace up for his sake. You hear me?" Catherine got up and did as she was told.

She didn't hear anything that was spoken

at the service until the preacher said, "King David had a son who was very ill. David fasted and prayed face down on the ground, pleading with God for the child to live. Even so after seven days, the child died. When David learned of the child's death, he got up, washed, put on clean clothes and asked for something to eat. His servants could not understand the change in him. David said in II Samuel 12:22 and 23, 'While the child was yet alive, I fasted and wept: for I said, who can tell whether God will be gracious to me, that the child may live? But now he is dead, wherefore should I fast: can I bring him back again? I shall go to him, but he shall not return to me.'"

Blake was never coming back. One day she would go to him. Catherine looked down at Tim. He was sitting all hunched over, trying to make himself as little as possible.

He looked so very sad and miserable. Tim was here and needed her. She had to brace up, as her mother-in-law had said, if for no other reason than for Tim. From then on whenever friends asked her how she was doing she would reply, "Fine." At night she would wrap herself in Blake's shirt and cry herself to sleep.

Chapter 24

Walt knocked on Catherine's door one evening about eight months after his return. She stood tall and stately, silhouetted in the door frame. Catherine had always been thin. Some women unkindly called her skinny. Today she weighed less than on her wedding day ten years before. Her features were sharp, partly due to the lack of any excess weight. Her dark hair was pulled back into a tight bun. Her dark brown eyes appeared large surrounded by her slim face.

Walt was holding a box of dried fruit. Catherine was surprised when she opened the door. "Walt, is everything all right? It seems late to be calling."

Walt spoke in a soft, gentle voice. Catherine thought it was so unlike his usual boisterous way. "Here, I brung ya these. Could we talk?"

"Well, yes. I'll come out. We can sit on the porch." There was a small table and two chairs near the end of the porch. "Would you like a cup of coffee or a glass of water?"

"Thank ya, no." He placed the box on the table between them.

"Catherine, I know yer grievin' fer Blake. When he married ya, I told him he'd gotten the pick of the litter. I've admired ya all these years. I know I'll never hold up ta

Blake or never take his place in yer heart. I don't aim ta. But I come here ta ask ya ta marry me. I've watched ya try ta carry on without him. I appreciate how hard it was for ya during the war and ta go on without him now. Ya need a man and little Tim needs a father. Like I said, I don't aim ta take Blake's place in Tim's heart. But I'll be the best father I can ta him and show him how ta be a good man. I promise ta love ya and always treat ya right. Maybe in time ya'll come ta care for me."

Catherine sat studying Walt. He looked much older than his thirty-two years. The dark clear eyes looking at her showed only sadness. The hair that had once been almost black was now nearly all white. What he had just said was the last thing she expected to hear. Her whole body protested against the idea.

"Don't say nothin' jest now. Jest think about what I said. If ya agree ta marry me, ya can tell me when ya decide. If ya don't want ta, ya don't have ta ever say so. I won't ever bring up the subject again. I'll be saying good-night now." He got up from the chair and walked painfully off into the darkness.

Catherine tried to put Walt's proposal out of her mind. But she couldn't. She had nothing. She lived at the benevolence of her father-in-law. She didn't believe he would ever put her out, except, things don't always turn out as they should. What about Tim? He should eventually get his father's share of the ranch. Surely, even if she didn't marry Walt, he would see that Tim got his rightful inheritance. After contemplating all of this for several days, she decided to talk to Walt again. She told Tim to find Uncle Walt and ask him to come by after supper that evening.

Walt came. It was obvious he had shaved and taken a bath. He also had on a clean shirt. This was unusual for the middle of the week. The night was turning cold and she had a fire going in the fireplace.

"Come in, Walt. Please sit down. Let me pour you a cup of coffee." Walt did not object. "I've given serious thought to your proposal. There is much truth in what you said. If you are willing to accept me, knowing I don't love you and there's no guarantee I ever will, I will become your wife. I promise to be a faithful wife to you and do the best I can."

"That's all any man could ask." They did not kiss, only smiled at each other.

The wedding was held in the same church

where Catherine had wed Blake. She couldn't help but compare the two. At her first wedding there was an air of jubilation. The first time, she wore a silk lavender dress with yards and yards of white lace over it. She had carried a bouquet of Texas bluebells. The sun had been shining.

This time it felt more like a dirge to her. Her dress was an old, faded brown one, without an inch of decoration. Her mother-in-law had given her an antique Indian turquoise necklace to wear. Catherine wasn't sure if it was a gift or if she was expected to return it after the wedding. She carried no flowers. It did not rain but the sky was overcast. Only the immediate family was present. Noticeably absent was Tim. He had repeatedly vomited the night before and was too sick to leave his bed.

Catherine had told eight-year-old Tim

about Uncle Walt and her getting married. He responded with a fiery outburst of anger. He threw himself to the floor, yelling obscenities and pounding his head. She had not expected that. Tim was usually very biddable. Catherine got down on the floor beside Tim and managed to get hold of him. She wrapped him in her arms, rocking him back and forth, talking to him softly. She tried to explain, "Tim, no one will ever take your daddy's place and he will always have a place in my heart just as you always will. We need to pull together, to go on with life. Please trust me. I only want what is best for us."

From that day on Tim became a more difficult child. He got into fights at school and sassed the teacher. It was a struggle to get him to obey at home. The only person who seemed to have any control over him was his grandpa.

Walt did his best, but Tim only resented him. Since riding a horse was extremely painful for Walt, he chose to drive a buggy. It was rare to see him astride a horse. Walt's father, Howard, gladly turned over the management of the ranch to him. It was not unusual for Walt to spend the entire day in his office. Tim thought this was sissified. He was too young to understand how severely Walt had been hurt in the war or how important Walt's management was to the ranch.

Chapter 25

In the immediate years after the Civil War there was an abundance of wild, unbranded cattle. During the war the cattle were allowed to roam because there had not been enough men left on the ranches to round them up.

Several ranchers went together on "cattle hunts." Each man carried his own grub – usually cornbread, bacon and some coffee. He also brought his own sleeping gear and an extra horse. Some of the cattle belonged to the Circle G. Walt was unable to help in the hunts. He was too weak and ailing to ride a horse or carry out prolonged hard work.

Mark, Walt's younger brother who had stayed home during the Civil War and Tim were part of the hunts. Howard Gibson also went with the boys, but he wasn't very strong at standing up for his rights. The Circle G often had difficulty proving which cattle were theirs. Because the boys were young, the older men from other ranches often bullied them. J.J. did his best to look out for Circle G interests. He, however, had his own brand, the Lazy J, to watch for and was not always around when challenges to the Circle G came up.

As the years passed, Catherine came to discover a special love for Walt. He was good to her. To this union was born a daughter, Ruth, and two sons, William and

Stuart. Sadly, they also lost two babies, one at birth and one at six weeks.

In 1877, Mark married a beautiful girl by the name of Sarah. They had twin sons, Matthew and John.

The main house built by Howard and Patricia Gibson was a large one-story building made of fieldstones. It had high ceilings, which helped keep the inside cool in the hot Texas summers. There were only a few small windows, since the house had been built for protection against raiding Indians and bandits. The homemade furnishings were simple and few. There were no luxuries.

When Patricia died in 1879, Howard exchanged homes with Walt and Catherine. They had been living in a smaller house a short distance from the main house.

Howard's youngest son, Mark and his wife Sarah lived in a third home on the ranch. Other buildings included a large stable, a bunkhouse and three adobe huts for married cowhands and their families.

In 1885 two of the huts were empty. Ramon and Teresa Mahoney occupied the third house. Ramon's father was Irish and his mother Mexican. Ramon had hired on to the Circle G in 1882. He and Teresa married in 1883.

The harassment by eastern and foreign syndicates became a problem for ranches. Several of the smaller ranchers gave up and moved further west. A number of the large ranches were owned by men from England and Scotland who had little interest in ranching other than to make money. The owners were seldom, if ever, around. They hired ranch managers to run the businesses. These enterprises were eager to control more and more land. As a result, several offers were made to buy the Circle G. Especially important were the grazing rights and the accessibility to water.

Howard Gibson refused to sell out. Other means were used to influence him to change his mind. The few cattle Circle G owned started disappearing. As soon as a calf was born, it either mysteriously vanished or was found wearing another rancher's brand. The cattle were stampeded. Several Circle G riders were injured. One man had died when he fell off his horse into the stampeding cattle. Men became hesitant to work for the Circle G. There were rumors anyone hiring on would soon be killed. Several cattle died from drinking poisoned water. The last year the

Circle G had had enough cattle to make it worthwhile for a cattle drive was in 1881.

Still, Gibson refused to sell. One day Howard Gibson was riding alone, checking his stock. He stopped by a wooded area near a water hole to let his horse drink and rest. A man sitting his horse a short distance away fired a single shot. Howard was found several hours later face down in one of the Circle G's coveted water holes. The sheriff said it was probably a hunting accident; no investigation was undertaken. Rumor was that the sheriff was on the payroll of the larger ranchers.

J.J. and Walt had remained fast friends since returning from the war. J.J. and his brother Elmer were each half-owners of the Lazy J. J.J. had never married.

After the Howard's funeral J.J. and another rancher, Dave "Slim" Barns, a widower with a twelve-year-old daughter, approached Walt, Mark and Tim.

J.J. spoke, "It 'pears the eastern syndicates are goin' ta win, boys. Slim and me are pullin' out. My brother, Elmer. and his family are movin' ta California."

"No, J.J., ya can't give up," uttered Walt in dismay.

"Well, we ain't exactly givin' up," put in Slim. "I jest got back from Montana. Beeves are sellin' high to the miners. And the government is handin' out free land, one hundred and sixty acres for every man and woman eighteen and over. It's a beautiful place. Good grazin' land. I sold my spread ta old Mr. Saunders jest a couple of days before he died. I feel I got a fair price. Ya got the water rights. I'm thinkin' ya could get a bit more."

J.J. suggested, "Talk it over with the women folk. If we pooled our interests, we could put together a herd of twelve, maybe fifteen hundred head. When we git ta Montana we can sell the three-year-olds to the miners and keep the young ones. Next spring we'd have a good start on some fine spreads. Why, with the women signing for land, your family alone would have hundreds of acres."

The Circle G family did not rush to a decision quickly. They debated for several days. The older men had remembered how hard their folks had worked to develop the ranch. Yet looking about them, they knew there was the real possibility of slowly being driven out and losing everything, no matter what they did.

Chapter 26

1885

One warm Sunday morning, a young man came running into the church disrupting the service.

"Hey! The Gibson's house and barn are on fire!" The worshipers ran out the door. In the far distance, black plumes of smoke were rising from the direction of the Circle G ranch. The people rushed to their buggies, wagons and horses and headed out of town to the burning buildings.

By the time the first people reached the ranch, the fire had totally consumed the barn. People quickly formed a fire line from the water trough to Mark's house and the bunkhouse. They wetted down those two buildings and were able to save the bunkhouse but not Mark and Sarah's home. The old family home was also completely gone. Tim was living in Catherine's former house and it had not been set on fire nor had the three small houses used for married cowhands.

Many community friends stayed on after the fires were out. Others left but returned later bringing food, small household items and clothing. Everyone, including children, helped clean the grounds as much as possible. Several men stood guard during the night to watch for hot spots.

That night the Gibson family sat in

the bunkhouse, overwhelmed. Finally, Catherine spoke up, "Walt, I'm for going to see young Mr. Saunders. Tomorrow talk to J.J. and Slim; see what their plans are. Go see Saunders. He'll be expecting you, I'm sure. Let's make plans for Montana."

"Are you sure, Catherine?" She nodded her head. Walt turned to Mark, "What are you thinkin'?"

"Walt, it's you that fought them Yankees. If ya think ya can live amongst them, then I say do it." Mark turned to Tim. "Speak up, Tim. Part of this spread belongs ta you."

Tim, now a mature twenty-eight, had conquered his hate and bitterness. He was well liked and respected. "The way I'm seein' it, there ain't enough here fer all of us. I've been thinkin' about movin' on anyhow. I guess Montana's as good a place as any."

Walt didn't have to go see anyone, including Mr. Saunders. By seven the next morning, J.J. and Slim were at the Circle G. The men sat in the yard on an odd assortment of chairs, around a partially burnt table, talking for a long time. Finally, Walt called to his wife, Catherine and Mark's wife, who was due to deliver her third baby, to come over.

Walt told the women what had been decided. "As soon as the spring roundup is over, Mark, Tim, J.J. and Slim will head out fer Montana. After the baby comes, the rest of us will go by train ta Denver. I believe there's a train line runnin' north ta Billings, Montana. From there we may have ta go by stagecoach or purchase wagons ta git ta where we're plannin' on settlin' in Montana. Slim's leavin' me a map showin' where ta go once we git ta Montana. 'Til we leave, the men can live in the bunkhouse and you women and kids can have Tim's house. I'll go see Saunders after lunch."

He had no sooner said this when young Butch Saunders rode into the yard. His presence made a strong impression: over six feet tall and quite handsome, he was broad-shouldered and solidly built. Old Man Saunders had died recently, and Butch had taken over. Butch was the same age as J.J. and Walt. His pa had paid another man to serve in his son's place during the Civil War and that man had been killed. No one in the district had good feelings for young Saunders. He only hired men who knew how to use a gun. It was rumored, he bullied his wife and children. Walt was concerned about dealing with young Saunders; he believed he would have gotten a fairer deal from Butch's father.

"Folks, I'm real sorry ta hear of your misfortune. If there's anything I can do ta help, jest let me know. My good wife jest made these rolls and said ta bring them to ya."

Catherine offered up a quick prayer before saying, "Thank you kindly, Mr. Saunders. Please thank Mrs. Saunders for me."

"Saunders, are ya still intent on buyin' our ranch?" This was asked by Mark rather acidly.

"Why, yes, Mark, I am. I'll be fair. I don't intend ta cheat you. I'm a good Christian man. I want you ta know I had nothing ta do with yer papa's death or this fire."

Before Mark or Tim could respond, Walt spoke up. "I appreciate that, Butch. Jest tell me when will be a good time ta come by and I'll be there."

"Y'all come by for dinner tomorra. Mrs. Saunders said to invite ya over. Come early and we'll talk before the meal. I got ta go now, but let me know if I kin help in any way." He tipped his hat to the women, turned his horse and started down the lane to the main road.

Chapter 27

At the same time the cattle were stampeding toward Rose and Doris in Nebraska, Mark's wife Sarah in Texas, was delivering their third child.

"Uhhhhh, ahhhhhh, oh, Catherine, won't this baby ever come?"

Catherine had just turned forty-four, three days ago. No one, not even her husband, had remembered, but that didn't bother her. She had been through too much sorrow to let a small thing like that disturb her. Today she was acting as midwife for her sister-in-law.

The laboring mother gave another yell. "I don't think he's ever going to get born. The twins came so easy."

Sarah was twenty-five, scarcely five feet tall and very pretty. Her chestnut blond hair was soaked in sweat. Her unusually short neck always bothered her. She felt it was unattractive. As the mother of two active twin boys, she frequently looked disheveled. She didn't have much time for herself, especially with Mark gone with the cattle drive to Montana.

"Sugar, I've birthed six young'uns. Each one was different. I can see the babe's crown. Push really hard when the next pain comes. He's ready to be born."

Sarah pushed as hard as she could with

the next contraction. Then she heard the sweetest sound. Her baby wailing.

"Sarah, it's a girl! She sure has got the lungs. My, she's pretty!"

"Let me have my baby, please. She is pretty. Oh, Catherine just look at her! I didn't want to say anything, but I so much wanted a girl."

"Give her to Teresa to bathe. You still have some work to do."

When Sarah was ready to have her baby back, Catherine asked, "Have you decided what to name her?"

"Yes, I'm calling her Rose Patricia. Rose was my momma's name and you know, Patricia was Mark's momma's name."

Three days later, Sarah had just finished nursing Rose Patricia when Catherine and her ten-year-old daughter, Ruthie, came into the house and set down a pail of berries and a pitcher of lemonade. Ruthie was the youngest of Catherine's children. She was fascinated by the new baby and would beg to rock Rose Patricia. She was always willing to help with the baby or to entertain her two cousins, Matt and Johnny.

Catherine told Ruthie to go back outside with her cousins for a few minutes. Sarah sat staring lovingly down at her daughter. Catherine came into the bedroom and smiled at the happy scene. She sat down beside Sarah. "How are you doing?"

"I'm fine, Catherine. Thank you so much for being there to help me with the birthing."

"I wouldn't have missed it for anything." Then remembering, "I made some lemonade before going ta pick the berries. Would you like a glass?”

“That would be wonderful.”

Catherine handed Sarah a glass. “Oh, Catherine, I do wish my momma was here ta see little Rose.”

“I’m glad you brought that up. If you don’t want to talk, it’s all right. But with us leaving soon, I’ve wondered about your papa and momma. Why didn’t you ever go to see them or at least let them know what happened to you?”

“I couldn’t. They died before I had a chance. I heard some young folks were living on the farm. I didn’t want to cause trouble with them. Causing them to worry I was going to run them out. I wish my folks could know how happy I am.”

"Maybe they do. God is good. Just trust Him."

They heard footsteps and a door slam. "Hey, what ya women doin'? Havin' a hen party?" Walt came noisily into the house with Ruthie and the twins following close behind. Walt didn't say much, but he was almost constantly in pain. He continued to manage the financial part of the business, but he was still unable to ride a horse for any length of time or physically help to run the ranch.

Catherine and Sarah came into the main room. Catherine found more glasses and poured lemonade for her husband and the children.

Walt informed the two women about the evening's plans. "Saunders is coming over after supper. We're making final arrangements for the sale of the ranch. He kind of has us over a barrel. He knows we want ta git out of here. He keeps trying ta lower the selling price."

Catherine answered her husband's pessimism hopefully. "He also knows the grazing rights we own are valuable. There are other ranchers more than eager to get them."

"Yes, but they may be afraid of bucking Saunders. Might be good for ya ta lift up a prayer."

"I've been praying about this move ever since Mark first suggested it."

"Speaking of movin', what's the idea of these three piles here?"

Catherine gave a hearty laugh. "One pile is things we must take with us. The second pile is things we might need. The last pile is things we don't need. I keep moving the items from one pile to another, depending on how I change my mind about our needs."

"Well, we'll be leaving as soon as the sale is final. Ya better make up yer mind and start packin'. When I'm in town, I'll contract with the freight company ta ship all the stuff we aren't taking with us. It can't be too expensive, as we lost so much in the fire."

"I'll do my earnest best to choose carefully and we'll be ready."

"I know you will, darlin'."

"Momma, kin I add anything ta the pile of things we need?" voiced Ruthie.

"Yes, dear, I'd never deprive you of your needs." She laughed again as Walt waved a good-bye and left the room, trailed by the children. Ruthie was the apple of his eye and the twins adored their Uncle Walt.

Later that evening, Catherine sat near a window enjoying the evening breeze. She could hear Walt and Butch Saunders sitting on the patio discussing the sale of the ranch. Ruth was asleep on a cot in a corner. Saunders was trying to lower the purchase price yet again. He maintained without the main house and barn, the property wasn't worth as much. She could tell by Walt's voice that he was upset.

Then Walt said, "Butch, I wasn't gonna bring this up, but I've had another bid for the place. When J.J. and I was makin' our way home after the war we stopped at a farm in Arkansas. It were owned by a nice widow lady. She'd lost her husband and two sons in the Late Unpleasantness. One son, Delbert was his name, survived.

Ev'ry wonst in a while he and I correspond. He's done all right. He knowed I've been thinkin' 'bout pulling out. In his last letter he said he wants ta move his family west and asked 'bout buyin' this place. He said that he'd meet any reasonable offer. If ya don't stand by yer pa's offer, I'm sellin' ta my friend."

Butch became very quiet, staring out into the night. "Does this Delbert know about the fire and the loss of the buildings?"

"He does. He still wants the land."

"Let me see the letter. How do I know yer tellin' me the truth?"

"Butch, are ya callin' me a liar? If that be so, ya can jest leave."

Butch looked at Walt like he wanted to hit him. He got up and paced about for several minutes. Walt became worried that he had gone too far and that Butch wasn't going to take the bait. Finally, Butch turned to Walt and said, "All right, Walt, you win. I don't know if yer tellin' me the truth or not, but I'll pay your price. Meet me in town tomorra mornin'; we'll do the paper work."

After Butch Saunders left, Walt came into the bedroom. "Did ya hear us, Catherine?"

"Yes, I heard. I don't recall you ever getting a letter from Arkansas."

"I never have. I don't even know if Delbert survived the prison camp." He looked at Catherine and smiled. Then they both started laughing. This woke up Ruthie.

"Why are you laughing, Momma?"

"Papa was just telling me about a funny dream he had. Go back to sleep, dear." She reached over and kissed Walt. The gesture surprised Walt. Catherine was not inclined to express her feelings.

"When do ya think Sarah will be ready ta leave? I don't want ta rush her. But I'm sure anxious ta git goin'."

"Could you give her one more week? She's young and strong. I can have Ruthie stay with her to help with the twins while Sarah packs."

"Sure. It'll probably take that long ta settle things with Butch. While I'm in town tomorra, I'll check on train reservations."

"That will be wonderful. I can't wait to see Tim and the boys. I still think the boys were too young to go on a cattle drive. It put an unfair responsibility on Tim."

"Well, what's done is done. No sense ta worry on it now. Besides, the boys are probably havin' the time of their lives."

Catherine fell asleep in her husband's arms, praying for her sons' safety, so far away.

The next day Catherine was hanging clothes on the line. She caught a movement in the corner of her eye. She looked in that direction and saw Teresa hunched down among a grove of cottonwood trees. Teresa was married to Ramon, a cowhand now on the cattle drive. Catherine dropped the shirt she was about to pin to the line, back into the clothes basket and walked over to Teresa. She had her face in her hands, sobbing quietly.

"Teresa, what's the matter? Why are you crying'?"

"Miss Catherine, I'm sorry. I did not think anyone would see me here."

Catherine knelt beside Teresa and put her

arm around the crying girl. "Tell me. What's wrong? Are you missing Ramon?"

"Sí, Miss Catherine. But that is not why I cry. I am, how you say, disgustada?"

"Distressed, upset?"

"Sí, I am distressed. Ramon wishes to stay in Montana. He says I am to come with you on the train and meet him there."

"Yes, I thought that was all decided before the men left on the drive?"

"Sí, but no one ask me. I am not sure I want to go. My madre, she cries. She says I never see her again. And I am afraid. I have never lived anyplace but here." Having said this, Teresa lowered her head into her skirt and began quietly weeping.

"Oh, Teresa, darling, I'm so sorry. You are right. Everyone just expected you to go along with the decisions that were being made. Texas is a wonderful place to live. I know how very difficult it is to leave people you love. But now you must decide what is the most important thing to you. Do you want Ramon to come back here and continue to work someone else's land? Do you want to continue to live in someone else's house and work in someone else's home? Or would you rather own your own land and live in your own house? You and Ramon are both citizens. Both of you can claim land in Montana."

"Me, señora? I can own land?"

"Yes, Teresa, you can. You could have an inheritance to leave your children."

"But what about mi madre? I do not want to leave her."

"Do you think she would come with

us? Would Ramon let her live with you in Montana?"

"Yes, sí. She lives with mi hermano, my brother. He will be happy to let her come with me. But I do not know if she will leave. Mi hermano has many children. She loves them so."

Catherine tenderly smiled at Teresa and used her skirt to wipe away Teresa's tears. "Darling, things are not always as bad as they seem. Talk it over with your mother and brother. And pray about it. God will help you make the best decision."

Teresa wasn't sure how to approach her mother. She decided to tell her some good news first. She told her mother she was expecting a baby. Her mother immediately insisted she come with Teresa to help with the baby, even before Teresa had a chance to ask her about coming.

The Texas Gibsons had no way to know that, as they prepared to leave for Montana, the men on the cattle drive were facing a life-changing decision.

Chapter 28

Rose turned the buggy in the same direction the cattle were running. "See if you can unleash the reins of them horses," she yelled at Doris as she guided the horse and buggy toward some tall bushes just passed the edge of the stampede.

Doris climbed into the back of the buggy and over the supplies. To her relief Molly was already loose and she was able to loosen Ginger's reins without difficulty. After what seemed like an eternity, the two ladies and their belongings were out of the main chaos and into the bushes. Milling around them were a number of bawling calves and some of their mothers.

Colby stood on his hind legs with his front paws on the edge of the dashboard, barking at the cows.

"Will you shut up!" yelled Rose. Colby looked at her before jumping out of the buggy. He sat down and continued to bark.

"Are ya all right?" asked a young, blonde-haired man. They had not realized anyone had ridden up. Before either had a chance to answer, two more trail hands rode up and dismounted. One was holding Ginger's reins. The other had Molly.

A fourth man galloped up. "Someone better shut that dog up 'fore I shoot it. It's goin' ta spook the beeves again. One stampede in a day is one too many. Any of you know what startled them?" They all stared at the fourth man, shrugging their shoulders and shaking their heads.

Doris jumped down and grabbed Colby, muzzling him with her hand. She carried him to the buggy and held him tight as he tried to wiggle out of her arms. Rose reached into the supplies and pulled out a bone and tossed it on the ground. Doris let Colby go. He pounced on the bone and was content to sit and chew.

"Now, who are ya and what are two women doin' out here in the middle of nothin'?" This came from Mark Gibson, part owner and trail boss of the Circle G and the man who had threatened to shoot Colby.

"What business is that of yers?" asked Rose in a most unfriendly manner.

"It's my business when ya run inta my herd."

"Just how were we ta know yer herd was goin' ta be stampeding over the hill at us?"

"Uncle Mark, maybe we should start over," put in Tim Gibson. "Ladies, this here's my uncle, Mark Gibson. He's the boss. The feller holding the ginger mare is Jim Johnson. We call him J.J. Dave Barns is holding the other mare. He's known mostly as Slim. I'm Tim Gibson. We four are partners in this herd."

"Howdy. I'm Mrs. Rose Elder. My friend here is Mrs. Doris Clark."

Tim gave Mark a startled look. Mark shook his head almost imperceptibly at Tim.

Mark asked "Would you be the Doris Clark the marshal's lookin' fer?" Mark was stocky and looked to be in his thirties. His face was round, with very light blue eyes and blond hair.

"How does everybody know about me? I haven't done anything wrong!"

"The marshal came ta see us when we were near Hays City. Asked us ta keep a look out fer ya."

"Hays City," both women said in unison as they looked at each other.

Doris continued, "What did he say to do if you saw me?"

"He didn't say ta do anything. Jest asked us if we'd seen ya. What have ya done anyway for half the country ta be lookin' fer ya?"

Doris sighed and leaned against the wagon. "My husband and five other men robbed a bank in Ardmore Bend. Two clerks were killed. Two of the outlaws were also killed. My husband was shot but managed to make it home. I didn't know 'til then that he was an outlaw. He died just after getting home. Before he died, he told me to leave because the three remaining outlaws would be coming to get the bank money. He had brought it with him in saddle bags.

"I was out in the barn getting ready to go when the other three arrived. While they were in the house I got on my horse and rode out. I hid in the woods nearby to watch them. They burned the house and barn. I was scared so I just rode, 'til I dropped.

"Rose found me. We've been riding together since then. We came across a sheriff that told us he had captured one outlaw. A second outlaw spotted us and tried to get me to tell him where the money is. We were able to get away from him. I think he was also arrested. I think there still might be one more outlaw around somewhere and he's probably looking for me."

"So why does the marshal want ya? Do ya know where the money is?"

"The last time I saw the saddle bags they were hanging over a chair in the kitchen."

"Would ya be a-goin' ta Ardmore Bend, Mr. Gibson?" spoke up Rose.

"We'll be goin' between Ardmore Bend and Ogallala. We don't plan on goin' into either place. Why ya askin'?"

"Mind if we tag along?"

"Yes, I do mind. We got no time for lookin' after a couple of women."

"Well, we'll jest ride a short way behind ya then."

"Suit yerself. Don't matter none ta me if ya eat our dust."

"Jest a minute, Uncle Mark. Could we have a word in private?" Mark and Tim walked out of earshot. They talked back and forth. Mark had a scowl on his face and his arms crossed. Tim had his arms close to his sides with his elbows bent, hands open, palms up and moving then up and down. Finally, Mark put both hands out in front of him, palms facing Tim and shrugged. They walked back to the wagon. Tim did the talking. "Do ya'll know how ta cook?"

"Sure, we do. Doris is the best pie maker in Nabraskee." Doris knew for a fact that was not true.

"Well, a while back our cook died from a snake bite. One of the men has been cookin', if that's what ya can call it. If ya want ta do the cookin', ya can come along 'til we get ta Ardmore Bend and hire on a new cook."

"Thank you kindly. I don't believe you'll regret it."

"Tim, drive them over ta the chuck wagon and introduce them to Gary. Give him the good news; tell him ta help the women fer today."

"Right, Uncle Mark."

Chapter 29

"Gary, these ladies are Mrs. Rose and Mrs. Doris. Boss hired 'em ta do the cookin' 'til we get ta Ardmore Bend."

"Does that mean I kin git back ta wrangling?"

"Tomorra. Fer today ya stay with 'em fer supper ta' show 'em what's expected."

Gary was only too happy to show the two ladies around. Gary, a young man of twenty-one years, was another very slim and tall man. He had a triangular-shaped face and a very pointed chin. His eyes were so dark brown they looked almost black. He was so attentive that Rose finally told him to get lost.

Gary gladly walked away. Doris with a worried frown on her face turned to Rose, "Do you know anything about cooking for cowhands?"

"What's ta know? We jest cook the same things, only more of 'em. Gary, come back here. What were you plannin' on fixin' fer supper?"

"Beans, that's 'bout all we got left."

Doris stood looking at Gary for a moment before turning to Rose. "Rose, our bacon's about gone. Let's fry it up and add it to the beans. Also, the potatoes are going bad. Gary can be put to cutting out the bad spots. I'll fry them with the rest of the onions. We can also fix hoe cakes and use the rest of the honey."

"Boy! Ya fix that and evera man will be askin' ya ta marry 'im. Even you, Ma'am." This last sentence was directed to Rose, who gave him a look that backed him against the wagon. "Sorry, ma'am, I meant no offense."

"Jest watch yer mouth or you'll be eaten' yer own cookin'."

"Yes, ma'am."

The cowhands came drifting in one by one. Doris thought they were as dirty as, if not dirtier than, the Indian children they had befriended earlier.

Two young boys rode in. They were covered in dirt and mud; Doris couldn't tell the color of their clothes or even their faces. They dropped down off their horses and unsaddled them. Both looked at the two women dumbfounded. The older boy shrugged his shoulders at his brother and handed over his horse's reins. This boy led the horses to the remuda. The area where spare horses were kept. When he returned, the two walked to the chuck wagon. Neither said a word as they each picked up a plate, and stared at Doris as she filled the plates with generous portions of food. They walked across to their saddles, sat down, ate and fell instantly asleep. Doris went to the sleeping boys and gathered up their dirty dishes.

Other cowhands were watching this and laughed. Doris noticed the other men licked their plates clean before handing them to her to wash. Gary told her that was what the hands were supposed to do. She wasn't expected to gather the dishes herself.

Doris placed the dirty dishes in a wash pan and asked, "Who are those two boys? They look too young to be on a cattle drive."

Gary smiled at Doris before speaking, "Those are Tim's half-brothers. See, Mark Gibson, the trail boss, is Tim's and the boys' uncle. They're part owners of these cattle with Walt Gibson, J.J. Johnson and Slim Barns. Mr. Walt is Mr. Mark's brother. He's Tim's step-father and the boys' papa."

Gary could see by the look on Doris' face, he was confusing her. He started again, "Tim's father, Blake, and his uncle Walt were in the Civil War. Mr. Mark was only a young'un, 'bout thirteen or fourteen when they left. So, he stayed home. Mr. Blake was kilt. Mr. Walt was bad hurt but was able ta make it home. Tim was eight or nine. Mr. Walt started courtin' Tim's ma. Sometime later Tim's ma and his uncle,

Mr. Walt, got married. Mrs. Gibson birthed Billy and 'bout two years later she birthed Stu. Little Ruthie was birthed eight or ten years ago."

"But why are boys that young on a cattle drive? Why didn't their papa, Mr. Walt, at least come on the cattle drive to look after the boys?"

"Shucks, they ain't so young. I started drivin' cattle when I was ten. And like I say, Mr. Walt got bad hurt in the war. He can't even set a hoss much. He mostly rides in a buggy. He knows his 'rithmetic real well and he's a knowin' man with words. He does the paper work for the ranch. He's parleyin' the sale of the ranch, too. When that's done and Mr. Mark's wife births her baby, the rest of the family will be comin' along to Montana."

"It's just the boys seem so dirty and exhausted."

"That 'cause they're drag riders."

"Drag riders?"

"Drag riders ride behind the herd and 're gittin' all the dirt. Their job's ta keep the slower beeves a movin'."

"It seems to me they could at least wash."

Gary laughed at this. "Why, what fer? They'd jest git dirty tamorra."

Doris sighed, finished washing the dishes then walked behind the chuck wagon. She was fascinated by it. She had never seen one up close. Behind the back gate, which came down, there were shelves for storing cooking supplies such as flour, sugar, salt, some spices and dried beans.

Gary had jabbed two poles a few feet out

on either side of the back of the wagon. He had then stretched a canvas between the back and the poles. This provided shelter for cooking and for the hands as they ate, in the event of rain.

All cooking pans were cast iron. There were four large frying pans and two good-sized kettles; the eating plates were enamelware. There was a field oven for baking. On one side of the wagon was a large barrel. Gary said it held enough water for two days. A large box on the other side held tools. Under the wagon an area had been built to store firewood.

The chuck wagon also carried the cowhands' bedrolls and personal belongings. Gary showed the women where to find mending supplies such as needles, thread and scissors. There were also several odd pieces of cloth, used for patching; they would be expected to repair tears in the men's clothing. In another box were basic medical supplies. As cooks they might be called upon to care for wounds, upset stomachs, general aches and hurting teeth. Doris looked into the medical box. She picked up a bottle. Coal oil was printed on a label. "What is this used for?"

"Lice," was all Gary said as he took the bottle from her and picked up another. "This is dried bachelor's buttons. It's used fer diarrhea. Beggin' yer pardon ma'am. And this smelly stuff is bison fat. It's fer piles. Beggin' yer pardon, again, ma'am.

"If'n a man don't know how ta read or write, he might ask one of yous ta write a letter fer him or read one sent ta him. Mmm, ya also might be called on ta pull a tooth." The women continued to stare

at Gary wondering what had they gotten
themselves into.

Doris spied a half-empty bottle of whiskey.
"What is that for?"

"That's what is called 'snake bite medicine'.
Now none of the drovers is allowed ta carry
a bottle. But sometimes it might come
in handy".

"It didn't help your cook much did it?"
voiced Rose.

"Well, Ma'am, it did ease his goin' some."

"Yes, it probably did. I'm sorry."

Next Gary showed the two women a large
pot. "Evera night, yer are ta put dried beans
and water in this pot. By the next day the
beans will have softened fer cookin'."

Gary went to check the coffeepot. It was
a large heavy one. Doris guessed it must

hold at least twenty cups. "Be sure ta' always have plenty of coffee on hand. The boys ridin' night guard will want it."

Doris had noticed a separate wagon which at present was empty. "What is that wagon sitting over there used for?"

"That's fer the baby calves that are born on the drive. Until they're able ta keep up with their mommas they get ta ride in the wagon. Right now, they's five. The boys put them in the wagon of a mornin' and at night parcel'm back to their mommas.

"Now ya best git bedded down as soon as possible. Our day starts about three come a mornin'."

"Three!" both women echoed.

"Yep. We need ta build up the fire ta make fresh coffee and start making biscuits. Come over here. This is the grinder and in this sack is the coffee beans. Do ya both know how ta use a grinder?" Doris and Rose nodded.

Oh, and here is the crock where the sourdough is kept. Ya jest pinch a bit off, add more flour and some water ta make biscuits. I'll come around in the mornin' and help ya get things started, if'n ya want me to." Again, both women nodded.

The rain that had been coming down intermittently all day, had finally stopped, at least for the time being. Cowhands who weren't on night watch were either talking in low tones or asleep.

Doris looked across the fire. Mr. Mark and his nephew, Tim, were having a conversation. Tim saw her looking at them. He winked and smiled; Doris felt her face burn. Feeling the glow, she rationalized that it was just the fire making her warm.

He got up and walked over to Doris and Gary.

"Are ya doin' all right, Miss Doris? I don't want ya to overwork."

"I'm fine. Please, don't concern yourself about me. Would you like a cup of coffee? There is a little left. I'm getting ready to make a fresh pot."

Tim accepted the cup then said, "The river's too high at this spot ta cross because of all the rain. Tomorra Uncle Mark and J.J. will ride up river ta see if they can find a shallow spot. Me and Slim will ride down river ta look. Gary, help the women ta make a list of stuff ya need. You and whoever ya want can go ta that town we saw this mornin' ta get supplies. Ya can use two of the mules that're used for pulling the chuck wagon ta carry supplies."

"Could you let Rose go with them?" Doris asked, surprising herself at this boldness.

"Why?"

"Ask her, please."

Tim stood looking at Doris for a minute. "She'll have ta ride a horse. Ya think you can do the cookin' by yerself?"

"Yes, I can do the cooking and she knows how to ride."

"All right. Gary, ask Mrs. Rose if she wants ta go."

"Sure, Mr. Tim."

"Thanks, fer the coffee. I have ta go on watch now." As he left, he gave Doris another wink and a smile. Doris was flustered. She hoped Gary hadn't seen the wink. Not knowing quite what to do, she finally asked Gary, "What did you mean when you asked about getting back to wrangling?"

"Josh, the feller asleep sittin' up over there, and me take care of the remuda. Most fellers have their own hoss and maybe one or two more. Each man really needs five or six ta do the job. Only a couple have that many. The ranch supplies most of the hosses."

"How often do the men change horses?"

"Well, it depends on what's bein' done. There's roundup hosses, cutting hosses and of course night mounts. They's the best seein' ones. A man might change hosses three or four times in a day."

"Do you like wrangling, Gary?"

"Mm, not really. I'd rather be with the herd. It's jest something that has to be done."

Doris had been hearing pounding near her wagon. She walked down to where it was parked. To her surprise she saw three cowhands extending a canvas over the back of the wagon. They had felled four pine trees, removed the branches and kept about five feet from each tree. They had nailed two of the poles vertically to the end of the buggy. They also nailed two poles vertically about two-thirds of the way towards the front. A rope was secured around the top of each pole. Over the poles they were now stretching a canvas from one side to the other side of the buggy. The covering wasn't high, only about three feet. But it would give her and Rose a smidgen of privacy.

Chapter 30

Overlooking the camp on a high ridge, Monte sat on his horse watching. He could see Doris at the chuck wagon. He was beginning to hate her. He blamed her for all his troubles. He'd never killed a woman and didn't want to now, especially one carrying a baby. He gave a mean laugh. **It being Nate's young'un, maybe it would be better if I did kill her. But what good would it do to harm her? I sure wouldn't find the money that way.**

Eventually he saw what he had been

watching for. A lone rider rode off from the main herd, working his way towards some brush where a cow stood. Monte followed; he knew this man. He and Monte had been in prison together. The man was older than most cowhands. He had deep-set eyes below a sharp forehead. This gave him the menacing appearance which he had rightly earned. He wasn't trying very hard to lasso the lonely cow. He pulled a bottle from his boot and took a long swig.

Monte called out, "Hey, Bob, hold up." The rider instantly stopped, pulled out his pistol and looked nervously around. As Monte approached, Bob relaxed.

"Oh, it's you, Sterling. Was that you that was part of that Ardmore bank hold-up? And say, Monte, don't call me Bob. I'm goin' by Arch now."

Monte laughed. He noticed Arch had lost

his two front upper teeth since they had been cell mates in prison. "Sure, Arch, I don't care what ya want yer handle ta be. When did ya git out of prison?"

"'Bout six months ago."

"How'd ya like ta make yerself a thousand dollars?"

"What'd I have ta do fer that? I ain't gittin' myself tangled in any killin'."

"Who said anything 'bout a killin'? I jest want ta git that gal by herself, away from that mother hen that's always hangin' 'round her. She knows where the bank money is. If ya can fix it so we kin talk and I git the money, I'll give ya a thousand bucks of it."

"Way, I heard it, there were over twenty-thousand taken. Seems ta me my part's worth more, say five thousand."

"Five thousand! What ya doin' besides gittin' her alone? I'll give ya two thousand."

"Make it another five hundred plus the two thousand and I'll do it."

Monte sat his horse staring at Bob. "All right, twenty-five hundred. Any idea how ya kin do it?"

"I'll think on it. Ya jest watch the camp. When ya see us ride out, follow." After saying this, Arch started after the cow, lassoed it and pulled it back to the herd.

Back in camp, Doris was checking the water barrel. It was almost empty. She didn't know what the procedure was for getting water. She hoped she wasn't expected to use the water from the river at the same place the cattle were drinking. She saw Arch come into camp. He come over to get a cup of coffee. "How do I go about getting the water barrel filled?"

"Here's my chance," thought Arch. Out loud he answered, "I'll hitch a horse to yer wagon and put the barrel on it. We kin ride upstream some ways ta where the water is cleaner."

He hitched a horse and helped Doris climb up. It crossed Doris' mind that perhaps she should check with someone to see if this was the proper thing to do. But who would she check with?

"It sure has turned out ta be a nice day after all that rain, ain't it, ma'am?"

"Yes. I'm so grateful for the sun." They continued with the small talk while they followed a winding creek that flowed into the river.

Doris didn't know Arch very well. She

thought he seemed like a nice enough fellow. Finally, Arch pulled to a halt, set the brake and jumped off. He held out his arms to help Doris down. When she reached the ground, she felt Arch's grip tighten. Fear filled her. "What are you doing?"

"Monte, Monte, where are ya?"

Doris realized she had been tricked. What a fool she was! "You can't do this. He'll kill me!" Then she had a thought. "My baby, oh my baby."

She bent her knees and appeared to faint. Arch moved his arms to catch her from falling. As he did this, Doris gave him a hard kick with her knee between his legs. He let out a yell and let go of Doris to grab himself. Doris took off on a run. The sides of the river were muddy and slick. She fell once and Arch almost caught her. He fell. She kicked him a second time in his groin this time using her foot. He doubled over, letting out a string of profanities.

Doris got up and started running again. She worked her way into a thick grove of trees. The low bushes were catching her divided skirt, tearing it in several places. Young tree branches slapped at her face and arms. She could hear feet crushing the ground behind her. Suddenly she fell face first into a deep gully. When she opened her eyes, she was staring at dirt and roots. The excess rain had caused a tree's roots to give way, felling the tree. There were a number of fresh fallen limbs from other trees lying about in the hole. She managed to cover herself with these branches before Arch reached the spot. She lay perfectly still, hardly breathing. The sound of voices came near.

"Well, where is she?" It was Monte's voice.

"I don't know. She has ta be close by, somewhere," answered Arch as he painfully walked beside Monte.

"Listen," shushed Monte as he held up his hand. Colby's barking could be heard in the distance. Then they heard several feet running towards the woods.

"Doris, Doris, where are ya?" This voice was Stu's.

"It's one of those boys. They must have missed the girl at camp, I'm gittin' out of here. Ya kin fergit the money; I'll git her myself."

Doris heard Monte's footsteps moving away from her hiding place. She heard the creak of the leather as he mounted his horse and then horse hooves fading away. All was quiet for several seconds.

Then Colby jumped into the hole,
barking nonstop.

Doris removed the branches and sat up.
Colby jumped on her and started licking
her face. Stu climbed in next and knelt
beside her. He began brushing dirt off.

"Arch, what's going' on here?" It was Tim's
voice this time. Besides Stu and Tim, Slim
and Ramon had arrived.

"Are ya all right?" Stu asked as he helped
Doris stand.

"Yes, I'm fine. Arch agreed to help me
get water. But it was a trick. That outlaw,
Monte, was waiting for us." She fell against
Stu, crying. He stood stiff beside Doris.
He wasn't sure what to do. No girl besides
his sister had ever been this close to
him before.

Tim, Slim and Ramon looked at Arch,

who had been standing nearby listening to Doris. "She's got it all wrong. She took it wrong."

Hearing this, Doris straightened up and shouted: "No I didn't! Arch grabbed me and started calling for Monte. I managed to get away."

Mark had arrived and heard Arch's comment. "Arch, you been nothin' but trouble since you hired on. Yer lazy. Ya sleep on yer watches, and when you do work, you do a lousy job. And I ain't sure you haven't been drinkin'. Ramon, take Arch back ta camp. See he packs his gear and is gone 'fore I get back."

"Does he get a horse?"

"Does he have one of his own?"

"Yeah, I got my own and I want it."

"Take yer horse. The next time I see ya, ya better be riding away. If I see ya looking at me, I'll shoot ya."

Arch rode Tim's horse back to camp, accompanied by Ramon. The other men had filled the water barrel and secured it to the wagon. Tim drove the wagon back, Doris sitting beside him. "I'm sorry, Tim. I never suspected Arch would be anything but helpful. I just don't seem to get anything right."

"You had no way of knowin'; none of us did. He took Doris' hand, placing it on his knee, and patted it.

Gary had started cooking supper when they reached camp. Arch was gone. "Miss Doris, go git cleaned up, I kin git supper."

"I won't be long. I want to do my share."

Doris hurried off. Before going to the

make-shift tent wagon, she wet a rag.
Once inside, she cleaned herself as best
she could. Then she removed her blouse
and divided skirt. She would have to see
about mending the tears. Some places on
her body hurt more than she wanted to
admit. She readjusted her undergarments
before putting on her only other piece
of clothing, a dress. As she exited the
wagon, the cowhands noticed the change.
One whistled. Tim, standing near the fire,
winked and smiled.

Chapter 31

Mark came up to the two women that evening after supper. "Miss Rose, do you know how ta use that six shooter ya been wearin' on yer hip?"

"Mr. Mark, I've never shot a revolver in my life. Why, this gun ain't even loaded."

Mark laughed. "How about you, Miss Doris? You shoot?"

"Mr. Mark, I'm really good with a shotgun. But, like Rose, I've never used a revolver."

"I figured as much."

Then he showed them a two-shot derringer he had been holding. "This is often called a lady's gun. You can carry it in yer pocket. It belonged to my ma. She always carried it in her pocket. She shot a skunk with it once. I've asked Slim ta show you ladies how ta shoot. He'll learn ya how ta use this and the six-shooter. Slim's a good shot and is real good at learnin' folks."

Before it got totally dark, Slim walked the women a good distance away from the camp and the herd. They were down in a hollow so the shooting wouldn't spook the cattle or a stray bullet hit anyone.

"This here gun ya got, Miss Rose, is called a single-action revolver. It won't shoot less'n ya cock the hammer back like this." He demonstrated the procedure as he spoke. "If it ain't cocked, ya kin pull the trigger over and over and nothin’ will happen.

“First thing ta remember is ta hold the gun tight. Tighter than ya think ya should.”

He had each woman hold the gun and practice cocking and uncocking it.

“Now how ya stand is real important if ya want ta hit what yer aimin’ at. ‘Course sometimes, all ya can do is duck and shoot quick. If ya git time ta aim, its best ta stand with your weight even on both feet, more weight on yer heels than on the front. Yer arms should be straight out in front of ya, relaxed, and your body leanin’ a bit forward. When ya shoot, the gun will kick back. Ya need ta be careful or the recoil will knock ya on yer as ... er…aw, put ya off yer balance. Beggin’ your pardon. Now jest try holding the gun like I done showed ya. It ain’t loaded so don’t try ta shoot.”

Each woman practiced as Slim had demonstrated. He had to bite the inside of his lip to keep from laughing as he watched Rose. She bent over at the waist with her knees almost bent to the ground.

"Miss Rose, ya don't have ta
bend so much."

"Well, I figure if I'm shootin' at someone, they'll most likely be shootin' back at me. The smaller target I make myself, the less likely I'd be ta git hit."

"Yes,'m. Yer right. Next, we need ta talk about yer aim." Slim pointed to a place on the front of the barrel. "This here's a sight. There's two of 'em." He pointed to the back of the barrel. "This un's is the other. Hold the gun tight and at arm's length. The front sight should be in between the notch of the rear sight and both sights should be level. Once ya brung 'em into line with each other, yer ready ta shoot at what yer aiming at.

"So, hold the gun tight. Close one eye and line up the sights on yer target. Begin ta squeeze the trigger without moving anything else. If ya do it right, ya'll hit yer target."

As Slim was talking, he demonstrated the process. The women practiced shooting without the gun loaded.

He enjoyed watching Doris. She was so pretty. He thought of his dead wife. She had been gone twelve years, but he still sorrowed for her. He began to wonder if he could interest Doris in himself. He knew Tim was sweet on her. **Shucks, Tim is younger, better lookin' and don't have a daughter almost growed. In a couple of years my Ivy will be old enough ta marry.** Though he thought these words to himself, he couldn't help lusting for Doris just a bit. He quit wool-gathering and came back to what he was doing.

"The next thing is how ta load yer gun. Be careful where yer pointin' it. Point it down. This is the ejector rod. It's used ta eject the fired cases from the cylinder." As he was talking, he demonstrated how the ejector rod worked.

"Yer gun holds six shells. It'll be safer fer ya if ya leave an empty chamber in the front of the gun's hammer. That way ya won't accidentally shoot yerself."

Slim pointed to a place on the side of the revolver. "This here is called the loading gate. Ya open it and half-cock the hammer. Now ya kin load one bullet at a time. Put one in the chamber, and move the cylinder to the next chamber. Skip this chamber. Continue to load the next four chambers.

Close the gate. Cock the hammer all the way back. Can ya see there ain't no bullet in the top?"

Each woman looked at the place on the gun where Slim was pointing. Then he pulled the trigger. "Now the gun's on an empty chamber. Ya ladies can practice loading and unloading."

When Slim was satisfied the women understood his instructions, he had them practice shooting, ejecting the spent shells and reloading. He hung a rag on a small tree some distance from where they were standing. Rose shot quickly. She didn't seem to aim. It was as though she was intent on emptying her gun as quickly as she could. The rag didn't move. Not one of her bullets hit the rag. Several times, her shots went into the dirt in front of the target. Slim decided Rose probably needed glasses.

Doris was a much better shot. She took her time aiming and, once on her target, she didn't move or even seem to breathe. Most of her bullets hit the rag.

Next, he picked up the derringer. "This little gun really ain't much good less'n yer close. And ya only git two chances with it. It works real simple. I'll show ya how ta load it. There ain't no safety on this gun." Once again as Slim talked, he demonstrated what he was doing. "This is the locking lever. Push it forward ta unlock it. Pull the barrel up ta open it. Make sure ya keep yer hands and fingers away from the end of the barrel. Ya don't want ta shoot any of yer fingers off. Put the cartridge edges of the shells on this here. It's called an extractor and it removes the used cartridges from the chamber. Slide the extractor down, inserting the shells into the chambers. Close the barrel and move the locking lever towards the rear of the gun. Yer ready now ta shoot."

The women practiced loading and shooting, this time using the derringer.

Rose only shot the derringer twice. "I don't like this gun. It's like a toy. I think I'll stick with my six shooter." The way she aimed, Slim decided that was wise. The more chances she had firing, the better for her.

"I kind of like this little gun; I'll just keep it with me." Having said this, Doris slipped it into her pocket.

"Be shore it ain't cocked," warned Slim.

"It's not. I checked it before I put it in my pocket."

Later that night, after Rose and Doris had gone to their wagon, Mark approached

Slim. "How did the learnin' go? Are they any good?"

"Miss Doris is pretty good. But that Miss Rose! She don't shoot straight and her aim is low. So, whatever she hits is goin' ta suffer a long time."

Chapter 32

By the following morning the water in the river had started to recede. Mark believed it was low enough to move the cattle across. He told Doris and Rose to cook extra bacon and biscuits to hand out to the men. There would be no time to stop at noon. The crossing was expected to take all day. The wagons and Rose's buggy were tied to logs to float them across.

Doris didn't know how to swim and was scared. She sat beside J.J. as he drove the chuck wagon across. Two extra horses had been lashed to each wagon to increase the pulling powder. A man rode on each of the extra horse to guide and encourage it. Colby sat beside Doris and started to bark. She picked him up and set him on her lap. He stopped barking and nuzzled his head between her side and arm.

Doris could feel when the wheels were no longer touching the bottom and the wagon was beginning to float. The wagon started to drift sideways, due to a swift current. Two hands moved next to the wagon and tried to steady it from drifting uncontrollably. Mark shouted, "Billy, get hold of them horses; keep them moving across!"

The wagon crossing seemed to take an hour, though Doris knew it was only several minutes. To her relief the crossing was soon finished. They waited until the second wagon and the buggy came across. The same process was used to move them. Mark was driving the buggy with Rose at his side. Once across, Mark told Rose to ride with Doris and help her with the chuck wagon.

J.J. jumped down and handed the reins to Doris. "Head up this ridge. At the top turn right. Keep going 'til someone comes to tell ya to stop."

Tim started moving the lead steer across the river. The rest of the cattle were used to following this steer and started across. Ramon and Stu were working together. Ramon couldn't help but ask, "Are ya scared, Stu?"

"I'd be lyin' if I said no. I jest wish tamorra was yesterday."

Ramon laughed at Stu's reply. "You'll do fine, my young amigo."

Unknown to Mark and the others, just north of where the wagons had crossed was a deep, narrow channel near the far side of the river. The channel caused the flooded river to run faster than usual. In just a matter of minutes, the first cows to start across were caught in the deep water and started drifting downriver. Ramon and Stu immediately took off after the panicked cows.

No sooner had they done this when Stu was no longer concerned about the cows drowning; he realized his own life was in danger. His horse struggled to swim out of the churning water. The fast-flowing current lifted Stu off his saddle. Somehow, he managed to hang on to the saddle horn and not float away. However, Stu started floating in a direction perpendicular to his horse. As he fought the raging river, the horse finally felt solid ground beneath him. Pulling himself out of the river, he could feel the heavy weight of Stu's tug on the saddle horn. Tim was instantly at Stu's side. He grabbed Stu and hugged him tight, embarrassing him. "Well, I declare, Tim, let me go!"

"I'm sorry, Stu. I tried ta reach you. I jest couldn't git to ya."

"I'm all right. My Aunt Hannah, Tim! Come on, ever one's lookin' at us."

Tim lowered Stu to the ground while Stu checked for injuries to his horse. Neither rider nor horse was injured.

Meanwhile, J.J. had started back across the river to help move the cattle, when he ran into a problem. A large logjam by the far shore had come loose. An unnoticed log from the jam came rushing down the river and slammed into J.J.'s back. It knocked him off his horse and he went under the torrential flow, swallowing a great deal of muddy water. He came up to the surface face to face with an angry steer. J.J. grabbed the horns and hung on. Luckily, the steer continued swimming across. Slim rode up beside the critter and dragged J.J. to shore.

J.J. was sure he had broken some ribs. He made it to a clump of trees and sat down. Cows were passing him on both sides. He heard the sound of a wagon; he was relieved to see it was Doris and Rose. They stopped and climbed down, somehow managing to get him aboard. His chest and side burned with pain. Rose helped him lie down as Doris drove the wagon through the stomping cattle and up the hill.

In a low shaky voice, J.J. whispered, "Miss Rose, I believe some ribs on my left side are busted." The bumpy ride had been no help. She did her best to wrap strips of cloth tightly around his chest.

Mark drove up to the chuck wagon still driving the buggy. "How's J.J.?"

"He thinks he's got busted ribs."

"I'll put Stu to driving the buggy. You stay with J.J. Doris about a mile northwest is a grove of trees. Go over there and make a big fire and git coffee brewin'."

"Yes, boss."

As she drove along the ridge, she looked across the river and saw a man lying on the shore. Milling around him were several cows.

It was Ramon, who slowly got to his feet.

When he had realized the danger he and Stu were in, he had the presence of mind to relax and let the water support him. The current carried him downriver, along with a number of cows. Once he was out of the channel, he had been able to swim to shore, safe but exhausted. At least a dozen cows were milling around him, bawling their displeasure. His horse stood several yards away quietly munching grass.

He turned his gaze to the river. To him it seemed half the herd was floating away. He managed to mount his horse, riding along the bank until he was ahead of the cows. He then returned to the river. Slapping his coiled rope on the top of the water, he steered the cattle to shore.

Once the cowhands realized what was happening, they moved fewer cattle across the river at a time. They rode on each side of those crossing, protecting them as they swam across. It took two days to get all the cattle across. A third day was spent rounding up the lost cattle. A number of the cows were found miles downriver. Some were lost in the surrounding brush and could not be found. About a dozen had drowned.

The first night of the crossing the crew took turns sitting around a roaring fire. Wounds were looked to; salve was rubbed onto bruised joints and much coffee was drunk. The one blessing from the day was a huge steak for each weary cowhand – a gift from drowned cattle.

Mark sat alone, hanging his head. J.J. walked over to him. "It weren't yer fault, Mark."

"Yeah, it was. I should have known about the channel. I should have checked the river out better. We could have waited another day or two. I could have gone further down the river to find a safer crossing."

"Mark! Sitting here blamin' yerself ain't doin' none of us any good. We jest have ta go on."

Mark was about to reply to J.J. when Tim and two other men came riding in. He quickly stood up, believing the two strangers to be Indians, although they were dressed as white men. Tim slid off his horse and walked towards Mark and J.J. Both Indians stayed on their horses.

Tim turned to the Indians. "Hey, fellows, come on. I want you to meet my uncle and friends." The Indians dismounted as Tim continued forward.

"Mark, J.J., ya ain't gonna believe this.

These two Injins jest brought back 'bout a hundred of our beeves. They saw them git away during the river crossing and rounded them up fer us. They told me they've been out lookin' for Doris and Rose."

"For us! Now why in heaven's name are Indians looking for us!" Feeling angry and perplexed, Doris walked towards the newcomers.

All the cowhands stood around, staring at the Indians.

"Good evening, Little Mother. I am glad we have finally found you. We have been looking for you for some time now."

Mark stepped between Doris and the Indians. We're mighty thankful for yer help bringin' back the beeves. Yer welcome ta stay and have some supper. Who are ya, anyway?"

"My name is David Silvernail. This is my brother, Paul. We are Santee Dakota of the Sioux Nation."

They were dressed in bright plaid shirts and denim blue jeans. Each, however, had on moccasins.

Rose handed both strangers plates of food. "Ya sure speak mighty good English."

David smiled as he and his brother accepted the food. "For an Indian, you mean." The two Sioux laughed. In a matter-of-fact tone David began, "In 1862 there was a great Santee uprising against the government. We lost, of course. The Santee were given the opportunity to become United States citizens in exchange for their tribal rights. My parents and about twenty-five other families chose to do this. Each family also received a homestead. It is near the Big Sioux River. My family became Christians. My brother and I were educated at the Flandreau Indian School. This fall I will begin my senior year at Yankton College. It is in the town of Yankton in the southern part of the Dakota territory."

Doris could understand why he spoke as though the words were memorized. She was getting weary of repeating her own story over and over. Nevertheless, it was an impressive tale. "Well, that doesn't explain why you've been looking for Rose and me."

David, the older of the two brothers, handed his dinner plate to his brother then walked back and reached into his saddlebag. He brought out a package wrapped in skins. "Do you recall helping a young Indian woman and her children?

"Yes."

"Those are my sister and three nieces. My father told my brother and me to find the little mother and grandmother who saved the lives of my sister and her children. Doris was about the same height as David. She looked into his black eyes. "I felt so sorry for her, out alone so far from her family and no friends."

Mark asked, "Why were they traveling alone?"

"My sister was married to a white man. He became sick and died. His family turned my sister out of her home. They never liked the idea of their son being married to an Indian. The white people of the town would not let my sister remain there either. She was trying to get back to her own people." David turned to Doris, "She came into your camp very hungry and tired. You fed her and her children. You gave my sister food to take with them and also a horse.”

“A horse!” exclaimed several men.

“You gave away a horse?” J.J. looked at Doris. She shrugged her shoulders and smiled.

“If you women had not been so kind, my sister and nieces may well have died. We have been looking for you since Grace, my sister, made it home. From questions we have asked while trying to locate you, it seems others are also looking for you.” David tilted his head to one side and grinned.

David turned to Mark and continued, “Two days ago, we were nearing your camp, we observed the difficultly you had while crossing the river. We watched as many cattle drifted downstream. With help from

God, we were able to round up some of the cattle."

Paul was busy eating, content to let David do the explaining. David continued, "Before I eat, there is one more thing I must do."

Rose was becoming exasperated that David was talking so much and letting his food get cold. "Son, roundin' up those cattle is enough. Now sit and eat."

"Please, I have this to give to the little mother." He reached into the skin bag and unfolded a little Indian blanket. "My mother made this for your little one. It will keep him warm." He handed the blanket to Doris. It featured a brightly woven design, showing children of various sizes playing among teepees.

Doris accepted the blanket. "Thank you; it's lovely. One day I will wrap my baby in it and he will be safe and warm." Then she began to cry.

Rose came over to her and put her arm around Doris' shoulder, holding her tight. Putting her mouth close to Doris' ear, she whispered, "Take a deep breath and quit bawling."

Doris only cried harder.

Rose squeezed Doris' shoulder so hard it hurt. "Doris, did ya hear me? Buck up!"

Doris heaved a great sigh and managed to stop crying. She walked to the chuck wagon, trying to hide her heaving, gulping breaths. None of the men knew what to think or say.

"I'm sorry if I upset the little mother." David looked very forlorn.

"Think nothin' of it. It's jest her way."

"This is from grandmother for you. She made it herself. Grandmother wanted to convey her gratefulness for the help you showed Grace." David handed Rose a beaded necklace with a gold, handmade cross.

"Why, this is beautiful! It is jest beautiful. Tell your grandmother, thank you very much. I will cherish it for the rest of my life. Now, please sit down and eat!" Rose's matter-of-fact change of voice make the cowhands laugh.

David finally sat down to eat. Rose went over to the back of the chuck wagon to find Doris. "Hon, are ya all right?"

"Yes. I'm sorry I acted like such a fool."

Chapter 33

Rose was about to reply to Doris' comment, when a weary young drover rode up. He slid off his horse almost falling in the effort. "Jim, you look plum tuckered out. Sit down, I'll fix ya a plate."

"Thanks, Miss Rose. I'm so tired. When this drive is over, I'm taking my pay and buying a ticket home. I don't ever want to see a cow again unless it's cooked and on my plate."

The two women looked at each other and

smiled. Rose continued, "I take it this is yer first drive. Where ya from?"

"My first and last. I'm from Pennsylvania and I sure wish I'd never left."

Rose handed Jim his plate, "Why did ya leave?"

"Oh, I read some of those dime novels telling about all the adventures and romance of the west. My mom and dad tried to tell me they weren't true. I wouldn't believe them. I had to come out here and find out for myself. I just hope my folks will let me come back home. I was so pig-headed."

Doris spoke up, "How old are you, Jim? Have you been gone from your home long?"

"I'll be eighteen in December. And I left Pennsylvania last year. My dad's a dentist and wants me to go to college and become one. He wants me to work with him. Being a dentist now doesn't sound so bad. I just don't know if they'll want me back. I said some pretty stupid things before I left."

Softly Doris said, "Jim, have you ever heard about the prodigal son? It's from the Bible."

Jim looked at Doris with a frown on his face. "Yaa, I remember something about him from Sunday School. What's that got to do with me?"

"The prodigal son said a lot of mean things to his dad before he left home. He lived a pretty bad life until finally he came to his senses and returned home. Before he even got all the way home, his father saw him coming a long way off. His father ran to him, hugged him and welcomed him back. I think your parents will be very glad to see you return also."

"Have ya been writtin' to yer folks?"

"No, Miss Rose I haven't."

Rose reached into a drawer and pulled out writing paper, a pencil and an envelope. "When ya finish eatin' ya write yer parents. Tell them what ya been doin' and as soon as yer job is finished ya'd like ta come home. I agree with Doris. I believe ya parents will be watchin' fer ya."

Jim finished eating and walked close to the fire to write his letter. Rose watched him, shaking her head. "Oh, how many youngsters have been lost lookin' fer what's right in their backyard?

"When my husband and I were on our ranch we'd get kids, some not more than babes, come looking fer work. Most were so hungry we had ta fatten them up first. Then some didn't stay more than a few days or a couple of weeks at the most. They didn't realize how hard ranchin' is. Like Jim, they had been fed a line from those dime novels."

Doris stood watching Jim, "I hope he gets home."

"Yes, so do I. Let me tell you about one youngster that came lookin' fer a job.

I was sittin' of the porch rockin' Saree. She was just a babe-in-arms. John, that's my husband, and this little thing, he'd jest hired that mornin', come ridin' up. John jumped off his hoss like it were on fire and ran ta the kid. He yelled fer the youngster ta git off. I asked what was wrong. He yelled, 'He ain't a he. He's a she!'".

"A she?"

Yes. It seems this girl, Julie was her name, had run away from home and pretended she were a boy. John got back on his hoss. As he was ridin' out of the yard, he looked over his shoulder and shouted, 'Do somethin' with her.'"

"Oh, my goodness. What did you do?'

"Well, first I took Julie into the house and fed her. As she was eatin', she told me she was fifteen and once again, had read the dime novels about how exciting it were to live in the west. Of course, she found out that it weren't true. Besides not knowin' anythin' about ranchin' or farmin' and even though dressed as a boy, it wasn't surprisin', she couldn't git a job.

"I got her cleaned up and gave her a dress ta wear. The next day she and I went ta town and sent her folks a telegram. Julie didn't think they would want her back. It weren't but two days later a man from town came ridin' out with a telegraph message from Julie's parents. Her ma was on her way ta git her."

"Children just don't know how much parents love their children, do they, Rose?"

"No, they surely don't. Julie's ma was scheduled ta arrive on the stagecoach a week later. And durin' that week, mind ya, I made Julie earn her keep. She helped me cook and clean. She even watched Saree fer me. I almost wished she could stay. I sure liked the help.

"Well, the stage carrying Julie's ma arrived early that day and we hadn't got ta town yet. She were standin' on the boardwalk waitin' fer us. It were jest like that story ya told ta Jim. When Julie's ma saw us commin' she jumped off the walk, almost gittin' run over by a hoss, and run ta our wagon. Julie jumped down from the wagon into her ma's arms. All three of us were cryin'."

"That is such a nice story. Did you keep in touch with Julie?"

"She wrote ta me now and then. That was until I left ta look fer Saree. Julie married and had a couple of kids of her own."

Chapter 34

Three days later, Tim rode up to the wagon Doris had been driving the last two hours. "Mind if I climb aboard?"

"Not at all, I welcome the company."

Tim tied off his horse, climbed onto the wagon and took the reins from Doris. There was an awkward silence for several minutes. Finally, Tim said, "How you fairin', Miss. Doris?"

"I'm doing fine, Mr. Tim."

"Look, why don't ya jest call me Tim?"

"I will if you'll call me Doris."

"That's a deal." Both gave a nervous laugh.

Tim looked at Doris and said, "I know ya had a terrible experience and some rough goin'. I jest want ya ta know that I'd like ta help ya, any way I kin."

"Thank you, Tim, but I don't know how you or anyone else can."

"I know Jesus can."

"Hmm! If He's so helpful, why didn't He tell me what to do when all this started?"

"Well, I've learned that God speaks ta us in different ways. Most times it's through the Bible. It's important ta search the Bible ta learn what God has ta tell us. He kin also speak to us in other ways. Sometimes He sends His help through prayer. Speakin' ta us in our thoughts. He might even use people ta talk fer Him, but it will always match what the Bible says."

"You really believe that?"

"Yes, I do."

Doris said nothing for quite a while. Then she looked at Tim and slowly said, "Before I married Nate, my best friend's momma tried to get me to wait. She offered to let me live with them. Later when I was talking to the pastor, he suggested I wait. His wife also said I could stay with them. She even volunteered to take me out to my farm once in a while to check on things. The night of Momma's funeral a woman from a saloon came to visit me at the hotel where I was staying. She told me Nate was no good and not to marry him. I figured she was just jealous and wanted him for herself. Do you think that was God using using those people to help me?"

"Might'a bin."

"I sure wish I would have listened. Now I would like Him to send me some kind of sign to tell me what to do next."

Tim smiled at her comment. "I'll pray fer ya. You kin pray too."

As he was saying this, Billy rode up. "Tim, Uncle Mark wants ta see ya."

"Thanks, Billy." Tim climbed on his horse. As he was riding off, he paused, turned toward her and gave Doris a wink and a smile.

Chapter 35

Monte rode into one of the many insignificant towns that dotted the trail. He was hungry, not having eaten since the previous morning. He had no money to buy any food. The stores were just closing as he rode down through the small town. He slowed as he passed the general store. A plump woman was putting items back into the store in preparation for closing. Another woman, wearing a silly-looking hat and carrying several boxes, was walking past the store.

"Evening, Alice."

"Howdy, Eunice. "

"How are you holding up with Charles gone? Isn't it a lot on you with a new baby and those spirited boys of yours?"

"Things aren't too bad. My Sally is old enough to watch the baby and the boys can mostly look after themselves. Charles should be home by the week's end."

"That sure was sad news to hear about his sister dying so young. I remember her living here. Such a pretty girl! Who's going to mother that babe of hers?"

"Judy's husband has four sisters. I'm sure one of them will take the baby."

"Sure, hope they do. Well, I've got ta get on home. That old man of mine will be wantin' supper. Let me know if you need anything. Give Charles my sympathy."

"Thank you, Eunice."

Eunice continued her journey home. Alice picked up the last few items and went into the store.

Monte heard her lock the door. He thought to himself, **A woman and a bunch of kids alone in a store.** He knew now how he was going to get some food and maybe even a few dollars.

Monte rode slowly out of town and waited for dark. He circled around to the back of the town, stopping behind the store. He could see a dim light on the second floor. He sat his horse waiting. Finally, the light went out. He waited another half hour, then dismounted his horse and tied it to a scrub tree growing between the store and the next building.

Cautiously he made his way to a side door. It was locked as he expected. He tried a window next to it. It too was locked. However, he noticed that the putty holding the pane to the sash was partly gone. He got out his knife and tried to flick out more of the putty. Before he could remove the pane, it broke and fell into the room. He let out an oath and waited. No one came. He reached in and unlocked the window, raised it, and climbed in. Since there was no moon, the room was totally dark. He took a chance and lit a match. He was in a storage room full of cans. He spied a gunny sack as the match went out. He filled the sack with cans, even though he couldn't read the labels.

There was a door between this backroom

and the store. He slowly opened it. A cash register sat on a counter just steps away. He walked the short distance and had just opened it when a voice said, "Daddy, is that you? Did you come home?"

"Shut up, kid. Git back ta bed."

That harsh voice brought a quick reaction: "Mommy, Mommy! There's a strange man in the store! He's taking our money."

Monte heard heavy footsteps on the stairs. He turned quickly towards the store room.

"Hold it right there, mister. This shotgun's loaded and I'll use it."

Monte saw the woman wearing a faded housecoat standing at the bottom of the stairs, her long hair in a braid. Throwing the bag of cans at her, knocking her off balance, he managed to grab one can off a shelf before climbing out the window.

He jumped on his horse and hightailed it out of town. Finally, he slowed down, letting the horse take his head. It was pitch dark.

It started to rain. Despondently, he said to his horse, "This will at least wash out yer tracks."

A lightning flash revealed some craggy hills. He followed a path in that direction. After looking around a bit, he saw an overhang large enough to shelter him and his horse. He removed the saddle and his gear, hobbled the horse and settled down. He used his pocket knife to open the can, the only can he was able to grab. It contained stewed tomatoes. "I hate tomatoes," he said aloud, but ate them anyway. Miserably, he lay on the hard ground and listened to a train whistle far off in the rainy night.

Chapter 36

Sarah sat nursing her newborn daughter, swaying with the rhythm of the train. Her twin boys lay head-to-toe on the opposite seat.

Sarah peeked lovingly under the blanket which covered herself and Rose Patricia. "Oh, darlin'. You are so beautiful." Rose Patricia had a little rosebud month and a tuft of blond hair on the top of her head. Sarah's heart was full. She was so happy and content. She thought about her blessings. She felt she didn't deserve her good husband, the two healthy twins and this sweet daughter. God had blessed her more than she deserved.

"Sarah, when you've finished nursing Rose, I'll hold her so you can get some sleep."

"Thank you, Catherine, I appreciate the kindness. Actually, we're done," she said as she wiped Rose's mouth and chin. "Here she is. She does need burping." Catherine took the baby and returned to her seat. Sarah made herself comfortable. The train slowed as Sarah was almost asleep.

"Momma, are we stopping again?" Johnny, the older twin, asked. Even though her boys were only ten minutes apart, sometimes Johnny seemed ten years older than his brother. Matt accepted things as they came; Johnny had to know why something worked this way or that, asking a hundred questions a day.

"Go back to sleep. We're pulling into another town." Sarah never realized how many small towns there were.

As the train started up again, three men entered the rear of the coach. They were dirty, rough-looking, cowboys. Each sat down in a different section, spacing themselves throughout the car. One stopped by Sarah, who by now was sleeping. He looked her over, and continued to the front of the car.

"Okay, ladies and gents, this is a holdup. Now jest do as yer told and nobody gits hurt."

Sarah opened her eyes. One cowboy was standing in front. One was near her. He smelled like he hadn't washed in a month. She turned to see the third one at the rear of the car.

"Mr. Smith here is goin' ta pass his hat
and ev'ry one is gonna be real generous;
wallets, rings, pins and any other jewelry ya
might have."

"Mr. Smith," the outlaw at the back, started
moving down the aisle. He came to
Walt Gibson.

"I—I don't have a wallet. It's in my suitcase,
in the luggage car."

"Now, why do I find that hard ta believe,"
replied Mr. Smith. He roughly pulled Walt's
coat open. The wallet was visible in the
left inside pocket. He snatched the wallet
and hit Walt across the face with the barrel
of his gun. Catherine screamed as blood
gushed from his open wound and into
his eyes. The other passengers did not
try to bluff the outlaws after seeing this
brutal assault.

The train slowed as it began climbing a steep hill. The three outlaws jumped off. One passenger commented in despair, "They must have known the train was going to slow. They probably have horses waiting."

Sarah and Catherine were tending to Walt's wound. Walt leaned back in his seat and moaned, "Why does everything have to be so hard? Why can't anything ever work out right? Our money! They got all our money from the sale of the ranch. I should have listened to you, Catherine, and put the money in the bank to be transferred to us when we reached Montana. We're broke. What're we goin' ta do?"

"Don't worry about that just now, darlin'. We'll figure out something."

As Catherine held Walt's head, Sarah wound a strip of torn petticoat around it. The boys were awake, looking wide-eyed and scared. The baby began to cry. Matt began to whimper. Sarah turned and whispered, "Johnny, Momma needs your help. Pick up baby sister and hold her tight. Talk to your brother. Tell him it's going be all right.

Catherine looked around. "Where's the conductor?"

An older man, traveling with his wife, went out to the platform. "He's here! They must have knocked him out. He's hurt bad. Mother, come out here. See what you can do for him." His wife did as he asked. She knelt by her husband, trying to comfort the conductor.

The train rolled on through the night, finally stopping at yet another small town. The man tending the conductor went after the sheriff. He came to the train and listened assiduously taking descriptions of the three outlaws.

"I hate to tell you this, and I apologize, but I probably won't be able to find those men or get your money back. Leave your name and destination with my deputy. If, by some miracle, we catch the desperadoes and find any of the money, I'll send it to you. But don't count on it." It didn't appear as if anything more was going to be done. The passengers settled back into in their seats to continue their journey.

For what seemed like the hundredth time, the train stopped at another small town. The passengers were told they had forty minutes to stretch their legs and to eat. Some of the passengers had a few coins they had been able to hide from the robbers. These people generously offered to buy food for the unfortunate passengers who had lost all their money.

Teresa and her mother, whose money was hidden in a cloth bag and pinned to the mother's slip, decided to stroll over to the Mexican barrio to buy something for their meal. The sound of a scuffle came from inside a cantina as they were passing. Mr. Smith came flying out the door, landing on his face in the street. Both women gasped. Teresa took her mother by the arm, propelling her away from the commotion.

As quickly as possible, they hurried back to the train station. They had to ask several people before learning where Walt had gone to eat. When they found him, they told him about seeing Mr. Smith. Walt displaying a bandaged aching head went to the sheriff and explained the situation.

The sheriff, who had read the telegraph

report about the train robbery, immediately deputized three men and handed out shotguns. Walt asked to be deputized as well, but the sheriff was reluctant at first. He could see Walt was not in the best condition to be facing a show down. However, realizing Walt was the only one who could point out the outlaws, the officer relented. The five men started towards the cantina. Walt saw the three outlaws lounging on a bench two buildings down from the cantina. "There they are, sheriff! That's them, sittin' 'gainst that hotel wall!"

The sheriff ordered the men to fan out across the street from the outlaws. When they were in place, the sheriff shouted, "All right, you three, raise your hands real slow and stand up!"

One man raised his hands and started to

stand as ordered. The other two reached for their guns and made a dive for cover. Five shotguns blasted the air before the two outlaws' guns had cleared their holsters. The third man, seeing what happened, started to shake uncontrollably, then fainted.

Back at the sheriff's office the surviving outlaw was placed in a cell. He told the sheriff he was only sixteen and that the train robbery was his first venture into crime. Most of the stolen money was recovered as well as money from the sale of the pilfered jewelry.

The sheriff questioned the teen-age delinquent. "You know, son, the judge might just go easier on you if you'd tell me where you and your friends sold these people's jewelry. I'll find out anyway. So, make it easier on me and I'll put in a good word to the judge."

The young man sat dejectedly in his cell. "You got to believe, sheriff, I really didn't want to rob nobody. My cousin, Arnold, made me. He was mean, just plain mean. I was afraid of him. All us kids were."

The sheriff felt bad for the kid. He was well spoken and seemed decent. "Where are you from, boy? I'll contact your folks. Maybe they can hire a good lawyer. Now tell me, where'd you sell the jewelry?" The sheriff already knew who in town usually bought such things. He wanted to get the boy's cooperation.

The boy sighed, "I don't know the woman's name. We went up some back stairs of a building across the street and in the next block. A real pretty lady opened the door. My cousin made me stay outside when he went in. That's all I know to tell you. I hope it's enough."

The sheriff knew the woman the boy was talking about. She was a middle-aged woman who had moved to town several years ago. There had been rumors for years she bought stolen items, but the sheriff had never been able to prove the allegations.

He made a list of the stolen valuables. He and a deputy were gone about twenty minutes. They returned with the fuming woman and a bag containing the stolen jewelry.

The money found on the outlaws was returned proportionally to each victim. The sheriff tried to be as fair as he possibly could. After identifying their pieces of jewelry, the travelers gratefully reclaimed their stolen items.

As the train started for Denver, Catherine approached Teresa. She hoped to encourage this courageous young woman. "Teresa, there is a verse in the Bible I want to read to you. It is from Romans 8:28. 'And we know that all things work together for good to them that love God, to them who are the called according to his purpose.'"

Teresa could not understand how the verse pertained to her. "How does that say anything about me, Señora?"

"I believe this verse means if we are in God's will, whatever happens to us, God can use that for our good. If you had not talked to your mother about coming to Montana, but had pressured Ramon to return to Texas, you and your mother would not have been near the cantina to see the outlaws. We would never have gotten our money back. God wanted you here to help us. Thank you from the bottom of my heart for coming with us. I pray that God will bless you beyond what you could ever imagine."

Chapter 37

"What are ya doin', Doris?"

"I'm practicing winking."

"Winkin'! My granny said, 'A girl who winks is like a hen that crows.' You jest let the men do the winkin'. And don't think I ain't been noticin' that young Tim winkin' at you." Doris blushed and turned her back to Rose, pretending to ready the frying pan.

Several days of hard driving had passed since the river-crossing incident. J.J. had been volunteered to help the women, since he could not comfortably ride because of his sore ribs. He overheard this conversation and chuckled to himself.

"J.J., do you know how to wring necks and dress chickens?"

"Yes, Miss Doris. My ma showed me how ta do all that 'cept fer fryin' 'em."

 Doris turned to Rose. "Rose, there are eight chickens left. I want to cook six of them for supper. They're kind of a nuisance anyway. We'll keep the two best layers. That way we'll have some eggs for cooking. I want to fix the men a really good supper. We'll give them fried chicken and dumplings. There is a jar of applesauce left. That is enough to make a couple of applesauce custard pies."

J.J. stopped in his tracks and declared,

"Applesauce custard pie! I've never heard of such a thing."

"It was my momma's specialty and my papa's favorite. J.J., come with me and I'll show you the six chickens to kill."

After the chickens were cleaned, Doris cut them up and put them in boiling water to stew. Later she would fry them in hot lard to make them crisp. As the chickens cooked, Rose made dumplings and Doris made the pies.

She needed milk, which she didn't have. The campsite was on a hill overlooking the cattle. She could see several calves being nursed and thought to herself, **why can't I milk one of the cows to get enough milk for the pie? I only need about a cup. I know no self-respecting cowhand would ever be caught milking a cow but I can. I've been milking cows since I could walk.**

She saw Stu riding up the ridge. "Stu, please, come here a minute. I need your help." Stu had a crush on Doris and would have tried to walk to the moon if she asked him.

He kicked his spurs into the horse and hurried up the hill. "Yes, Miss Doris. What kin I do fer ya?

"I need a milk cow. Can you fetch one for me and tie it to that tree beside the back of the chuck wagon?"

"What ya need a milk cow fer?"

"Why do you think? I'm going to milk it."

He shook his head but would never deny Doris anything. He rode back down the hill and lassoed a calf. Its mother followed, mooing in protest, as Stu pulled the calf up the hill. He jumped down from his horse and tied the calf to the tree. Taking another rope, he lassoed the mother and tied her to the tree. "Miss Doris, these beeves ain't exactly tame. Ya try milkin' her; she's likely ta kick ya."

"Can you hobble her? Would that help? I only need a very little bit. Stu hobbled the cow as the calf stood close by. Doris cautiously approached and petted the cow on her head.

"Now Bessie or whatever you're called, I'm only going to get a little of your milk. Then we'll let you go and you and your baby can leave." Stu stood close by with a stick, watching carefully. She squatted down, put a pail under the cow and started to milk. The cow looked back at her and pushed her rump towards Doris. Doris leaned in and pushed hard against the cow. "Bessie, don't get rough with me. I'll be done faster if you cooperate. Just a couple more squirts and I'm done.

"There, Stu, unhobble her and let them go back to the herd. And, thanks, awfully much."

"Yer welcome, Miss Doris. Anythin' you want, jest ask." Stu freed the cow, mounted his horse and herded the cow and her calf back down the hill.

Back to her pie-making, she hoped she could remember the proper amounts for each ingredient. First, she made the crusts, using flour and lard. That was the easy part. In a bowl she mixed the last quart of applesauce with some sugar. She added the milk to the mixture along with two eggs, some flour, a little cinnamon and a couple teaspoons of vanilla. This made enough filling for two pies. Dividing the pies into fourths would be enough for the eight men. There was a portable oven which J.J. had made ready for Doris to use; in went the pies along with a prayer.

The cowhands began coming in shortly after Doris had taken the pies out of the oven. Along with the chicken and dumplings, there was the ever-present beans. The men were very pleased and surprised at what they were seeing and smelling.

Rose quietly told J.J., "Yer in charge of the chicken. Make sure each man gets a fair share of the chicken. I don't want the first men to take all the best parts, leaving jest backs and necks for the ones coming in later."

Since each man was given one-fourth of a pie, that didn't leave any for Doris or Rose. Billy noticed this when he was given his piece, as he was one of the last to eat.

"Miss Doris, y'all ain't gettin' any pie. That ain't fair."

"It's all right, Billy. Women don't care for pie like men do." Actually, she really wanted a piece. He left but returned about five minutes later, holding a plate with a number of tiny pieces of pie.

"These are fer ya. I collected them from the men that hadn't eaten all theirs yet."

Doris thought she was going to start crying. "Thank you, Billy. You are so kind to have done that. We surely will enjoy them."

Billy hurried off; a bit embarrassed. It was obvious he also had a crush on Doris.

The next few days passed quietly. The days were long and hot. The lead cows seemed content to move forward without much effort on the cowhands' part. The most work was tussling with the same few cows who attempted to wonder off from the main herd.

Late one afternoon Stu rode in as Doris and Rose were setting up camp for the night. "Have ya seen any screwworm medicine in the wagon?"

"No, Stu I ain't. Doris ya seen any?" Doris shook her head.

"Well, I guess I'll have ta use manure". This was shouted by Stu as he turned his horse and rode out.

"Rose, I don't think I'd know what screwworm medicine was if I saw it." Rose chuckled as she told Doris about screwworm. "First, I'm surprised they're having a problem this far north. Screwworms are usually only seen down south. The drovers have ta watch the cows for open sores. Big flies called blowflies can get in'm and lay eggs. The eggs hatch and are called screwworms. They eat on the flesh of the cow and can do a lot of damage. Most of the cowboys carry a bottle of remedy with 'em."

"What is Stu going to do with the manure?"

"He'll take some crushed cow chips and pack it in the sore to cut off the air to the worms and then they'll die."

"My-o-my, there is so much more to driving cattle then I ever realized."

At night before drifting off to sleep, Doris would lie in the wagon listening to the night riders singing to the cows. The night riders worked in pairs. They rode in opposite directions around the outside of the herd. First one man would sing a verse of a song; then the second man would sing another verse. Doris' favorite was one they called <u>Night Herdin' Song.</u>

**Oh, move slow, dogies; quit
rovin' around,
You have wandered and trampled all
over the ground.
Oh, graze along, dogies, and feed
kinda slow,
And don't forever be on the go.
Move slow, little dogies, move slow,
Hi-o, Hi-o-o-o-o**

**I've circle herded and night
herded too,
But to keep you together! That's
what I cain't do
My horse is leg weary, and I'm
awful tired,
But if you get away, I'm sure to
get fired.
Bunch up, little dogies, bunch up,**

on the go.
Move slow, little dogies, move slow.
Hi-o, Hi-o-o-o-o

Oh, lay still, dogies, since you have
laid down,
Stretch away out on the big
open ground.
Snore loud, little dogies, and drown
the wild sounds
That will all go away when the day
rolls around.
Lay still, little dogies, lay still.
Hi-o, Hi-o-o-o-o, Hi-o, Hi-o-o-o-o

Sometimes the men made up their own songs or words. Occasionally they were rather racy. The men probably thought the women were sleeping, but they sometimes weren't.

Night herding was typically quiet and

peaceful. A man would decide which of his horses was the best night seeing and surest footed to use. However, there were times when night herding was not quiet or peaceful. It didn't take much to disturb the cattle, a strange noise, a clap of thunder or a bolt of lightning. Two men on night watch even with their best seeing and surest footed horses were not always enough.

Chapter 38

Two nights later those sleeping were awakened by angry shouts coming from the direction of the herd. Several shots were fired. Rose and Doris awoke confused and got out of the wagon. Men were up and urgently saddling horses.

"It's rustlers!" shouted Rose. Colby took off after the horses. "Colby, git back here." The dog ignored Rose. She and Doris stood by their wagon.

Rose went to the chuck wagon and got

out the medical supplies. "Doris, git as many rags as ya kin. We'll need 'em for bandages."

Doris hurried and gathered rags. When she got back to the chuck wagon, Rose was building up a fire. Doris quickly poured water into a large pot and hung it over the fire. Rose began to make coffee. Stampeding cattle, men yelling, and gun shots charged the air.

The rustlers had planned their operation well. They came in from the east, dividing the herd in two. On the north side of this divide, some of the rustlers drove the cattle they intended to keep to the west. The other rustlers turned the remaining cattle south, spreading the cattle out, yelling and shooting off their guns. Terror and panic were the result, as the south-moving cattle stampeded.

In just a matter of minutes Circle G men reached the mayhem. The rustlers, who had stampeded some of the cattle south now turned and rode off west, driving many cattle before them. Tim, J.J. and Slim saw them heading away and followed. The sky was overcast, with only a sliver of a moon; it was obvious the rustlers knew the area. The Circle G men could only follow by listening to the moving cattle.

Suddenly a volley of shots sounded. Tim was hit and fell from his horse. Slim was also shot, but managed to stay in his saddle. J.J. did not see Tim fall so rode over to Slim. "How bad ya hit?"

"Not bad. Go see to Tim. I heard him groan."

"Tim! I didn't know he was hit."

"He's down. Find him. I'm goin'
back ta camp."

J.J. got off his horse and looked around.
He finally spotted Tim several feet in front
of him. J.J. bent over Tim, "Tim! Can ya
hear me?"

There was no answer. J.J. could see that
Tim's face was covered in blood. He felt
Tim's head and discovered a wound at
the left edge of his forehead. J.J. was
not totally healed yet from the injury
he received when crossing the flooded
river. Despite his excruciating pain, J.J.
managed to get Tim on J.J.'s horse. He
then mounted behind Tim and trotted back
to the camp.

Rose and Doris were tending Slim when
J.J. arrived with Tim. Rose looked up as
she saw them ride in. "Slim, can you hold

this bandage against yer side while we see ta Tim?"

Slim did as Rose instructed, lying back against a wagon wheel. J.J. got off his horse. Rose and Doris helped him pull Tim down and over to the make-shift nursing area. J.J. got back on his horse and returned to help with the rounding up the scattered cattle.

Doris saw Tim's head wound and was petrified. Rose understood. "Doris, finish bandaging Slim while I look after Tim." With no response, she added volume: "Doris! Do as I say!"

This startled Doris into action. Fortunately, the bullet had only skimmed Slim's side. Doris poured alcohol over his wound before applying a bandage. Rose cleaned Tim's head as Doris fearfully watched. She began silently praying. **Please,**

God, please, don't let Tim die. Please, please, please.

"Oh, he ain't hurt bad. The bullet only burned across the outside of his head. The head always seems ta bleed a lot," Rose said as she applied pressure to the superficial wound.

Mark rode in as Rose was wrapping a bandage around Tim's head.

"J.J. told me Tim was shot! How bad is it?"

"Not bad. The bullet jest plowed and burned a row across the side of his head. He'll have a bad headache fer a couple of days is all."

Doris fought hard to keep from crying. She hadn't realized how much she cared for Tim. Still, she tried to focus on the others; she picked herself up, poured a cup of coffee and, with a shaking hand, offered it to Mark.

"Thanks, Doris," Mark sighed. "I never thought I'd say this, but I'm grateful you ladies joined up with us."

"Could I have a cup of that coffee?" Tim surprised them as he tried to sit up.

"How ya feeling, nephew?"

"I'd be doin' much better if y'all would stop prancin' around like yer at a square dance."

Rose chuckled and said, "It's not us that's doin 'the dancin', son. You jest lay still and take it easy.'

Mark mounted his horse and looked down at Rose and Doris, "I got ta git back ta the herd and find out how bad the damages are. It's almost dawn. We'll be stayin' put for today, ladies. The men will be comin' in, a couple at a time, fer breakfast."

"Uncle Mark, wasn't Billy on night watch? Is he okay?"

"I don't know, Tim. We ain't seen him yet." Tim lay back and closed his eyes as the sun was coming up blood red.

Rose put her hands on her hips and said, "Red sky in the morning, sailors take warning."

"What's that mean?" asked Slim.

"It means we're gonna have bad weather." Rose heard Tim trying get on his feet. She ran to him. "You jest stay put, Tim Gibson! Anythin' ya need either Doris or me kin get fer ya."

"Well, Miss Rose, 'lessen ya let me git up,

ya better bring me some of them rags so I kin use 'em for diapers."

Doris' face turned beet red. She turned so no one would see.

Rose looked over at Slim, "Hey, Slim. Do ya feel up ta helpin' Tim see ta his needs?"

"Yes, Miss Rose. I could use a walk myself."

No sooner had the men walked away when Stu came riding in, holding Billy in front of him. Doris and Rose ran to help lift Billy off the horse. Billy was a large boy for his age, and both women struggled not to drop him. Rose grabbed hold of Billy's arm. He gave out a sickening cry and fainted. Rose then saw his terribly misshapen arm. Stu jumped off his horse and helped the women carry Billy over to the nursing area. Besides the broken arm, Billy's face was so bruised he was scarcely recognizable. His left eye had a long cut across the lid and was swollen shut. There was dried blood all over of his shirt and dungarees.

Tim and Slim came walking back to camp. Tim saw Billy and started to run towards him but had to grab Slim's arm to keep from stumbling. Doris went over to Tim. "Billy is all right. He has a broken arm and several cuts and bruises. But he's all right."

Tim bent down next to Billy. "Billy, it's me, Tim." Billy opened his right eye.

"Tim, I'm sorry. I tried ta stop the beeves. I jest couldn't. I'm sorry I failed ya, Tim."

"You didn't fail me, Billy. It was rustlers. There wasn't nothin' ya could do. Jest rest and git better."

Rose continued to nurse Billy as Tim watched. Doris went back to preparing food for the cowhands.

Slim came over to her. "Miss Doris?"

"Yes, Slim."

"If there's anythin' I kin do ta help ya, jest point me in the right direction. I cain't ride jest now ta help round up the beeves. I want ta do what I kin."

"Thank you, Slim. Could you slice some bacon?"

Before Slim had a chance to answer, Mark came back to the camp. He jumped off his horse. "Stu, I heard you brought Billy in. How bad is he?"

"Miss Rose says he ain't bad. He has a broken arm, though."

"Thank God, that's all."

Tim asked, "How many you think we lost, Uncle Mark?"

"Could be half the herd, 'pendin' on how many beeves are scattered in the wilds. The rustlers sure knew what they was doin', real professionals. What beeves are left could be miles south, east and west.

"Ain't we goin' ta go after the rustlers, Uncle Mark?"

"No, Stu. We only got five able riders. The rustlers are long gone. It'll be at least another day, 'fore we git the cattle what's left rounded up." He made a fist with his right hand and pounded it over and over in his left palm, swearing under his breath.

Doris handed him a cup of coffee and a buttered biscuit. "Thanks, Doris. Stu, you and me need ta git back ta work."

Rose walked up to Mark and said, "Mr. Mark, I've wrangled many a cow. Doris is able ta take care of things here. Saddle me a horse and I'll go with ya."

"No, Rose. I couldn't ask ya to do such a thing."

"You ain't askin'. I'm offerin'. I'm a good cowhand. I know what I'm doin'. When me and husband first started ranchin', we couldn't afford any cowhands. I strapped my baby daughter on my back like a papoose and rode with'm ta round up our cattle."

"I won't pretend we couldn't use the help. Speakin' of which, that dog of yers sure has been workin'. I reckon he's had some experience in drivin' cows. Doris, you and Slim all right handlin' things here?"

"Yes, Mr. Mark. We'll be fine."

"I'm goin' out too," spoke up Tim.

Slim laughed. "You kin hardly walk. Ya jest look after yer brother and watch that I behave myself around Miss Doris."

Even though his head was bandaged, everyone could still detect Tim blushing.

Just after lunch Mark and J.J. rode in leading Joe Unger's horse with his body draped across the saddle. Joe had been a quiet, older man who had worked for the Circle G for several years. He had never married. "We found him about a mile east, looks like he was trampled."

Tim forced himself to his feet, "So them thieves ain't jest guilty of rustlin', but also killin'! Uncle Mark, we got ta let the law know."

Doris was listening to the men talk. "Mr. Mark, Billy really needs to be seen by a doctor. If his arm isn't set right, he's never going to be able to use it."

"Both of you are right." Mark turned to Slim, "Slim, since ya came through here last year, can ya remember any town in this area?"

"No, I don't, Mark."

"I do," spoke up Rose, who had just ridden from helping to herd the strays. "I've been through this area a couple of times in the last five, six years. If my memory serves me right, 'bout ten or so miles due northeast is a good-sized town. I can't rightly remember its name."

"Rose, tomorra mornin', you and Slim, take Billy to that town usin' yer buggy. We'll start the herd heading north. Right now, we need to get Joe buried."

As he finished saying this, it started to rain

again. All but Ramon and Rose gathered for the burial. They stayed with the cattle. Joe was wrapped in his saddle blanket.

Mark read Psalm 23.

The Lord is my shepherd; I shall not want.
He maketh me to lie down in green pastures: he leadeth me beside the still waters.
He restoreth my soul: he leadeth me in the paths of righteousness for his name's sake.
Yea, though I walk through the valley of the shadow of death, I will fear no evil: for thou art with me; thy rod and thy staff they comfort me.
Thou preparest a table before me in the presence of mine enemies: thou anointest my head with oil; my cup runneth over.

Surely goodness and mercy shall follow me all the days of my life: and I will dwell in the house of the Lord forever.

Tim prayed, "Our heavenly Father, our hearts are heavy and we're sorrowin'. Joe was a good hand and brave. He never complained and was quick to give a smile. He was our friend. We ask that You favor him with lettin' him enter heaven where his ma and pa are waitin' fer him. We ask that You comfort his sisters when they learn the bad news. We also ask that You comfort us. We bring these requests in Jesus' name. Amen."

"Amen," was repeated by the others present. All stood around the grave. The gentle rain continued to come down.

To everyone's surprise Stu started

singing <u>Be Still, My Soul.</u> He had a clear, sweet voice.

> Be still, my soul; the Lord is on thy side.
> Bear patiently the cross of grief or pain;
> Leave to thy God to order and provide.
> In ev 'ry change He faithful will remain.

As Stu began the second verse J.J. pulled out his mouth organ and accompanied him.

> Be still, my soul; thy best, thy heav'nly Friend
> Thro' thorny ways leads to a joyful end.
> Be still, my soul; the hour is hast'ning on

**When we shall be forever
with the Lord,
When disappointment, grief, and
fear are gone,
Sorrow forgot; love's purest
joys restored.
Be still, my soul; when change and
tears are past,
All safe and blessed we shall
meet at last.**

Billy was the last to leave the grave; he walked very slowly back to the camp site.

"Are you all right, Billy?"

"I guess so, Tim. I can't help but think that could have been me."

"Yes, yer right. But it wasn't. We cain't always understand God's ways. And we don't know what tomorra holds. We jest have ta make sure we're ready ta face God when our time comes. Are ya ready, Billy?"

"Yes, Tim, I am. I asked Jesus ta forgive me of my sins and ta come inta my heart in Mrs. Crosby's Sunday school class last year."

"Good for you." Tim ruffled Billy's hair and smiled at him.

Doris and Slim started fixing supper as soon as they returned to camp. Doris asked, "Do you know if Joe had family back in Texas?"

"Yes, Miss Doris, he's got a couple of sisters. One's married ta a cousin of J.J. The other's a schoolteacher. J.J.'ll probably write 'em when we get ta a town."

"Life is sure hard."

"Yes, Miss, Doris, it sure is."

Mark came to camp near sundown. He and Tim sat talking by the chuck wagon.

Doris wasn't eavesdropping, but couldn't help overhearing the conversation.

"Tim, we'll be movin' out at first light. Reckon we lost half the herd from what the rustlers got and the cattle we jest can't find. Also, remember we had ta pay the Indians in the Territory fifty head when we crossed their range jest after we started this drive." Mark finished totaling up their loses and stared into his coffee cup.

Tim nodded in agreement and added, "What are we goin' ta do about sellin' ta the miners? We need the cash ta improve the land and build. Do ya think we'll make it?"

"A lot is goin' to depend on how well Walt did sellin' the ranch. Jest hope he got a good price. How ya feelin', anyway?"

"I'm doin' much better. I plan ta ride tomorra."

"We'll need ya on the line, especially with Slim and Rose plus Billy gone. Git a good night's sleep."

"Who's got the first watch?"

"Me and J.J."

"Wake me 'bout midnight. I'll be ready."

As Doris and Rose were bedding down that night, Doris asked, "Rose, have you ever heard about cattle drives having to pay Indians to cross over their land?'

"Sure have, dearie. Injins are pretty smart. They decided instead of raidin' and scalpin' the white man, they'd jest charge him for crossin' their territory."

"Ranchers actually agreed with the Indians to pay? Isn't that extortion?"

"Well, I guess it's better than losin' yer scalp and all the cattle to boot! Now, go ta sleep. Yer in for a busy day tomorra."

Chapter 39

Before the sun was up the next day, Rose, Slim and Billy left for town in the make-shift wagon. They rode across the prairie for several miles. The wagon, having no springs made a very uncomfortable ride for Billy. He was laying in the bed of the wagon on Doris' and Rose's blankets. The trio had only gone a short distant when Billy tugged on the back of Slim's shirt, "Slim, I hurt awful bad." He was covered in sweat. "My arm hurts so much from all this bouncing I feel like I'm about ta cry." Slim stopped the buggy, turned and looked at Billy.

Rose glanced at Slim and said, "Help'm git up here on the bench. If I help support him maybe the pain will let up." Slim climbed into the bed of the wagon and with Rose's help lifted Billy onto the bench. Rose put her arm around Billy. She cupped her other hand for Billy's elbow. This helped ease his pain.

About an hour later they came to a dirt road. The ride smoothed out. Billy rested his head on Rose's shoulder and was soon asleep. "Poor kid! He didn't sleep much last night. I sure hope the doc can help him."

"He will, Slim. That is if'n there's a doctor in town."

The sun was hidden by ominous looking clouds as the wagon entered a fair sized, prosperous looking town. "Surely, there's a doctor in this town. Rose, ask those two ladies talkin' by that fence." The ladies told them to turn right at the second street. The doctor's office was in the middle of the block, three houses down.

On the corner of the street, where they turned, was a blacksmith and livery stable. The last renegade outlaw, Monte, had gotten a job helping to shoe horses. He seldom did any honest work. His plan was to earn enough money to see him through to Ardmore Bend and wait there for Doris. Monte watched as the ramshackle wagon turned the corner. **That's the old woman that's been ridin' with Nate's wife! I wonder if she knows where the bank money is hid?**

"Hey, I ain't paying you to lollygag watching traffic. Get back to work." Monte gave his boss a malicious look before continuing to clean out a stall. At the same time, he watched as the wagon stopped in front of the doctor's office. He saw the old woman and the driver help a kid into the building.

They were greeted by a middle-aged woman at a desk in the small waiting room. There were two other people present, a woman obviously very pregnant and an older man with a very washed-out complexion. The receptionist looked at Billy, got up and opened a door to an examination room. "Bring the boy in here. I'll tell Dr. Mockler to come. He won't be long."

Once Billy was seated and as comfortable as possible, Slim rested his hand on the door knob, "Rose, will ya be all right if I leave and find the sheriff? I want ta tell him what happened."

"Go ahead. We'll wait here fer ya." Billy was resting on the examination table as

Rose paced back and forth. The day had turned very warm and humid. It had yet to begin raining. She heard an odd noise at the partially open unscreened window. She walked over to it and leaned out and was grabbed by Monte.

"What'a ya doin'. Let me go!" A large dirty hand was placed over her mouth. Monte dragged Rose into the doctor's carriage barn behind the house. The tip of his knife nicked her neck and she felt blood trickle down on to her shirt.

"Ya feel this knife?" Rose nodded ever so slightly. "I'm goin' ta take my hand off yer mouth. If ya yell, it'll be the last time ya ever do." He removed his hand from her mouth but not the knife from her neck.
"I know who you are. And I want ta know where yer friend hid the money."

"I don't know what yer talking about. My

grandson was hurt. Me and his pa brought him in ta see Doc Mockler."

Monte pushed Rose against a buggy. She stumbled and fell. He grabbed her arm wrenching it behind her as he lifted her and pushed her face into the buggy seat. Holding her pressed against the buggy seat with one hand and holding the knife to her throat he continued, "Look lady, I don't want ta kill ya. I jest want my money."

Rose was thinking fast. She saw the buggy whip leaning against the buckboard. "All right, I'll tell you what I can remember. Please, jest take that knife away from my throat so I can think."

Monte eased back on the knife but continued to hold her pinned to the seat. She tried to straighten up. "Ya don't have ta move ta think."

A man and his wife, were walking down the street. They happened to look into the carriage house and viewed the odd scene. "Look George. What's going on in there?"

Startled by the woman's voice, Monte moved just enough for Rose to grab the whip and ram the hard end into his belly. Momentarily stunned, Monte dropped his knife. Upon entering the building, the man shouted, "Are you accosting that woman?" Monte swore and ran out a side door.

Rose collapsed on the building floor as the couple came in. She was shaking with fury. Blood continued to trickle ran down her neck staining the collar of her new shirtwaist. "He's a murderer. Get the sheriff, quick!" After a nod from his wife, the man turned and ran down the street in the direction they had just come. The woman put her arm around Rose and led her back to the doctor's office.

"I thought you were in the examination room with your son? stated the receptionist, her eyes the size of saucers. "How did you get out?"

Suddenly, Rose was very tired. She sat down with the help of the stranger. The washed-out complexioned man handed her his blue and white handkerchief without saying a word. She placed it over the nick in her neck. "Thank you."

Rose was given a glass of water by the receptionist, who then left and went into the examination room. The pregnant woman said, "Take some deep breaths, Sweety. It's always helped me."

For some reason this struck Rose as very funny. She started laughing, "I'm not pregnant! I was bushwhacked by someone who tried ta kill me!"

The front door opened at the same time as the examination room door. Slim and the sheriff came in. They started talking at the same time as the doctor. Dr. Mockler held up his arms, "Stop! This woman needs attention. Sheriff, you can question her later."

Rose wanted to tell the sheriff what had happened so he could look for Monte. Instead, she let herself be led into the room where Billy lay sleeping with a cast on his arm. Her two rescuers told the sheriff what they had witnessed, then left.

"This won't need suturing. I'll just clean and bandage it." When he was done, Dr. Mockler gave Rose instructions about taking care of the wound. "Keep the dressing on a couple of days. Then let it air. Keep it clean."

Rose had been watching Billy. He seemed to be in a very deep sleep. "Is Billy okay?"

"Your young friend is fine. I gave him a pain medicine before I set his arm. In six weeks remove the cast. He can leave as soon as he awakens." Rose got up from the chair she had been sitting in. She and the doctor returned to the waiting room. The washed-out man was sleeping with his head on his chest.

Rose turned to the pregnant woman. "I'm sorry for what's happened. You have been waitin' so long."

"Ma'am, I don't mind one bit. I've got five youngsters at home. My mother-in-law is tending to them. It's nice and cool in here. Except for getting a little hungry, I could sit here all day, even if the magazines are the same ones, I read last month. I ain't enjoyed so much excitement since the day my second was born.

"My husband came running into the house and fell through the open cellar door in the kitchen floor. He ended up in worse shape than me. My mother-in-law had left it open. Thank goodness it wasn't me." She had a bright smile on her face as she relayed this information. The doctor beckoned her into a second examination room.

The sheriff moved forward stating, "If it's not too much trouble, I'd like to find out what's happened. Slim, here, has already told me about the cattle rustling, the death of the drover and the boy's broken arm."

Rose took the seat the woman had just vacated and looked at Slim. "Did you tell the sheriff about Doris and me?"

"No. I ain't. Why don't ya start from the beginnin'."

Before Rose could say another word, the sheriff spoke. "You're not talking about that woman, Doris Clark, are you?"

"Why, yes, I am. What do ya know about her?"

"Only that half of the country is looking for her. She's somehow involved in the bank robbery in Ardmore Bend. I expect a bounty to be put on her any day now."

Rose stood placing her hands on her hips and leaning towards the sheriff. "Look here sheriff, Doris had nothin' ta do with that robbery. It was her husband. She knew nothin' about it until he wandered home, half-dead."

"Word has it, she knows where the money is. What about you? Do you know?"

"That is what this—this Monte person wanted. If Doris does know where it's hid, she hasn't told me. All she has said is that the last time she saw it, it was in saddlebags which were hanging over a chair."

"So why is she running and hiding? Why didn't she go to the peace officer in her town?"

"For one thing, when I found her, she was runnin' fer her life from the outlaws. She was lost and I'm not sure she knew what she was doin'."

"That doesn't answer the question why she is still running and evading the law."

Rose looked at the sheriff, "Truthfully, I don't know. I guess you'll jest have ta ask her, when ya see her."

This exchange came to an abrupt end

when a man came running into the doctor's office. "Sheriff, your deputies told me to come get you. They have that man you're looking for cornered in a shed behind Widow Stevens' house." The sheriff bounded out the door almost knocking the informant over.

The door to the second examination room opened. The pregnant woman exited, followed by Dr. Mockler. He walked over to Rose and Slim. "You two go have lunch. Your young friend will probably awaken soon. Have the café fix him a sandwich."

Rose turned to the lady. "Please, join us fer lunch. I feel it's the least we can do."

The woman hesitated. "I really would like to. But I'd better get on home and rescue my mother-in-law. There's only so much one can expect. She'll be hotter than hot cakes by now."

Rose and Slim were about to enter the café when they heard gun shots and a lot of commotion. Monte came bounding into the street from an ally across from the café. He saw a saddled horse standing at a hitching post. Leaping onto it he pulled the reins loose and sped out of town. The two deputies were close behind. They got on their horses and followed the outlaw. The sheriff, who was past his prime, came breathlessly into view. Bending over with one hand on a knee and the other hand propping up the side of a building, wheezing, he called out in a faint voice, "Go get'm, boys." He realized half the town was watching him. He regained his self-respect and walked across the street to Rose and Slim. "I could do with some lunch."

The trio sat by the front window eating ham sandwiches. Slim and Rose were truly enjoying this change in menu. "Look, it's your deputies, Sheriff," declared Slim.

Between the two sat Monte on the stolen horse with his hands tied to the saddle horn. All three appeared as though they had been wallowing in a pigs' pen, covered in sweat and dirt. Each sporting torn shirts. One deputy's pant leg was ripped from thigh to ankle. He had a bruised and swollen cheek and a black eye. The second deputy was holding his arm ever so gently across his midsection.

Monte looked the worst of the three. One eye was swollen shut. His shirt resembled a large rag. He was half bent over, breathing hard. The sheriff got up. As he walked out the door he looked back with a smile, "I knew they'd get him!"

The jail cell where Monte was housed had never been breached. Built in the basement of the court house, it was made of quarried stone on all sides with no windows. The door had an opening only large enough to pass a plate through. Monte lay on a thin mattress over a cement block bed. He was fuming. His side hurt every time he took a breath. Dr. Mockler had come to look at him and taped his midsection. He told Monte to take it easy as he had several cracked ribs. Well, what else could Monte do but take is easy?

Slim and Rose headed for the doctor's office to check on Billy. Billy sat in a chair on the front porch holding a slice of chocolate cake in his good hand, enjoying every last crumb. Rose smiled as the two walked up. "Well, will ya look at him!"

"Hey! Slim, Miss Rose, look what Mrs. Mockler gave me!"

"I take it yer feeling better?"

"Sure am, Slim. Say, Doc said there was some real excitement while I was sleepin'. I'm sorry I missed it."

"That's quite all right. But, we're all kinda' tired. So, Rose and I've talked things over. We've decided to stay here for ta night and head back in the mornin'."

"Are we gonna stay in a hotel? I've never stayed in one before."

Before Slim could answer Dr. Mockler opened the door followed by his wife. She was carrying a tray of lemonade and glasses. She placed them on the table and poured lemonade for each one. "Could I interest you in a piece of cake?"

Rose smiled at Mrs. Mockler. "That sure looks good. But, none for me. Thanks just the same. I'm very full from lunch."

Slim had been eyeing Billy's cake, "Well, I

sure won't turn down a piece. That cake looks mighty fine."

When the sheriff had Monte safely put away, he went looking for Slim. He found him sitting on the Mockler's porch. "Slim, I want to talk with you some more about the cattle rustling. You hear about the other bit of cattle rustling that took place here abouts?"

"No, when was this?"

"About a week ago. The owner, a Wilbur McNeill, brought in his nephew and two other drovers. His nephew died just after arriving. Doc treated the two other men.

"The boy was buried three days ago. It was really nice how the community treated McNeill as if he were one of our own. He was some broken up over the death. He's staying at the Bergman Hotel. His men aren't fit to travel."

Dr. Mockler interrupted the sheriff. "I have a couple of rooms I use, kind-of like a small hospital. The men are still patients here."

Once the cake had been eaten and the lemonade finished, Slim, Rose and Billy drove the unique wagon to the Bergman to register. After they were settled in their rooms, Slim went in search of Mr. McNeill.

Chapter 40

Slim, Rose and Billy caught up with the herd the follow afternoon. Riding beside them was a stranger. Mark rode over to greet them. Slim got down from the wagon as Mark and the stranger dismounted. Slim introduced the man.

"Mark, this is Wilbur McNeill. We met in town. He's drivin' a herd ta Montana from Kansas. Wil, this is my friend and part owner of our herd, Mark Gibson."

Mark and Wilbur shook hands. Slim

continued: "We've got a lot ta tell ya. First, he looked at Doris, "You'll be glad ta know that the last outlaw was caught, thanks ta Rose."

"What! Tell me what happened."

Rose spoke, still sitting on the wagon beside Billy. It's a lot ta tell. Let's hear from Mr. McNeill first. I'll tell ya all about catchin' that rascal later. It's a long tale."

Wil McNeill looked at Mark, "All right. Like Slim said, I was driving a herd of about fourteen hundred head from Kansas to Montana. I got a contract to deliver a thousand head to a mining camp up there. About a week ago a band of rustlers attacked our camp. Probably the same ones that hit yours. They run the cattle right through the middle of our camp. Killed my nephew; he was only fifteen.

His ma, my sister .... didn't want him ... to come along."

Wilbur paused several times while speaking. It was obvious to everyone that Wilbur was having difficulty controlling his emotions. He pulled a big red and white handkerchief out of his back pocket and wiped his face before continuing. "His pa... said it would do the boy good."

Rose jumped down from the wagon. "I'll go fetch ya some coffee." She and Doris hurried off to get coffee for the men.

Doris noticed the bandage on her neck. Rose, what happened to you?"

"In a minute, Doris, in a minute."

Wilbur took a deep breath and carried on. "I don't know how ... I'm going to be able to tell my sister. It's going to break her heart." He sighed, then resumed. "The stampede also killed our cook and destroyed the chuck wagon. Two of my men were shot. That's why I was in town. They're still at the doctor's house. The doc said they aren't in fit shape to go on with the drive. I told 'em that I'd stop by on my way back to Kansas to get 'em."

Rose arrived with cups of coffee. Doris followed with a pan of biscuits.

Mark asked, "How many of your cattle did ya lose, Mr. McNeill? We may have some of them. When we rounded up what we could find of ours, there were a few with an odd brand. We figured we'd jest let them mix with ours until we could find out who they belong ta."

"Please, just call me Wil. We started with fourteen hundred, give or take a few. The four hundred extra I'd planned to sell to the new homesteaders in Montana. Trouble is, I'm shy of seven hundred."

Slim spoke up, "Wil, sit down and rest. I'd like ta talk with my partners."

He and Mark walked a short distance away. Slim called J.J. and Tim over. He explained to them about McNeill, and then said, "I've been thinkin'. What would ya think about our two herds joinin' up? We're short men and so is he. He doesn't have a chuck wagon anymore or a cook. He's in need of more cattle ta fulfill that contract. We need a buyer fer our cattle. Together I think we'd all come out on top."

Tim said, "That sounds good ta me. Have you said anything ta him?"

"No, I haven't. I thought I'd best talk it over with you other owners first."

J.J. responded, "Thank ya, Slim. I 'preciate that. If Mark is fer it, I am too."

Mark looked at his three partners. "This jest may be the answer to our prayers, boys. Let's see what Wil has to say."

Wil was keen to agree. "I got to get back to my camp. My men will be wondering what's become of me. If you keep heading northwest, you'll see my herd just on the other side of that rise yonder. We'll wait for you. If you leave at first light you should be there by late morning."

Doris was a little provoked that cows seemed to be more important than Rose's injury and catching the outlaw. But instead, she asked Wil, "Do you have food for your men until we arrive?"

"Yes, ma'am. One of my hands went to

town with me. I sent him on ahead with supplies. But thank you for your concern."

Wil got back on his horse and headed in the direction of his cattle. Slim passed on what the sheriff had told him, "He said the rustlers have been on the prowl fer some time. They're well organized and know the territory. He don't have much hope of catchin' the men or gettin' any cattle back. I left him our information about our destination. But the best thing about goin' was gittin' Billy's arm fixed and catching that feller that's been stalkin' Doris. The doc says the arm should heal fine without any problem. And...and." He looked straight at Doris. "The last outlaw was caught. Rose was mostly responsible fer that.

Doris smiled at Billy. "That's real good news, Billy." Suddenly she was light headed and weak in the knees. She realized she hadn't eaten all day.

"Catch her! Don't let her fall", shouted Slim, as Doris' knees gave out. Tim caught Doris before she had a chance to hit the ground. He carried her to the wagon. Rose followed him. "She'll be fine, Tim. She's jest relieved it's over. Go back ta the men. I'll see ta her."

Doris was coming around as Rose was speaking. "Is it really over, Rose? Really?"

"Make yerself comfortable. I've got a whopper of a story ta tell ya."

That evening Billy was up and about as though nothing had happened except for the cast covering his arm. He saw Mark drinking a second cup of coffee. "Tamorra' I'm goin' back on the line with ya."

Mark looked up at Billy, "I'm not sure that's

a good idea, Billy. I wouldn't want ya ta fall and be hurt more."

Doris was washing up the dishes, "Billy, I was hoping you could help me. This driving all day, then having to fix the meals is a little too much for me alone." In truth, it wasn't too much for her. She was enjoying herself more than she had in a long, long time.

"Aw shucks, Miss Doris. I suppose I kin, if ya really need me."

"I do, Billy." Without Billy noticing, Mark mouthed a thank-you to Doris.

Chapter 41

After two days of infuriating sameness a janitor came to mop the hallway in the jail section of the court house. He was accompanied by a deputy. Monte sat up. The janitor was Bob or Arch, or whatever his name was. He was the man Monte had hired in the failed attempt to get Doris alone.

Monte couldn't help but notice that Arch was wearing the same clothes he had the day of the incident. They looked as though they hadn't been washed. Nor did Arch appear to have bathed or shaved.

The deputy was young and inattentive. He seemed to be day-dreaming. Probably thinking about what his plans were after work. Arch threw some water from his bucket toward the deputy, wetting his boots. "Hey! Watch it!

The deputy was looking at his wet boots not paying attention to Arch, who moved closer to him. He said, "Sorry, son," and pulled out a short-rounded club from his pocket. It was a rule that no weapons were allowed in the cell area. Not even the deputies carried them. The deputy looked up at Arch and saw the club coming down. One of his last thoughts, as Arch smashed the end of the club onto his head, was that he hadn't checked the janitor for a weapon.

Arch grabbed the keys from the prone

officer's pocket. Before Arch opened the cell door, he looked at Monte and said, "We go fifty-fifty on the money. Right?"

Monte hesitated for only a second. "Sure, sure Arch. Fifty-fifty. Jest git me out of here."

Arch hastily unlocked the cell door. They proceeded down the hall and cautiously opened the door leading to a larger corridor. Hanging on a hook on the outside of the door was the deputy's holster containing his gun. Monte quickly buckled it on. The two crept up the stairs into the main part of the court house. It was early evening and no one was present.

"I've got a couple of hosses tied up in back. Follow me."

They continued to a rear door and out into the gathering dusk. So as not to arouse attention, they slowly walked their horses out to the edge of town before kicking them and launching into a gallop. Monte let Arch lead the way for several miles. Only when they were far into some foot hills, where no one would hear, he pointed the gun at Arch, shooting him in the back.

Monte continued to ride. "Share my money! Hah, not after what I've been through."

The bullet meant to kill Arch did not do its job. He lay where he had fallen throughout the night drifting in and out of awareness. Just before dawn he heard black birds starting to sing, high in a pine tree. Funny, he hadn't paid attention to the singing of birds for many a year. Just as the sun was coming over the horizon the wrens started their cheerful calling to each other.

Arch sat up. His shoulder ached something fierce. He didn't think it was bleeding anymore. Worse than the ache was his raging thirst. Standing under the pine tree was his horse. She came at his whistle. "Good girl. I can always count on you." Hanging onto a stirrup Arch managed to pull himself to a standing position. Suspended from the saddle was his canteen. He grabbed for it as a drowning man might grab a thrown rope.

His thirst quenched, he contemplated mounting his horse and looking for Monte. But he knew he didn't have the strength or inclination to go after him. Over the chirping of the birds came the pounding of hooves. The sheriff and a deputy came upon Arch standing by his horse hanging onto the saddle horn, his head resting on the seat. He raised his head. Sad eyes looked at the sheriff, "Help me, please." He fell to the ground and back into unconsciousness.

Arch opened his eyes and looked around. He was in the same cell from which he had helped Monte escape. His shoulder was bandaged and his arm was in a sling. Again, the thirst was worse than any pain. "Water. Please, I need water."

He turned his head as he heard the cell door open. "Here, son. Let me help you sit up." Strong arms lifted him to a sitting position.

"Thanks Sheriff. How long have I been here?"

"Not long. Only a few hours. Tell me what's your name? It's not Mike, is it?"

At first Arch just sat, sipping the water. "Oh, what's the use? My real name is Bob. Or rather Robert, Robert Sadakis."

"Are you wanted for anything? Anything

that is, besides clunking my deputy over the head and helping a prisoner escape?"

"No. But I've done time in the state pen."

"Well, rest for now. I'll have some supper brought to you."

The sheriff started to leave. "Sheriff?"

"Yes."

"How is the deputy? He's not dead, is he? I've never killed nobody."

"He's not dead. He has a big knot on his head and a roaring headache."

"Do ya suppose I could have somethin' for pain? My shoulder sure is hurtin'."

The sheriff yelled, "Doug! Get that medicine the doctor left for the prisoner and bring it in here." Doug came, opened the door, and walked to the cell carrying a

small brown bottle. He gave Arch a dirty
look. There was an ugly bruise along the
right side of his face. He handed the sheriff
the bottle and a large spoon through
the cell bars. The sheriff poured a bit of
the liquid into the spoon. Arch opened
his mouth and swallowed it. The sheriff
walked out the door, closed it with a loud
clink, then locked it.

Chapter 42

When supper was finished and the dishes cleaned up, Tim came over to Doris and asked her if she would care to take a walk. They walked to a ridge overlooking a narrow stream and sat down on a fallen log.

"Is the drivin' of the chuck wagon and cookin' too much for ya, Doris? Maybe Rose ought ta come back and help."

Doris gave a laugh. "Goodness me, no. I just said that to keep Billy from going out with the herd."

"I'm glad ta know that. I cain't help but notice that sometimes ya look so sad. If ya want ta talk 'bout it, I'll be glad ta listen."

Doris was silent for several seconds. Tim became concerned that he had overstepped his place and was about to apologize when Doris said, "At times I feel so much hate in me. I'm angry about what happened to my family. I hate Nate so much. I even hate his wife. That doesn't make sense. I'm also afraid. I'm angry at God and that scares me."

After a pause, Tim began, "A long time ago I learned it's all right ta be angry at God. He kin take it. I once heard a preacher say 'God is worthy to be praised no matter what happens'. I believe that's true. Ya know, don't you, that Billy and Stu are my half-brothers?"

"Yes, Gary told Rose and me when he was

helping us. He said that your papa had died during the war."

"That's right. I was eight when he and my Uncle Walt left ta fight. They didn't go 'til near the end of the war. Then about eight months later Uncle Walt came home. He had been hurt bad and could hardly walk. He said that he'd walked most of the way home, only gettin' a ride once in a while. That was the first Ma and I learned my pa was dead.

"I guess I started gettin' angry at the world and everyone in it right then. I was mad Uncle Walt came home and not Pa. I was even mad at Pa for dyin'. It wasn't but 'bout five, six months later when Uncle Walt and Ma got married. That really riled me. I started frettin' and gettin' in fights at school. I sassed back at Ma and Uncle Walt and even the teacher, who happened ta be the preacher. One day Ma told me she was gonna' have a baby. I hated that baby at first. It was Stu, but don't ever tell him." Tim gave a shy smile at Doris.

"You still don't hate him, do you?"

"Oh, no. I couldn't love him more, if'n he were my own son. What happened, was, Pastor Pritchard, made me stay after school one day. He said, 'Tim, yer very angry at what's happened to you. You've got ta let go of yer hate. I want ya ta take this paper and write yer pa a letter. Tell him exactly how ya feel.'

"I shouted, 'Why, he's dead! He won't git it!'

"Pastor replied, 'Jest do it!'

"Well, I did. I told my pa jest how I felt. Then Pastor gave me another sheet of paper. Now those were hard times and paper were scarce. He said, 'Now, write a letter to yer Uncle Walt. Tell him yer feelings. I promise he won't ever see it, so be honest.' I wrote it out. I even used some swear words.

"Next, he gave me a third sheet and told me ta write ta my ma. I asked were he sure she weren't ever goin' to see it. He said, he was sure.

"Then we went outside. There was a bit of woods nearby. He had me git some branches and twigs that were lyin' about so we could build a fire. When it was goin' good, he said ta tear the letters inta little bits and put them in the fire. He explained it were my sacrifice of praise ta God. He warned me if I didn't give God the hate and anger, I was harborin' in my heart, it would make me an evil, sad man. I did as Pastor Pritchard told me even though I didn't understand it all. As the smoke went up ta heaven, I gave all my sorrow and hate ta Him and told Him I didn't want it back."

"Did that work?"

"I won't lie and tell ya everythin' were peaches and cream after that. I was still sad at times. But God helped me see how Uncle Walt was really tryin' ta do right by me and my ma and how important he was ta our ranch.

"One day I walked inta the house and heard my momma crying in her bedroom. I looked in and she was holdin' a shirt. It had been packed in a chest. She saw me and smiled, 'This was your pa's favorite shirt. I loved him so much and sometimes I still miss him so.

"'I hope you understand I had ta marry yer Uncle Walt. There wasn't nothing else ta be done. You needed a papa and I needed a husband. Yer uncle will never take the place of yer papa. But he's a good man. I can't say I really love him. I'm trying to. Someday I will. I'm sure of it. I don't believe I'll ever love him like I did your papa. But someday I'll love him. There are times I jest feel I need ta take out yer papa's shirt and hold it. Walt knows and understands. I'll keep this shirt fer you. When yer a little bigger, it will be yers.'"

"Do you have that shirt now?"

"Yes, I save it fer special times." Tim moved closer to Doris. She thought he might kiss her. She stood up and suggested they return to the camp.

That night she lay on her bedroll crying gently. Rose patted her arm. "What's the matter, child?"

"I'm sorry, Rose. I didn't mean to wake

you up. It's just that I feel so guilty about keeping my secret. I believe Tim really likes me. And I like him, too. I'm thinking I should tell him and Mr. Mark my secret."

"No, I don't think you should. You and them are safer if ya don't tell. We'll be in Ardmore Bend in jest a few more days. Then everythin' will be over."

Doris curled into a tight ball. She was scared. "Yes, everything will be over," she whispered softly.

Doris didn't sleep very much that night. Finally, about midnight, she got up. Quietly she found paper and a pencil. Sitting near the burning embers of the night's fire, she started to write. She poured out her heartache and sorrow to God. Next, she wrote to Nate. It was awful, hate-filled language. Finally, she wore herself out. Silent tears rolled down her cheeks. She stood up, walked closer to the fire and slowly dropped pieces of the paper into the fire as she tore it up.

"God, I give my hateful sin to you. I don't want to carry it anymore. Please come into my heart and give me peace. I forgive Nate for all the lies and hurt he did to me. Help me to follow You. Please, Jesus, don't let me take it back!"

Off in the shadows watching stood a tall young man, having just returned from night duty. He also prayed, "God help Doris in her struggles. Give me wisdom in my decisions."

Chapter 43

The two drives met up late morning the next day. Two days later Mark commented to Tim how agreeably the two outfits worked together. It seemed as though they had been partnering all along, not just for a couple of days. Tim replied, "Well, I guess we both were in need of a blessing."

"Tim, tonight I'm goin' ta tell Rose about Sarah. I want you ta be there."

"Sure, Uncle Mark, I'll be there."

Mark rode up to the chuck wagon. Billy

was driving while Doris mended a man's shirt. "Doris, tamorra we'll be as close ta Ardmore Bend as we're goin' ta be. Tim can take ya in. I want him ta git some supplies and check fer mail. He's also goin' ta look fer a cook."

"You'll be out two very good workers if we leave the drive."

Mark gave a hearty laugh at Doris' comment. "I won't deny that, little lady. There's somethin' I need ta talk ta Rose about. After supper I'd like the two of ya ta come see me."

After cleaning up from supper and getting ready for the morning, Rose and Doris met the two men. The four walked to a grove of trees some distance from the camp. Mark began, "Miss Rose, there is somethin' I need to tell ya. It's kind of a long tale, so it might be best if you and Doris have a seat on this here log."

Mark breathed a deep sigh and began his tale. "For a long time, my ma was a sickly woman. She had what the doctor called arthritis. She got real crippled up. So much so, she weren't able ta do much fer herself. There was a good lady that my pa hired ta be like a nurse. Well, this lady, Miss Rita was her name, worked fer my ma 'bout two years. She and one of our hired hands got themselves hitched and moved further west. So, pa sent me ta town ta find another nurse.

There weren't any women in the area that weren't already married or jest too young. I'd been askin' several town people, most of the day, if anyone knew of a gal that might be willin' ta come ta the ranch as a nurse.

"I was goin' past the dry goods store as this pretty little thing was comin' out. She was as lovely as she could be without bein' an angel. She was carryin' a passel of boxes and dropped a couple right in front of me. I picked 'em up and introduced myself. I asked if I might carry them fer her. She replied she would 'preciate the help. I ventured she was new in town. She answered, she was, jest havin' arrived two days before. I inquired if she had come with her family or maybe a husband. She didn't say anythin', jest stood in the middle of the boardwalk. I told her that I didn't mean ta be impolite. I told her about my ma needin' a nurse and would she be interested.

"She looked at me real sad and said, 'Oh, Mr. Gibson, if ya only would have asked me yesterday. I've signed a five-year contract ta work for Miss Tilly.' Well, now,

Miss Tilly's ain't the place for any innocent young woman ta be workin'. If ya know what I mean?"

"Yes, Mr. Mark, I know what ya mean." Rose was unusually quiet and thoughtful. "Please go on." If anyone had looked, they would have seen two large teardrops on her checks, but it was too dark to see.

"She said right now she was only helpin' the other gals ta get themselves ready fer visitors. But Miss Tilly planned ta teach her more. I asked her if she'd like me ta talk ta Miss Tilly 'bout gettin' out of her contract and come ta be my ma's nurse. She looked at me with such sorrowful eyes. I'll never forgit that look. 'Course she said yes, and the only reason she had accepted the job at Miss Tilly's was 'cause she hadn't eaten regular and no one would hire her.

"We goes over ta Miss Tilly's. I talked ta

her. She said she had a contract and it would cost me five hundred dollars ta buy it. Well, this young thing gasped and said she only signed it for one hundred and fifty dollars. But Miss Tilly said it would be five hundred dollars and by six o'clock that night. It was then 'bout half past three. I said I'd be back. I left pretty low. There weren't no way I could get five hundred dollars. I went ta the bank but Mr. Ferguson, the president, jest laughed at me. Well, I told the Lord if He wanted me ta buy that contract, He'd jest have ta send me the money.

"At about a quarter ta six, I was ready ta give up when this kid came up ta me and said a dude from back East is looking fer me. He wants ta buy my horse. I told the kid ta git lost; I weren't sellin' my horse. Then the dude walked up ta me and asked how much I wanted fer my horse and rig.

I said six hundred dollars. He looked at me like I was loco. He said it was a good horse and a nice saddle but not worth six hundred dollars. He offered me four hundred. I come back with five hundred. He said all right, it were a deal. He opened his carryin' bag and counted out fifty ten-dollar gold pieces into my hands. I ran ta Miss Tilly's and dumped them in her lap, grabbed the gal and left."

"You redeemed her!"

"What'd ya say, Doris?"

"You went into the place of sin and redeemed her."

"I guess ya could call it that. I never thought about it that a way."

"How did the two of you get home?" Doris asked. Rose just sat listening.

"My uncle owned the livery stable. He loaned me a horse and buggy.

"Now that gal was a right good nurse and friend fer Ma. She was there about two years when Ma called me ta her room. She said, 'Son, there's a passel of men eyein' my nurse. If ya don't get up the nerve ta ask her ta wed, she'll be gone jest like little Rita was.'

"After supper me and the gal were sittin' on the porch. It were a warm night. I tried six ways ta Sunday ta git up enough nerve. I don't know why but I was durn scared. Finally, she looked at me. 'Mark, is there somethin' you want ta ask me?'

I somehow said, 'Will ya marry me?' She laughed and answered she didn't think I'd ever get 'round ta askin'. Rose, that gal was..."

"My Saree! I figured that out right away, Mark."

"Yes, yer Saree. Here's a picture of her with our two boys. They're twins, four now. The picture was taken two years ago." Mark lit a match so Rose could see the picture.

"Look, Doris, ain't she beautiful? And the boys, so good-lookin'."

"You're a grandma, Rose."

"Why, yes, I am. What's their names, Mark?"

"John and Matthew. They're named after our fathers."

"My husband's name was John."

"And my pa's name was Howard Matthew. He never cared fer his first name and asked us ta name the boy Matthew."

"Why didn't Saree ever let me know? I've been lookin' fer her fer ten years."

"A man that knew ya came through lookin' fer a job 'bout seven years ago. He told Sarah you and her pa had died. He said the ranch had been sold ta a young couple."

"Oh, my husband did die jest after Saree left home. I let out the place and started lookin' fer her. I still own the farm. They sharecrop. They're doin' right well; my brother tells me. He collects the fees and goes ta see 'em regular for me."

"I'm sorry, Rose. We should have tried harder checkin' things out. Sarah had her hands full carin' for the twins and we've had so much trouble with the big ranchers tryin' ta take over."

"It's all right, Mark. I understand. And I've had one heck of a time lookin'. Why I never would have met Doris if I hadn't been on the trail. But why didn't ya say somethin' before now?"

"I jest don't know. Well, at first, I had ta be sure. I can't explain it. But I want ya ta know I'd like ya ta come ta Montana and live with us. Sarah will be so happy ta see ya. And Doris, I know ya plan ta go ta your sister's place. If yer plans should change, there'll always be a place at our table fer ya. There's one particular person I know fer sure who would be real pleased if ya'd come with us."

Doris was glad it was dark so he didn't see her blush. "Thank you, Mr. Mark."

As the four walked back to camp, they passed Stu, Bill and two young hands from the McNeill drive sitting under a tree, laughing and joking. Wil was drinking a cup of coffee near the campfire. "What are you youngsters jawing about over there?"

The two hands from McNeill's drive got up and walked over to Wil.

"Mr. McNeill, we were talking 'bout girls." This initiated a laugh from the rest of the men around the campfire.

"Charlie here is sweet on Cora Ann Douglas."

"Charlie, you won't go wrong hitching up with Cora Ann. She's right pretty and her pa says she's a good worker."

"Yeah, Mr. McNeill, but she doesn't seem to care for me. Mrs. McNeill ever say what made her take to you?"

"She said she just fell in love with my dark, curly hair."

"Dark, curly hair? Shucks, boss, you're about as bald as an egg!"

With a twinkle in his eye, Wilbur answered Charlie. "Son, I sure wasn't when I was twenty-one!"

Chapter 44

Tim, Doris and Rose left the cattle drive and rode into Ardmore Bend. The first place they visited was the post office. Two letters were there that Doris had hoped for. The first letter was from Mr. Dodd. It contained a check for several hundred dollars less than she had anticipated. Mr. Dodd had included a short note expressing his condolences for all that had happened to her. He added the farm wasn't worth as much as he first offered because the house and barn were gone. He was now only buying the land.

Doris gasped when she looked at the amount on the check. Tim thought something was wrong and quickly came to her. "Are ya all right, Doris? Is it bad news? Do ya need ta sit?"

"I'm fine. It's just this letter. It's ... it's a ... surprise." The second letter was from the bank president and held a second check for the amount in her parents' savings account.

As she was pondering what to do with this money, a man walked up to her. "Are you Mrs. Clark, Doris Kepler Clark?"

"Yes."

"I'm the sheriff. I need you to come to my office to answer some questions."

"Could we go to the bank where the robbery happened? I believe I can better answer your questions there."

"Well, I guess that'd be all right."

The four crossed the street and walked into the bank. A clerk looked up. "Can I be of help, Sheriff?"

"We come to see Drake."

"Mr. Kershaw is having lunch with his wife presently. Would you care to wait?"

"No, we wouldn't care to wait."

The sheriff walked behind the gated area and knocked once on the door. Without waiting for an answer, he opened it and went in. "Drake, I've got some folks to see you."

Mrs. Kershaw was sitting on her husband's lap, caressing his beard. She jumped up and smoothed the front of her dress. Mr. Kershaw, clearly annoyed, shouted, "What's the meaning of this, breaking into my office uninvited?"

"Let me introduce you to Mrs. Clark." As the sheriff said this, he stretched out his arm, waved it toward Doris, and bowed slightly.

"The robber's wife?"

"The same."

Mrs. Kershaw looked at Doris, "Why, where are your manners, Drake? Get Mrs. Clark a seat. When is your baby due, dear?"

"In about a minute."

"What!" This was echoed by the three men. Rose laughed.

In a take charge manner, Mrs. Kershaw looked at her husband, "Drake, we need to get the doctor. Quick, tell one of your clerks to run and get him."

"That won't be necessary. Is there a room I could use?"

"Yes, yes." The president hurried to open a door. Behind it was a very small bedroom. It held a single bed, a nightstand and a straight-back chair. Doris gave him a strange look on seeing the "bedroom."

Somewhat red faced, he volunteered, "We live several miles out of town. During inclement weather or if I have to work late, I sometimes stay over."

Mrs. Kershaw started to follow Doris into the room. "Let me help you, Mrs. Clark. I've birthed four children, all boys." She said this as though her helping Doris would ensure a male birth.

"That won't be necessary, Mrs. Kershaw; I'm all the help she needs." Rose pushed Mrs. Kershaw to the side with an elbow and followed Doris into the room. Mrs. Kershaw put her hands on her hips, indignantly harumphed, and stared at the closed door.

They were in the room only a couple of minutes. To the four people waiting it seemed like hours. The door opened and Doris walked out carrying a dirty gray pillow case. She turned it upside down onto the president's desk. Hundreds of bills in various denominations came floating out along with a number of rags.

"Here's my 'baby', the money taken from your bank."

Mrs. Kershaw plopped herself down on the chair that had been originally brought for Doris.

Tim stepped forward and looked at the

money, then at Doris' flat stomach. "You mean there ain't no baby?"

"No baby." Doris thought Tim actually looked disappointed.

"Why do you have these rags in with the money?" asked Mr. Kershaw.

"Well, every-once-in-a-while I added more stuffing to the pillow case so it looked like I was getting bigger."

The sheriff spoke up. "Mrs. Clark, do you know there's a twenty-five-hundred-dollar reward for the return of this money? It appears it's yours. And by the way, there's also a thousand-dollar reward on your husband. That's yours, too."

"My name is Kepler."

"Kepler?"

"Yes. Nate Clark or Clarkson was already

married when he married me. I understand our marriage isn't legal. Please see that the thousand is sent to his legal wife. Her name is Rachel Clarkson. She lives in St. Louis. There is also a son. I don't know his name."

"What about the twenty-five hundred? You want her to have that, too?"

"No, I'll keep that." Doris turned to the bank president and said, "I'd like to deposit these two checks. I need to keep some of the money to buy some personal items."

There was a bit of small talk. Finally, the sheriff said, "This has been a real surprising and interesting day. But I've got to get back to the office. Stop by later. You'll need to sign some papers." The sheriff turned and left, heading for his office.

Doris was about to leave the room when she looked at the pillowcase. It was one Momma had embroidered with beautiful yellow flowers and little blue birds. It was the only thing she had left of Momma. She picked it up gently folding it, and took it with her.

Chapter 45

The trio stood outside the bank. No one knew quite what to say. Doris could feel the hurt she had caused Tim. Finally, Rose spoke up.

"Tim, if yer mad at anyone, it's me. Doris wanted ta tell ya. I told her not to. I still think I was right. It was safer fer her and the rest of ya not knowin' the truth."

Tim looked at Rose, then Doris. "Yeah, sure, I see what yer sayin'. It's okay, I understand. Right now, I've got ta find a cook willin' ta join our drive. How 'bout I meet ya fer supper in the hotel dinin' room?"

"That would be fine." After Tim left, Rose looked at Doris. "Don't be a'frettin' yerself. Just give him time ta cogitate for awhile and ta simmer down. I'm headin' over ta the hotel. You comin' with me?"

"No, I want to do some shopping. I'll be there in a bit." Doris watched Rose walk away. She could still see Tim in the distance. Maybe her planning and dreaming wasn't going to come about. She realized she was at peace. Well, God, I told You I was going to let You handle things. It's up to You.

Doris walked to the "Lady Pemberton Ready-Made Clothing Store for Women." As she entered, she saw several styles of dresses. She had never had a readymade dress in her life. Both she and Rose needed new clothes. She saw a really pretty, delicate sky-blue dress.

The owner, Mrs. Pemberton, walked from behind a counter. "Isn't that a lovely dress? I so enjoyed making it. Would you like to try it on?"

Doris was about to say yes when she figured if her plan came about, she really wouldn't need such a fancy dress. In the end she bought a light green gingham dress for herself and a dark blue gingham for Rose. The clerk assured her if Rose's dress didn't fit, she would alter it for her or Rose could exchange it. Doris also bought new undergarments for both of them, as well as divided skirts, and two shirtwaists each.

She was walking back to the hotel thinking how a nice warm bath would feel when a strong arm grabbed her about the waist and a dirty, rough hand covered her mouth and most of her nose. She dropped her boxes as she was pulled into a narrow alley between two buildings. The hand partially covering her nose made it hard for her to breathe. She was feeling faint. She knew that somehow it was the last outlaw, Monte. They came to a porch at the back of a store. He whirled her around and shoved her down onto the wooden porch. He straddled her, pinning both of her arms to the floor.

"Lady, ya scream, and yer dead. You understand?" Doris nodded. "I've had it with chasin' after ya. Yer goin' back with me ta show me where ya hid that money."

Doris realized he didn't know the money had already been returned to the bank. She struggled to get loose, but Monte was too strong. She suddenly had terrible memories of Nate holding her similarly and was terrified. Abruptly she relaxed and sent a swift prayer to heaven.

"That's better. Now we're gittin out of here. Remember if ya yell, I'll break yer pretty neck." Doris bobbed her head. Monte roughly pulled her to her feet.

"I don't have to go back with you. I have a map. I was taking it to the bank to give to them. It's in my pocket." Doris put her hand in her pocket before Monte had a chance to. She felt the derringer. She was so scared; she didn't want to shoot anyone, even Monte. But she believed he would kill her if he found out the money was gone.

"Come on, give it over!"

She didn't take the derringer out of her pocket, but cocked the hammer and pulled the trigger. Monte let out a horrific yell and fell to the ground. Doris took off on a run towards the main street, screaming as loudly as she could, and slammed smack into the sheriff.

"What's going' on here? What was that shot about?"

Doris pointed to Monte laying in the dirt, holding his leg and swearing. "That's the last outlaw! He tried to get me to tell him where the money is!" The sheriff moved Doris out of his way and ran down the alley to arrest Monte.

Doris began to shake uncontrollably. Several people had heard the shot, Doris' screams and Monte's yelling. Soon the alley was full of men. Doris felt strong arms gently embrace her. Tim whispered in her ear, "It's over, sweetheart. It's all over, yer safe."

"Is he dead?"

The sheriff was walking back toward Doris, half dragging Monte, who continued his vile rant.

"No, as you can see, he isn't dead, Miss Kepler. You got him in the thigh. He'll live long enough to hang. Cecil, go get the doc."

Monte had been groaning. He heard the sheriff. "Hang! I ain't done nothin' ta hang fer."

"You killed two bank clerks."

"That weren't me." He pointed to Doris and added, "That were her husband. I ain't never kilt nobody."

"Well, that will be for a jury to decide."

Tim spoke up. "Sheriff, I'm taking Miss Kepler to her hotel room. Could a couple of you fellows get her boxes and come with us?"

The sheriff had one last comment: "Don't forget to stop by my office. There's also a thousand-dollar reward on this fellow. Maybe you ought to go into law enforcement, Miss Kepler."

Doris only gave a weak smile as she and Tim started for the hotel. She was still shaking. The second time she stumbled; Tim picked her up and carried her the rest of the way. Doris put her arms around Tim, laid her head on his shoulder and closed her eyes. She didn't ever want to let go.

The hotel clerk looked up when he saw Tim carrying Doris, followed by two men bearing a number of boxes. "I heard a shot. Is that Miss Kepler? Has she been shot?"

"Yes, this is Miss Kepler. And no, she wasn't shot. What is her room number?"

"Twenty-five. Her friend Mrs. Elder ordered a tub of water for herself and one for Miss Kepler. I just finished filling Miss Kepler's. It's nice and hot. Room twenty-five."

Doris opened her eyes and lifted her head, "Thank you, I'm sorry I don't know your name."

The clerk smiled. "Dan. Dan Jennings."

"Thank you, Dan."

The group walked up the stairs, Tim still carrying Doris. She continued to think how comfortable she felt. They stopped at number twenty-five. "Will you be all right if I put you down, darlin'?"

"Yes, I'm better now."

Tim opened the door. "Jest put the boxes

on the bed. Thanks, fellows." The two men tipped their hats and left. Rose could be heard singing and splashing in her room. Tim looked into those lovely shining, blue eyes and thought, Holding her felt so good. I want to hold her forever. Why can't I say the words that are in my heart?

Instead, he quietly uttered, "Guess I'll be goin'. Do ya still want ta have supper?"

"Yes, of course. Tim?"

"Yes, Doris."

"I've been thinking about what to do with the money from the rewards and for selling the farm. I also have the money from my folks' savings. All together it amounts to quite a lot. I suppose I should send some to Susan. But, even so, there will still be a good amount left. I really don't want to go to California. I'm thinking of investing in something. What would you think of my giving the money to you, to use to get the Montana ranch started?"

Tim didn't say anything at first but put one arm around Doris, drawing her close to him. He looked deeply into her eyes. Once again Doris could hardly breathe. This time it wasn't because of lack of air.

Then he said, "I don't know. Montana can be pretty cold in the winter. We could lose everything. And ya'd be out all yer money. It would be real chancy. Ya'd be takin' an awful risk." As he was saying this, it was clear his mind was elsewhere. His other hand played gently with the hair that had come loose from her bun.

Shyly Doris whispered, "I'm willing to take the risk. There is just one requirement that comes with this offer."

Surprised, Tim moved his hand from her hair to her shoulder and eased back just a bit. "Requirement? What would that be?"

Doris bowed her head and took a long, deep breath. She couldn't believe she was doing this. Very quietly she said, "A husband."

Doris had spoken so softly Tim wasn't sure he had heard her right. For a second time, he pulled her closer, lifted her chin with his cupped hand and asked, "What did you say?"

Doris looked at him with mist in her eyes. "A husband," she repeated louder.

"Sweet, sweet, Doris. You don't need ta buy yer way inta my heart. You already own it. I've longed ta take you in my arms since that first day, I saw you standin' beside that silly-lookin' wagon.

"Like I said, the winters in Montana can be pretty cold. And it would be real pleasurable ta have a pretty gal like you ta snuggle up to. As a matter of fact, it would be real pleasurable ta snuggle up ta ya on a warm summer night! Doris Kepler, ya'd be doing me a great honor by becomin' my wife. Will you marry me, and we'll keep each other warm durin' those cold Montana winters?"

"There is nothing more I'd like than to be snuggled next to you on a cold winter's night. Yes, Tim, I'll marry you."

He lowered his head to hers and kissed her. For the third time that day, Doris thought she was going to faint. Then Tim gave out with a loud whoop!

"I'll be back in fifteen minutes with a preacher. Meet ya in the parlor."

Doris laughed. "Make that an hour. I want to use that water Dan has hauled up these stairs."

"Come ta think on it, I could use a bath too. See ya in an hour. Bring Rose!" They both laughed.

He turned to go. As he reached the stairs, Doris called, "Tim?"

"Yes?"

Doris gave him a wink and a smile!

Chapter 46

The wedding was delayed for several hours. The minister was out of town but was expected back on the 7:25 evening train. When Doris found out there would be a delay, she and Rose walked to Mrs. Pemberton's store.

Mrs. Pemberton was sewing on a ribbon to a christening dress. Beside her sat a girl of about ten, sewing buttons on a white blouse.

"Good afternoon, Miss Kepler, it is so good to see you again."

Doris was pleased Mrs. Pemberton remembered her and proceeded to introduce Rose who was more interested in focusing on the little girl. The girl looked up and smiled.

"And this little girl is my granddaughter. I'm teaching her to sew. She is very bright. What can I show you?"

Doris smiled at the little girl, "I'd like to try on the blue dress. I'm getting married this evening."

The dress fit perfectly; it was made for Doris. Fashioned of light blue silk, Doris said it reminded her of a bright, cloudless day in March. She dearly remembered the day a year ago when she and her father had lunched along the road on their way to town. She was beginning to fondly remember her family without tears. The healing had started.

Doris stood looking at herself in the mirror. Delicate white lace was attached to the V-shaped collar. There were tiny blue buttons down the front terminating at the waist. The tight sleeves had lace cuffs. The skirt was slightly gathered.

Mrs. Pemberton excused herself for just a minute and left the room. She returned carrying a veil. The veil was made of white lace and held in place by a ring of tiny, rather worn, yellow flowers.

"This was the veil my mother wore at my wedding. My daughter also wore it at hers. I'm hoping someday my granddaughter, Gladys will wear it with her bridal gown. I would be most pleased if you would wear it. That could be your 'something borrowed.'"

Doris thought it was lovely except for the yellow flowers. She decided she didn't want to hurt Mrs. Pemberton's feelings, "It is lovely Mrs. Pemberton. I'd be pleased to wear it.

"Gladys, please, go to the box of flowers and bring back some blue ones about the same size as these." Mrs. Pemberton replaced the worn, yellow flowers with blue ones and placed the veil on Doris' head. The front part of the veil came to Doris' fingertips, while the back of the veil reached the floor. The border of the veil was trimmed with satin braiding. The offer of this veil was more than Doris could have hoped for.

Mrs. Pemberton, not to miss a sale, asked Doris, "Do you have appropriate shoes for the wedding?" Doris looked down at her much-worn boots. "Let me show you some very nice ones." Mrs. Pemberton said this, as she led Doris to a row of stylish shoes.

Doris rejected fancy ones preferring instead a pair of white high buckle shoes with a slight heel. In her practical mind, Doris reckoned if she couldn't keep them clean, she could always dye them black.

On the way to the counter Doris observed an acorn-colored two-piece traveling suit. It had three rows of dark cording around the bottom of the skirt and the same cording going down each sleeve. With her recently acquired funds, she was sure this suit would make a good wardrobe addition. "I'd like to try this on."

"Of course, it may be a little short but has a large hem. I can have it adjusted by tomorrow morning. There is also a light-colored suit top that matches the skirt." She stated this as she reached for a beige jacket.

Mrs. Pemberton walked over to some

hats. "You'll need a hat and gloves to complete the costume." By the time Doris was finished, she had bought the wedding dress, shoes, a three- piece suit, two hats and two pair of gloves.

Rose had been oohing and aahing over each purchase. She laughed, "At this rate yer goin' ta have ta go to the bank ta withdraw more money."

Mrs. Pemberton wasted no time starting the alterations: "Gladys, take this skirt and carefully remove the basting thread for me. Try not to break the thread. Wrap it around this spool."

"Yes, Grandma."

Doris wondered what the situation was with Gladys. She decided there was probably an interesting story there—a good reason as to why Gladys' grandmother took her under her wing.

Rose was not as inhibited as Doris. "Gladys sure is a good little helper. Does her ma work fer ya, too?"

Mrs. Pemberton looked to be sure Gladys had left the room before replying. "Gladys isn't really my granddaughter. As-a-matter-of-fact, we aren't even related. Her mother was a dance hall worker. Gladys was only six months old when a fire burned down the saloon. A couple of the girls died.

"A day or two after the fire, Gladys' mother came into the shop. I'd made many of the clothes for the girls. She told me she was leaving town and asked me if I would keep Gladys until she got another job. She said she would then send for her. That was eight years ago."

"Didn't the girl's mother ever contact you?"

"No. She never did. Three years ago, I hired a lawyer. He made several inquiries. Finally, he located the mother in another state. She has married and has other children. She said her husband knows nothing about her former life. She didn't want Gladys back. The lawyer drew up papers, so I now have legal custody. I couldn't adopt Gladys because I'm not married. It seems a woman can have her own baby and not be married but cannot adopt one.

"Gladys knows nothing about this. I've told her that her mother died when she was born and her father died fighting Indians."

"Gladys is a very lucky little girl." Said Rose most sincerely. "I admire ya.

"And, I'll need something nice ta wear to the weddin'. I've been eyein' that kinda purple dress hangin' up over there. Can I try it on?"

"Yes, certainly, the color is called mauve. The material is muslin. I think, with just a few tucks and shortening the hem, it will fit you perfectly."

"Can ya have that all done in time for the weddin'?"

"Yes, I have a couple of ladies I can call on to help me get these items altered. I'll bring the things you need for the wedding to your room about half past six. The other garments I'll have ready in the morning."

Waiting for Doris at the church was the pastor, Rev. Henderson with a beautiful bouquet of white roses held together with deep blue ribbons. Tim had placed a note on it which read, "When I saw these ribbons, it reminded me of you."

A messenger was sent to let the men on the cattle drive know about the wedding. Wilbur McNeill and his men stayed with the herd so that the Texas men could attend the wedding.

Doris didn't know if she should ask one of the men to escort her down the aisle, but she didn't want to hurt anyone so she decided to walk alone.

When Stu heard she was walking by herself, he found her and asked, "Miss Doris, I really would very much like ta walk ya down the aisle. I don't think it's right for ya ta go by yerself. It'd be an honor if ya'd let me."

Doris knew Stu had a huge crush on her. "Stu, I'd be very grateful to have you escort me."

Only a few people besides the cowhands

were present to witness the exchange of vows in the candle-lit church that evening. The sheriff and his wife came, as did Mrs. Pemberton and Gladys. The pastor's wife, Mrs. Henderson and their four youngest children sat in the front row.

Trying to add to the festive occasion, the pastor's oldest daughter played the organ, unfortunately rather badly. But Doris didn't notice; her heart was so filled with happiness. As she walked down the aisle to meet Tim, she thought her heart might burst. She couldn't imagine being happier than she felt at this moment. The picture was complete with Rose as the matron of honor and Mark as the best man.

Mrs. Henderson surprised the couple with a reception at the parsonage. Lemonade and sugar cookies were served. She apologized for not having had time to bake a wedding cake, but Doris couldn't have cared less. She smiled and smiled until her jaws were sore.

Doris was amazed when she saw some gifts on a table for her and Tim. It hadn't even entered her mind that anyone would give the couple presents. The children were anxious to see them unwrap the gifts.

"Open them up, open them up!" A very pretty girl of about six or seven hounded Doris.

"That's enough," cautioned her father, though he also wanted to see the gifts. "Mrs. Gibson, if you'd like to open them, we all would like to see what you've received."

Doris looked at Tim and smiled; she had been called Mrs. Gibson for the first time. How nice it sounded!

"Go ahead, honey. I'd like ta see, too."

The first gift was from the sheriff and his wife. It was a small, off-white book with fancy black lettering that read "Guests." Doris had not seen one before and wondered what it was.

A little boy spoke up. "What's that for? Is she going to go to school?"

Mrs. Henderson sensed that Doris wasn't sure what the book was for either and spoke up. "Ralph, that is called a guest book. It is for people to sign when they come to your home for a visit."

The next gift was from the Henderson family. It was a large family Bible featuring biblical pictures. Doris almost cried. Her family Bible had been lost in the fire. She reached up to Mrs. Henderson who was standing nearby and hugged her. "Thank you, thank you so very much."

The last gift was from Rose. It was a slender hand-painted white porcelain vase trimmed at the top and bottom in gold. The middle was covered with chrysanthemums in shades of pink and yellow, with leaves of green and gold. "Ya keep that safe 'til ya git yer garden like ya told me yer momma had. Then ya'll have somethin' ta put the flowers in." Rose's message brought back emotions Doris thought she'd left behind, and she started to cry. Tim hugged her.

"Boy, what some women won't do for a hug," declared J.J. with a smile.

Mark took Tim aside during the reception. "Tim, there's enough men ta handle the cattle with the two herds combined, so ya can leave the drive and go by train ta meet up with yer ma and the others if ya've a mind ta. I'll send a telegram ta Walt, one ta Denver and another ta Billings. Hopefully, he'll get one of them. If things work out fer the best, ya could go the rest of the way together. I'm sure he would appreciate the extra help. I'll tell him ya'll will meet up in Billings. If he should happen ta get ta Billings before ya, which is very unlikely, I'll tell him ta leave word for ya and go on.

"Thanks, Uncle Mark. I appreciate that. I know Doris will too."

So it was that he and Doris traveled by train to Montana. They extended an invitation to have Rose go with them. Rose would have liked to accompany them, as she was anxious to see Sarah, but she decided three people on a honeymoon was one too many and stayed with the cattle drive.

Rose and Doris had a serious talk the next day before the newlyweds boarded the train for Denver. Doris was uncomfortable about meeting Sarah. She wasn't sure what to tell her about Rose.

Rose tried to encourage her friend. "Doris, I think it'll be difficult ta explain yer presence on the cattle drive without also telling about me and how we got hitched up with 'em. Just tell the truth. Tell her I love her and can hardly wait ta give her and my grandbabies a big hug."

Mark hired a cook, Mike Finnegan, who had been working at a local café but wanted to try his luck in Montana. Rose and Mike squabbled about the food preparation all the way to Montana. Frequently, Mark had to step in between them. He was afraid that if he didn't, they might come to blows. The rest of the crew thoroughly enjoyed the entertainment. Without this amusement, the remaining drive to Montana would have been just plain boring.

Epilogue

Doris and Tim joined Walt and the rest of the family in Billings. They purchased two wagons and followed Slim's map to the homestead area. The cattle drive arrived near the end of September, 1885. The mining company bought the thousand cows as contracted. Wilbur McNeill returned to Kansas, picking up his injured men on his way home.

Tim and Doris established their homestead, naming it Journey's End. Mark and Sarah's ranch, which also included

Rose, was east and south of Journey's End. They called their ranch Promise Valley. J.J. and Slim continued to use the same names as they had in Texas, the Lazy J and the Diamond S.

The remaining stock after the sale to the miners was divided among the four owners. Ramon purchased a few head from each man.

The winter of 1885-86 was a terrible initiation to Montana. It drove some newcomers to give up and return to their former homes. Tim, Mark, J.J. and Slim did not give up.

In the summer of 1886, an old-timer hired onto the Diamond S. He advised the newcomers to put up hay and plant barley for feed. He also said to fence their grazing ranges to keep the cattle from roving and to build three-sided shelters with the open side facing southeast. The old timer's help was truly beneficial.

The winter of 1886-87 was one of the coldest in Montana history. Temperatures dropped to minus sixty degrees. Some ranchers lost as much as ninety percent of their stock. Tim and Mark each lost about one third of their cattle. Whereas J.J.'s losses amounted to a fourth of his stock, Slim faired the best, losing only a couple dozen. After the disastrous winter, each man started to improve the condition and size of his stock by selective breeding.

Ramon lost most of his cattle. He learned that raising sheep might be better for him. When he became aware that sheep were able to withstand the cold winter better, he sold his remaining cattle stock to Tim and became a successful sheep herder.

Catherine and Walt

The winter 1886-87 was hard on everyone. Walt strived to do his part for his family. He struggled just to stay alive. He lost that battle in the early spring of 1887.

To everyone's surprise, Catherine and J.J. married in 1888. Even more surprising was the birth of two children to the couple. Catherine died peacefully many years later at the age of 87, surrounded by her family. Two years after Catherine's passing, J.J died.

Rose Elder

Rose made her home with Sarah and Mark. She loved her grandsons but doted over her namesake, Rose Patricia. Rose Patricia became a nurse and served in France during the Great War. While there she met and married a Scottish officer. After the war, they settled in Scotland.

Rose visited Rose Patricia twice. On her second visit she decided she liked it so much that she chose to stay in Scotland.

She met the grandfather of Rose Patricia's husband when she was eighty. He was ten years her junior. The two fell shamelessly in love and were married six months later.

One of Rose's greatest joys was having her great-grandchildren visit. They would gather around her chair spellbound as she told of her life in the United States. It didn't matter if she told the same story over and over.

Just before her ninetieth birthday in 1931, her husband asked her what gift she would like. Rose thought back over her life. She had crossed the prairie in a covered wagon. She had ridden a horse with a baby strapped to her back, helping her first husband herd cattle. She had roamed the west in a homemade buggy, searching for her daughter. She had cooked for a cattle drive with the help of her good friend. She had even helped drive those cattle. She had learned how to drive a car and had crossed the ocean twice on a ship. The thing she hadn't done was to fly in an airplane.

On her ninetieth birthday she and her husband drove to a nearby aerodrome. They were flown around the community and over their home. Next, they flew to Glasgow and stayed at the Grand Central Hotel, dining in the Tempus Restaurant. The menu included leek and potato soup, pan-seared trout fillet, tomato and basil gnocchi with a pimento dressing. The dinner was topped off with a glazed lemon tart and raspberry coulis. Rose never dreamed she would enjoy such luxuries. The next day they flew home. The Lord blessed her with another five years of a genteel life. She was buried clutching her braided Indian necklace with the gold cross.

Doris and Tim

After five years of marriage, Tim and Doris had yet to be blessed with children. They had been living in their new home for about a year when a delegation of area mothers arrived. Doris welcomed the company but wondered why so many women had come to visit at the same time. Among the women was her mother-in-law, Catherine, who never seemed to stop having babies.

Catherine was the spokesperson for the group. "Doris, you're the only one in these parts that has finished high school. With

so many children about, there is need
of a school. We've come to ask you to
start one."

Doris was stunned. All she could think of to
say was that she would pray about it and
discuss it with Tim.

Doris started the school. At first it was
held around her dining room table. Within
two years, it became obvious more room
was need. Tim donated land and the
community fathers build a large building.
On weekdays it was used as the school.
On Sundays it was the church. Evenings
and Saturdays, it became the community
meeting and party building.

Doris continued to teach in that building
for the next thirty-two years. Some children
came from too far away to travel back and
forth each day; they boarded with Doris
and Tim. Their fathers would bring them

on Monday morning and return on Friday afternoon to take them home.

There were other times when all the children had to stay overnight, and sometimes even several days, when a winter storm prevented them from going home. Those were fun times. Corn was popped, games were played and songs were sung.

Tim and Doris had been married almost ten years and still there was no baby to be kept warm in the Indian blanket. Late one afternoon Dr. Langston, the local physician, accompanied by his wife, rode up the lane. As they climbed out of their buggy, Doris noticed Mrs. Langston was carrying a baby. To Doris' knowledge Mrs. Langston had not been expecting. Goodness, Mrs. Langston was older than Catherine.

Doris called to Tim, who was working at his desk.

After exchanging pleasantries, Dr. Langston explained that a colleague of his who practiced in Billings had contacted him for help. He told Doris and Tim there had been a thirteen-year-old girl working as a maid for a prominent family in the Billings area. The man of the house had taken advantage of this girl. Mrs. Langston was holding the result: a baby boy, now seven weeks old. The girl wanted to keep her son, but at thirteen she was much too young to be a mother and had no way to support herself or the child. Tearfully, the girl signed adoption papers knowing the child would have a better chance of a good future in a more stable environment.

Dr. Langston had thought of Doris and Tim. Mrs. Langston handed the baby to

Doris. Doris looked at the tiny infant and knew in her heart, she loved this little boy as her own.

That was how Little Tim came to be part of the Gibson family. Doris found the little Indian blanket in her storage chest. At last, she had her baby to wrap in it. She would sit for hours in her rocking chair, singing and rocking Little Tim.

Little Tim became very attached to his "bankie." He dragged it everywhere with him in the house. Doris wouldn't allow him to take it outdoors. Occasionally Doris wrestled the banket from Little Tim to launder and repair it. Those nights when he got it back, he would lay in his bed licking it until he was satisfied, it once again smelled like him.

When Little Tim was almost four, Big Tim decided it was time for the bankie to go. It had become little more than a rag. He rode up to the house leading a coal-black pony. He told Little Tim he would trade the pony for the bankie. After a bit of hesitation, Little Tim agreed. That night Little Tim asked for his bankie back. Big Tim said it was gone.

Doris listened as Little Tim cried himself to sleep. Big Tim wanted to burn the blanket to be sure it never surfaced again. Doris wouldn't let him. She cleaned it and gently folded it back into the storage chest. She knew one day, Little Tim would find it and fondly remember his "bankie."

Little Tim grew to be six inches taller and fifty pounds heavier than Big Tim. But even as an adult he was forever called Little Tim. Friends sometimes asked him how he liked being an only child. He would laugh and say that there had always been so many other kids in the house he was about six before he realized he was an only child.

Little Tim served in the Great War. He returned home with a French bride. Doris loved learning French. Big Tim chided her, saying she was supposed to be teaching her daughter-in-law English, not the other way around.

The "Old Man's Friend," pneumonia, came to visit Big Tim in the spring of 1943. He had had a long and exciting life and was ready to go.

Three weeks later Doris sat looking out the window thinking about something her father had told her, so many years ago. She had been upset about something. She couldn't even remember what it was. She knew it had something to do with how we lived and what we did. She did remember he told her that whatever she did, do as if it is for Christ. Only what's done for Christ matters.

A spring snow gently fell on jonquil buds. She thought back upon her life. Had her life mattered? Some people said what luck it was that she had been able to escape the outlaws that were after her. She knew it wasn't luck. It was God's prevenient grace. It wasn't luck or coincidence finding Rose. Or was it Rose who found her? No, once again it was God's guiding hand. The adventures they'd shared traveling across the prairie was by God's direction. Although, at the time, she hadn't realized it. And how, with so many cattle drives crossing that wide prairie, was it possible for them to run into the very herd that would change both their lives forever? It wasn't luck, coincidence or just good fortune. Doris knew it was God's hand guiding them all the way.

She wondered if her life had been
a worthwhile life. Were the children
she taught any better, for her having
instructed them? She hoped so. Wasn't
that the reason for living, to have made
a difference? To leave this world a
better place because you lived! She
hoped she had.

Her eyes became heavy and she drifted off
to sleep. She awoke in Heaven. She saw
Jesus, and standing next to Him was Tim.
He walked to her, young and strong, with
a full head of beautiful blond hair. Just
before he enfolded Doris into his arms, he
gave her a wink and a smile.

The End

Acknowledgements

I wish my dad were still here so that I could thank him for initiating me to the love of westerns. I remember sitting with him "watching" the radio as we listened to cowboy shows. I even had a Dale Evans six-shooter. I went to all the Audie Murphy, John Wayne, Hop-Along Cassidy and as many other western movies, as I could as a child and a teen-ager. It was a wonderful childhood. I read all that Louie L'Amour had to offer plus many other western authors. I still watch westerns on television. My husband puts up with them.

Speaking of my husband, John, I want to especially acknowledge him. He has encouraged me, supported me and cheered me on, in this undertaking. He read the first manuscript finding mistakes, making corrections, questioning authenticity of some sections and suggesting changes. He has read, reread and read again the book as changes were made. God really did a wonderful thing when He gave me John.

Dianne Ferris, who does academic editing, did the initial editing. Colleen Konop is a retired English teacher, now doing free-lance editing. I want to thank both ladies for the many suggestions they offered.

There are many other people that need to be thanked. I am sorry if I forget to thank someone. I really appreciate all those who helped me. Two friends I unquestionably want to remember are Tod (with one d) Pritchard and Vianne Van Cleave. Both are retired teachers, and avid readers. They read the novel with red pens in hand. Vianne told me that she loves using a red pen! Both she and Tod offered excellent suggestions. Any remaining inaccuracies are surely mine.

The idea for the shooting lessen came from the time my dad taught me to use a shotgun, but never a revolver. Two people that contributed to this chapter are Cindy Gonzalez and David Alford. Cindy is a retired police officer, and David a retired security officer. They helped me understand the basics of shooting a revolver.

While exploring authenticity for this book I perused numerous encyclopedias, instruction manuals, and reference books

on western folklore. I really enjoyed
that activity.

This book would not have been published
without the outstanding help of the team
members at Typewriter Creative Co. I
cannot say enough about how much I
appreciate them. Taryn Nergaard and
MaryBeth Eiler skillfully guided me through
the process. Cassidy Wierks designed
the attractive front cover and Sara
Ward the appealing back cover. Finally,
Janna Wilson created the interior of the
book. It far surpasses what I expected.
Thank you, team, so very much, for the
outstanding work.

Most of all I want to thank my Lord, Jesus
Christ. When I was thirteen years old, I
confessed my sins and accepted Him as
my Savior. It is the best decision I have
ever made. There have been times when I

failed Him. He never has failed me. He was with me when my daughter, Deborah died. I know she is now with Him in heaven. One day I will see her again.

The dream I wrote about is one God gave me about Debbie, just after her passing. This book is dedicated to her.

About the Author

Marsha Pester grew up looking at the radio with her dad while listening to western stories. She has never lost her love of westerns. Now she watches old western movies on television. She even convinced her husband, John, to like them. They have been blessed with a daughter, Deborah, a son, Timothy and are the grandparents of eight and one great-grandson. Cancer claimed lovely Debbie in 2016. Marsha began writing after retiring from thirty years of nursing. She also spends time leading a women's Bible study, helping John with a nursing home Bible study, writing, sewing and weeding her garden.

marshapester@gmail.com

www.ingramcontent.com/pod-product-compliance
Lightning Source LLC
Chambersburg PA
CBHW060558300726
48975CB00005B/1366